THE TRAIN JUMPER

GWEN BANTA

ALSO BY GWEN BANTA

Novels

The Remarkable Journey of Weed Clapper

Inside Sam Lerner

With Wanton Disregard

Children's Books

The Monster Zoo

Plays

The Fly Strip

Dedicated to the towns of:
Wabash, Indiana
Franklin, Indiana
Kansas City, Missouri
and
New Orleans, Louisiana
To all the railroads that connect great cities, and to the generations of
folks who travel the rails in search of adventure.

PROLOGUE

Wabash, Indiana

WHEN JAKE JACKSON'S DAD PULLED INTO HIS DRIVEWAY IN A FORD Crestline Sunliner convertible one July afternoon back in 1952, people streamed out of their houses so fast you would have thought they were giving away free corn dogs at the Indiana State Fair. It was a veritable Hoosier stampede. The vehicle was such a bright yellow that it announced its arrival while still a block away. A few neighbors grumbled about the effect of such a "loud" color in a small, quiet Indiana town like ours (no doubt the paint awakened a few denizens of the local cemetery), but to quote Mr. Jackson, the Ford Sunliner was like "Marilyn Monroe in a yellow negligee ... and she purrs just as pretty."

Jake's dad promptly instructed his rapt audience to touch the car with eyeballs only. "No fingerprints please. This here's a Larado Da Vinci paint job." (Mr. Jackson was famous for screwing up words.) I was transfixed by her shiny chrome trim and whipped cream white leather seats. Jake and I walked around the car, looking at every angle of her sleek chassis.

Jake was my best friend. I had a closer sensibility with Jake than with any of the girls in the neighborhood. Everyone called

1

me a tomboy, and I guess I was. I preferred the nickname "Kat" rather than my given name of Kathleen Marie Caswell, a label which may have sounded more feminine but seemed foreign to me. My dark hair with cropped bangs was too short, and my sartorial choice of loose trousers and dirty sneakers often made me a target for derogatory comments. But I didn't care - all I required was comfort. And Jake claimed I looked like a young Audrey Hepburn which was good enough for me.

My closeness to Jake was about more than my disinterest in dresses and lipstick. He and I enjoyed doing the same things - trainspotting, listening to Yankee games on the radio, wading in the nearby creek, or watching trains speed overhead from beneath the river railroad bridge. We knew the entire Yankees roster and all the numbers of the Wabash trains that traversed our town - as familiar to us as every bend in the creek. I loved Jake's family too. My world was full of endings, but to me, Jake and his family represented a world of sunshine-bright possibilities.

During that memorable July of our thirteenth year, not many days passed before Mr. Jackson honored Jake and me with the task of washing the magnificent Ford convertible for him. "Wash her real gentle - like you're washing a baby's ass." The accompanying circular hand motion - like a man trying to find his way through the fog – was hypnotic. "And take some toothpaste to those white walls. They should be whiter than Wonder Bread."

Just one sign of bird droppings on the windshield would send Mr. Jackson into a spasmodic gait as he raced across the yard to the crime scene. If a flock of well-fed, hapless birds flew overhead, he would charge out with his BB gun aimed at the sky while indignant neighbors screamed out their windows, "Shut the hell up, Jackson!" Quite often, "you jackass" was added to the admonitions for both emphasis and assessment. For us, the entertainment never ended.

On rare occasions, George Jackson even let us fire the BB gun into the elm trees, much to the dismay of Jake's mom, Gladys, who always cowered behind the door with one fist clutched to her apron and the other hand pressed to her face as though her efforts might somehow stifle the sound and make her invisible. Of course, every time we fired a shot, the nervous birds reacted by emptying themselves again, but the abundant discharge just added to the excitement and the justification to keep the gunfire going.

Just for fun, Jake frequently yelled out in warning even if there were no birds in sight. "Hey Dad, I see a well-fed flock circling. They look like monster crappers!" I think George Jackson sometimes knew Jake was pulling his leg, but he always came running anyway, if only to entertain us. Gladys put a stop to it when he ran outside wearing only his boxer shorts - to our enthusiastic applause.

Most summers, Jake and I loved to spend our idle days on the outskirts of town where we could lie in the warm, grassy field watching the Wabash Cannonball speed down the tracks in all her majesty as she transported goods and mail from one end of the country to the other, linking with tendrils of other railways along the way. The Cannonball was a constant flow of energy.

Whenever the Cannonball came our way, we ran alongside her in hopes of garnering the attention of the travelers. To our great delight, woefully misdirected cattle sometimes required the Cannonball to slow down almost to a stop. On those occasions, passengers often opened windows to wave and shout greetings to us as we sidled up to the train.

Jake always wanted to know where the passengers were going. Sometimes he fell deep into conversation with any passengers who would engage with him long enough for him to rattle off details about destinations of interest along the line. He was an encyclopedia of facts. As the train started to speed up again, he would yell things like, "Send me a postcard from Kansas City," or "Tell St. Louis that Jake Jackson is coming!" We attached a lot of rituals to that pastime, including sharing our dreams of where our lives would take us - always together, fearless, and hell-bent on a good time.

The summer of 1952 and that bright yellow Ford convertible proved to upend our usual routines, as we were content to stick around the neighborhood more often in hopes of an opportunity to wash the Crestline Sunliner and to "Start 'er up." We were so obsessed that we even went to the library to learn everything we could about Fords.

Our car services involved no pay, but Jake and I agreed it was the ultimate privilege to be near an object of such workmanship and beauty. Periodically Mr. Jackson hosted a joy ride around the neighborhood, the three of us nestled happily into her cushy seats. We didn't go far - just across the railroad tracks and back. I had never ridden in a convertible, so it was thrilling to experience the wind in my hair and to have a chance to yell to the neighbors as we drove by. In my mind, I was Princess Grace Kelly parading through the streets of Wabash-Monaco.

Sometimes we had to wait for trains to pass by. It was always a big thrill when the duly impressed travelers waved from the windows at the three of us traveling in a vehicle almost as wondrous as the Wabash Cannonball. Our status in our little world was elevated to new heights in that car.

Although the seats were luxurious, we really couldn't feel them. They were smothered with clear plastic seat covers that Mr. Jackson had ordered from the same seat cover maker who had designed all the plastic protectors for Mrs. Jackson's living room furniture. She said he was a true artisan. (The guy had turned the couch into a water impermeable floating device.) The man's name was Freddy Ashton, but Jake and I nicknamed him "Furniture Assassin," because his covers were painfully uncomfortable and remarkably hideous. (We also determined that he must be a commie from Russia. After all, the Cold War was in full swing.)

When we scooted across the Assassin-designed convertible seat covers, the friction on the plastic made farting sounds, so we entertained ourselves by making as many rude noises as possible. "The joker who made these is a real Fartisan-artisan," I whispered. Jake loved the new nickname.

During one of our joy rides, Jake and Mr. Jackson were dressed in long pants, but I was wearing summer shorts, so my bare legs stuck to the sun baked seat covers like adhesive bandages.

When Jake saw me wince, he tapped his dad on the shoulder. "Kat is stuck to the backseat, Dad." Jake rolled his eyes and popped his Juicy Fruit gum as punctuation. "I think we're gonna have to surgically remove her."

Mr. Jackson was unflappable. "Oh here, honey, try this." He reached under his seat and then tossed a towel to me.

It took me several minutes to gingerly un-stick myself from the seat that held me captive. "I think I left half my thigh on Fartisan's evil seat wrap," I groused.

"Dead skin will only enhance the beauty. Don't worry. The Fartisan-artisan can cover anything."

"Do you think Fartisan can design plastic skin grafts?"

My snide remark somehow struck Jake's funny bone, and with a loud guffaw, he spewed forth his chewing gum. I gasped when I saw Jake's expression and realized he had no clue where the gum had landed. In total panic, we began searching the backseat, convinced the gum had fallen somewhere inside the car.

"What's going on back there, kids?" Mr. Jackson stared in the rear view mirror in an attempt to check out our suspicious activity.

"Um, nothing, Dad. Kat just dropped her, uh, her comb."

"No way! Kat has a comb?"

"Very funny, Mr. Jackson." My voice was overly animated as I tried to disguise my consternation.

The gum was nowhere to be found on the seat or on Jake. For a minute, we thought we had avoided disaster, but then Jake's eyes grew wide as he silently pointed toward his feet. The chewing gum was on the floor mat. Well, not exactly on it, but *in* it – thanks to Jake's foot.

I moaned when I saw the rubbery mess clinging to Jake's shoe. "Oh no, Jake! You're deader than Jacob Marley."

Without hesitation, Jake picked up the mat and nonchalantly tossed it out of the convertible. For a brief moment, I forgot how to breathe. I was so horrified that I was ready to bail out over the side of the car myself, but Jake was calmer than a day-old corpse.

When we were at least a block from the scene of the crime, Jake called out to his father, "Hey Dad, did you know you're missing a floor mat back here?"

"That's impossible!"

"I'm sorry to say, but it's true."

"Well I'll be a son of a-"

"It's pretty easy for things like that to happen. The prep guys were probably making sure your car was extra clean and forgot to put all the mats back. You can get another one though, can't you?"

"I'll have to go back to the dealership and try to locate it. Or I can just get Freddy Ashton to make up some clear plastic protectors for those nice carpet mats. You remember him, Jake – he made those terrific seat covers you're sitting on."

Jake and I started laughing so hard that I had to squeeze my legs together so as not to baptize the Fartisan's seats. We had such a great time that day that even those tortuous seat covers did not damper our spirits. Everything about that Ford made us happy.

———

Eventually Mr. Jackson allowed Jake to start the car just for thrills, and the response of the engine seemed to excite Mr. Jackson as much as it did Jake. "Gas it, buddy!" Mr. Jackson would yell as he surreptitiously glanced about to assess the ongoing admiration of the locals. "That's it - good job. Now let Kat give it a try."

That was the moment I found religion. When I jumped into the driver's seat and depressed the gas pedal, the roar of the V-8 engine excited me more than the time Lee Engstrom kissed me behind the art easel in the third grade. Both events were transformative.

Even though my dad was usually drunk, and my mom had died, those were idyllic days. I had a lot of chores to do at home, but at Jake's house, life was my idea of normal. Mrs. Jackson baked pies and yelled at Jake to clean his room. Mr. Jackson sneaked cigarettes in the garage and hung fake owls on the trees to fend off "those damnable woodpeckers." And Jake and I walked to Charley Creek on weekends when Mr. Jackson was off somewhere cruising in the Ford.

One night I asked my dad why we couldn't replace our own beat-up old Chevy pickup truck with an automobile like the Ford. "For God's sake, Kat, we could if you would just steal the damn keys from Jackson. He won't miss it. He's got more convertibles down at the dealership." That was the way my dad looked at life - the world owes a break to its humble masses just for sticking around this dismal place, so you better grab what you need before somebody else does ... larceny notwithstanding.

I was an idealistic, optimistic kid, so I didn't agree with Dad's philosophy about life. At least back then I didn't. In my imagination, I was a Ford Crestline Sunliner convertible streaming down a highway of Technicolor vistas, heading for exotic destinations - places where moms weren't dead, dads weren't drunks, and the world pulsated with promise. But soon I discovered a world that was not black and white, much less Sunliner yellow.

BOOK I

INDIANA

CHAPTER ONE

I ALWAYS UNDERSTOOD MY DAD'S IRRITATION WITH PEOPLE LIKE George Jackson. Jake's dad had graduated from high school and had completed two years of college education at Purdue, thanks to some money left to him by his own father. He owned the biggest car dealership in Wabash (also inherited), and a "mighty fine house with custom-made furniture covers," according to evaluations often overheard at Chet and Bea's Barbershop (secretly referred to as the "Chop-n-Bleed"). Dad, however, worked long, tedious shifts at the Wabash Paper Company over on Factory Street. He shuffled like a man who had been beaten. He had a constant cough from breathing in paper fiber, and he often gagged from his futile attempts to push the sputum back down his ragged throat.

My mom died when I was two - or so I was told at the time. At the end of each day, Dad found solace from his loneliness and troubles in foul whiskey and the Camel cigarettes he dragged on as though sucking in his last breath of air on earth. I swear there was less action in an accordion. We often sat out on the weather-beaten porch in silence (save for his occasional gagging and subsequent spitting) before he finally grunted a word of good night before shuffling into the house. One time he even stumbled right through the screen door. We never fixed it. It remained torn until Dad died - his own story imprinted on a house of emptiness.

Nothing much ever excited Dad, who wore defeat like an ox yoke, but that summer the appearance of the Sunliner in our neighborhood was probably the biggest event we had experienced in the past four years. Even my dad got off the porch to run down to see the Ford convertible, which would later become known as simply "Marilyn." My dad's presence made the event even more unforgettable to me. His arrival was an awkward moment, but the unexpected smile on his face is etched deep in my memory.

The neighbors were also surprised to see my dad, who had avoided most people since the great chicken incident of 1948. Unfortunately, the embarrassing fiasco was still brought up in conversation at public events such as church pancake dinners and basketball games. As time passed, the recounting of the events became even more detailed and colorful, resulting in abject humiliation that clung to my memories and never let go.

One night my dad had decided it was better to polish off the whiskey than to save the fumes, so while fully inebriated, he set our old wood shed ablaze. No one knows how he did it, or even if he *intended* to do it, but the flames burst into the air like arthritic orange fingers clawing at the nighttime sky. The shed was small and would have burned out quickly - save for the maple tree that sheltered it. Soon the tree was also aflame. It was truly shocking ... and it was downright mesmerizing as well. It reminded me of the Olympic torch destined for glory, albeit heading towards Sam Goodwin's house, where no glory awaited.

The noise was so loud that a deaf person would have thought the Horsemen of the Apocalypse had arrived in Wabash, Indiana, to wreak their havoc. The sound of the collapsing shed and blistering fire was simply a backdrop to the ear-splitting ruckus of panicked chickens. Yes, chickens. We didn't have a working farm, but my dad always had chickens. He loved the dang things, and he always proclaimed that an egg would cure anything. That summer, however, he discovered that eggs are no cure for a fire. The chickens, smelling smoke and no doubt fraught with visions of becoming someone's dinner, scattered across the yard like buckshot, lifting several feet off the ground in a flurry of feathers.

Neighbors came running from every direction, as Hoosiers are wont to do. In their efforts to be helpful, they frantically dashed about in an attempt to corral the hysterical chickens who continued to scream and wrest themselves from the clutches of all would-be rescuers. The neighbors were squawking as loudly as the chickens. At one point, Mr. Jackson, one of the enthusiastic fire-fighting volunteers, ran head first into the side of our house in a race with a panicked chicken who was clever enough to stop just short of contact. It was a sight to behold.

By then, my dad was in a heap on the porch steps, his head hanging down while he talked to his empty whiskey bottle. Finally, he yelled to no one in particular, "Somebody save Marie." If there could be a silent moment in the middle of chaos, that moment was it. Everyone who heard his comment was dumbfounded ... including me. Marie was my deceased mother's name.

We all stared at my father while his plea hung in the night sky like a discarded appendix. No one wanted to touch it, but it was impossible to ignore.

Sam Goodwin was the first to gather his wits. He dropped his frantic chicken captive, and then he walked over to my father and placed a tender hand on his shoulder. "Take it easy, Frank. Calm down. Marie passed away - remember?"

Out of the blue, my dad popped up like a maniacal clown in a carnival game. "I know my wife is dead, Goodwin. I'm not daft!" he growled. "I'm talking about Marie, my rooster - the fat cowardly one over there that is molting so fast he looks like a bowling ball."

Everyone was taken aback – even me. No one had ever heard my usually laconic father put so many words together at one time.

"The rooster? Don't you mean the hen?"

"No, I mean that damn half-naked rooster, Goodwin. Are you deaf? That's Marie!"

"Marie? I think you're a little confused, buddy. Roosters are male. You know that, don't you?"

"Of course I know roosters are male. But not that stinkin' bird. No, sir - that rooster was castrated, or whatever you do to foul to neuter them. A man's name don't suit that bird. I found out he's sterile after I got him. He's as worthless as a turd hat. All he does is make noise and eat nonstop. He's costing me a fortune. He's so blubbery I could use him as a footstool."

"I agree he's unusually large. And balder than a Thanksgiving turkey."

"He ain't normal! That rooster can hardly move. I shoulda named him 'Doorstop.'"

"So why in the heck do you keep a capon with the mange, Frank?"

"Sam Goodwin, I may be more confusin' to you than a Sunday preacher, but even I know this here situation is not the best occasion to be discussin' my choice of foul. But for your information, I keep that useless bird so he can wake up the neighborhood every damn morning just like he always has. Y'all need something to keep on bitchin' about."

Sam shook his head, shrugged, and then headed back to help wrangle Marie, who continued to leave piles of feathers all over the yard. After the chickens were lured into the basement and the fire was put out, I went upstairs and buried myself as deep into my bed as the mattress would allow.

I was overcome with humiliation and guilt. I knew I should have kept a better watch on my dad, and I also knew I should have quietly disposed of the can of gasoline he always kept in the shed. Shame kept eating at my conscience during a long and restless night ... until Marie woke me up with a crowing volume that verged on sonic.

Marie had escaped from the basement and was standing in my dad's room. That rooster had about two feathers left and was out for revenge. Marie was there to make the old man with the monstrous hangover pay the devil his due. Fortunately, I was able to hide my dad's shotgun before he was able to roll out of bed onto the floor. Which he promptly did.

After the chicken fiasco, as if it wasn't embarrassing enough that my inebriated father had set fire to the shed, the piles of feathers left in our yard then blew throughout the neighborhood with every breeze. I winced when I overheard Sam Goodwin complaining down at the Chop-n-Bleed one afternoon. "My house reeks of smoke, and I can't even open my windows or I wake up with feathers in my mouth. Damn that Frank Caswell and his bald ass capon!" Much to my humiliation, the jokes circulated faster than the feathers. No doubt fat Marie secretly enjoyed his/her revenge.

CHAPTER TWO

I HAD TRIED TO FORGET THE CHICKEN INCIDENT, BUT IT BECAME A
fresh wound the day my dad showed up to see Mr. Jackson's
Ford. However, the embarrassment was something I was able to
swallow just to see the light return to my father's eyes, if only
momentarily.

July dripped into early August, and Jake and I were dreading
the start of school which was looming ahead. The Indiana
summer days were long, hot, and humid, but I could sense
autumn sneaking around the bend.

One morning, I was sitting at the table eating bacon when
Jake walked through the front door. We never needed to knock at
each other's houses. Jake was like a brother to me, although Dad
referred to him as "a bland fixture who was easy to trip over."
Jake wasn't bland - he was just pale and unremarkable in his
appearance. His hair was the color of cornflakes, and his face
had been seasoned with paprika freckles. I liked Jake's appearance - he reminded me of the rural Indiana corn fields. He was
small in stature, so I towered over him by four inches. I was
stronger too, although I sometimes let him win at arm wrestling
because he claimed that the humiliation of always losing was
stunting his growth.

Jake was not into sports as I was. I had a good arm for baseball and could pass and catch as well as any of the boys at school. Jake did not excel in any physical activities, but he never missed one of my games. His dad and mom didn't either. They often sat in the stands to cheer me on. I knew they were attempting in some way to make up for my nonexistent family life, although they never talked about it. Their presence filled me with a confidence that I wish Jake had. However, even though sports were of no interest to Jake, when it came to knowledge about things like railroads and the stars, architecture, wildlife, and cooking, he was chock full of interesting, random facts.

That morning I shoved a piece of bacon under his nose, but he shook his head to refuse it. "No thanks – bad for the heart."

"That's a rumor that was started by pigs."

"Proof enough they're too smart to eat. Com'on Kat, we're gettin' outta here."

Bacon in hand, I silently got up and followed. I never asked questions because Jake always had a day of untold adventures planned for us. We wandered through the field behind my house, navigating the tall grass and inhaling the delicious aroma of Indiana corn ripening for harvest.

Jake and I always carried long sticks in case an ill-mannered snake might cross our paths. He refused to walk with me unless I also carried a stick. "Did you really fend off a rattlesnake last summer, Jake?" I asked as we traversed through the rows of corn. "Or was it more like a little earthworm on crutches?"

"Yes, it was a man-eating snake, and I was quite heroic. But I may have screamed the whole time … and I may have also soiled my trousers. I'm not sure because I went home and promptly passed out."

Jake had a way of embellishing that always entertained me. He once complained of diarrhea that was so bad it was shooting out of his butt like bottle rockets to the tune of 'The Star-Spangled Banner.' I'm not sure anyone appreciated his humor as much as I did.

On that August morning, Jake stopped to stare at me, as he often did. When we were younger, he had poked fun of my pale green eyes, claiming the unusual color indicated I was possessed by the Devil of Lettuce, and nicknamed me 'Lettuce-stopheles.' I named him 'Saltine' like the cracker and told him to stick out his tongue more often so people could see him. I knew he thought I was pretty, and his opinion was the only one I cared about.

"You've got bacon in your teeth, Lettuce-stopheles," Jake abruptly announced, "but your teeth are perfect." He shoved back my lip with his thumb for a better look.

"Get your dirty thumb out of my mouth!"

"I have a slow tooth." Jake pointed to one front tooth that slightly overlapped the other. "I think it's slowly ruining my James Dean looks." Jake distorted his face, knowing he could get my attention with just a curl of his lip. He raised one eyebrow and made it walk around his forehead, a move he had perfected just to delight me. When I tried to mimic him, I only succeeded in looking like a lunatic. Words were never necessary between us - we could entertain each other with our faces.

After cutting through the cornfields, we settled in our favorite spot to wait for the Wabash Cannonball. No matter how many times we waited for her, it was always thrilling when she streamed into view. Others took her for granted, but we under-stood the power and the promise of that exalted locomotive.

Her soothing sounds forced the cacophony of my own life into the background as we worshiped her from afar. She anchored me to the land, and her consistency gave me the comfort I never had at home.

Jake was on his feet immediately when he heard her bellowing from way around the bend. "Here she comes, the 10:10 - right on schedule heading west from Lafayette to Logansport!" He called out the same thing every time we saw her, but each time it filled me with excitement. I jumped up to join him as we both ran closer to the tracks, gathering discarded glass bottles as we made our way.

Soon I spotted her shiny blue dome approaching, her prominent cowcatcher jutting forward like a finely waxed silver mustache. Her face was adorned with a red flag with a dark blue rectangular inset bearing big yellow letters that identified her majestic arrival - WABASH. "Follow the flag!" we yelled the second we were able to see the train. That was her slogan - and a mighty good one we thought, because in our imaginations, we followed her everywhere.

On the last bend before the Wabash Cannonball reached us, the engineer sounded her whistle again, which was our signal to move in. As the train crawled closer, we started firing the empty soda bottles at her embossed flag. Of course, the object was to hit our target, but we seldom ever got close enough to make contact. I had managed a few times, but Jake could never land one. It didn't matter because it was all part of the greeting process. No disrespect was ever intended. To us, it was exactly the opposite - we wanted her to know we were there for her as her faithful following.

Jake saw a man in the window of the passenger car as the mighty Cannonball streamed by. He immediately launched into a wild tale because we loved to create a story for every face.

"Look! That man with the mustache is meeting his long-lost wife in San Francisco, where they plan to stay at the exclusive Fairmont Hotel."

"Why was she lost?"

"She took the wrong train," he explained, rolling his eyes in hyperbolic exasperation, as though I was expected to know the plot to his story. "The poor thing has been wandering around Salt Lake City for over a year. The husband doesn't know she has been Mormon-ized."

"'Mormonized,' huh?" I took my turn next. "See that lady in the blue hat? She's going to have tea with her friend in the Grand Hall of Union Station in St. Louis. Afterward, they plan to visit the Missouri Botanical gardens-"

"Where her hand gets stuck in a mutant Venus Flytrap!"

"Hey, whose story is this? But you're right. Her friend has to chew the lady's hand off to free her from the ravenous plant."

"So they take the hand home in her matching blue handbag."

Delighted with our own humor, we followed with a round of slapping and shoving each other.

Based on the mood we were in, our conjectures were either funny or dramatic. But Jake always made everything colorful and added a happy ending.

After counting the cars and gathering a few more bottles to return for money for Popsicles at the IGA grocery, we both lay down in the warm grass and focused on the iridescent blue sky. As if on cue, we began singing the first and last verses of the song "The Wabash Cannonball" - made popular by a singer named Roy Acuff, according to Jake's research. We only sang two verses (the only ones we knew, and the only two we cared to know) because the lyrics expressed it all for us:

'Listen to the jingle, The rumble and the roar, as she glides along the woodland through the hills and by the shore.'

We always sang the last line with gusto, belting out the words, *"On the Wabash Cannonball."*

We had learned the tune while hanging out at the Chop-n-Bleed Barbershop. A lot of the old timers in there enjoyed singing, and four of the men were part of a – you guessed it – barbershop quartet. They sang at all the local functions, but they always practiced at the barbershop.

I couldn't afford our local beauty shop, so I usually cut my own hair over the kitchen sink, but once in a while I saved up enough babysitting money to get my hair cut at the barbershop with Jake. It was cheaper than the beauty salon, and the big draw was the singing.

Jake referred to us as the "barbershop duet." Singing was simply another way to honor the rails. After a second chorus of "The Wabash Cannonball," we launched into another Hoosier favorite, "On the Banks of the Wabash":

"Oh, the moonlight's fair tonight along the Wabash ..."

The song's sonorous notes blended into the balmy air with ease. "Do you know a guy named Paul Dresser wrote that tune?"

"I do now. You're going to wear out those encyclopedias of yours. Hey, wait a minute! Did you go to the library without me, dang it?" He knew I loved to go to the library with him. It was our magical clubhouse. "So did you go there solo, Jake, you traitor?"

"Guilty. Dad was lecturing me again about sports, so I ducked out. He still somehow thinks signing me up for baseball will give me abilities that are just not in my genes. In spite of my dazzling good looks, I will never be Mickey Mantle."

"More like Mickey Mouse."

"Hilarious."

"Com'on - we both know you're a world-class klutz, but you make up for it in smarts."

"He definitely does not agree with your evaluation of my acumen. Just because my grades last year were spectacularly inadequate, he thinks I'm mentally deficient."

"No way, Jake. He does not."

"I keep trying to explain how I'm just a painfully slow reader, but that at least I remember most everything I read. I told him I could recite the entire back of the Cheerios box for him, but he wasn't impressed."

"The only thing 'slow' about you is that tooth of yours."

"You're a riot today. I was just concerned because I always feel like I let him down."

"Did he say that?"

"No. But you know how his face does all the talking. It's like a silent movie without the organ music. Anyway, it was too early to wake you, so I slipped out."

"It's okay. We can go later."

We trudged through the grass a bit longer, but my irritation was growing because the gnats were attacking my legs as if they were breakfast sausages. "It's already getting hot," I groused as I slapped another hungry carnivore off my leg.

"Yeah, I'm getting eaten alive too."

"Let's get out of here. You wanna walk to the creek or go hang out under the river railroad bridge?"

"Maybe a little later. Right now, I have something else in mind."

"Oh yeah - what?"

"Let's wait for the next train and hop it."

"Yeah. Right"

"I mean it. Let's hitch a ride."

I looked at Jake in disbelief. I couldn't believe what I was hearing. "You better be joking."

"No, I'm more serious than a five-foot hole in a six-foot boat."

"Have you lost your marbles? Hell no, we are NOT jumping a train! You know train hopping is incredibly dangerous!"

"I'm gonna try, Kat."

"Shut up, Jake. People die hitching rides on trains! What's wrong with you today?"

"You always play it so safe, but being safe won't get you anywhere. Risk has its rewards. Let's live a little."

"Yes, that's my point - let's LIVE, not die!"

"I'm not going to die. If you don't want to jump, it's okay by me. You can stay here."

"Please stop talking, Jake." I covered my ears and started walking ahead of him.

"Kat, don't you think I can do it?"

"I don't care if you can do it! Where is this coming from? Have you gone brain-dead? If you're trying to prove something, just forget it. I'm not going to listen to this ridiculous nonsense!"

"I think it'll be easy. I'll board where the grass is high, so if I fall, I'll have a cushion. We've watched other train jumpers do it. It can't be that hard. That hobo guy Joe only has one arm, and old Doc comes and goes all the time."

"Joe's arm is really strong, and Doc may be old, but he has experience."

"He had to start somewhere."

I could see Jake was revving himself up. I always knew when he was talking himself into something he really didn't believe in. "Jake, you could get maimed - or even paralyzed! Just drop it, dammit!"

He paused for a moment and stared down the rails to some unknown destination. I didn't know what was going through his mind, but when I heard a distant steam whistle, I knew we had to get out of there.

"Com'on, Jake. We're leaving."

As I was turning back toward the pathway to the street, Jake suddenly shouted, "I've gotta do it, Kat! Here she comes!"

My jaw dropped open in shock when Jake started racing toward the tracks. For a split second, I watched him in disbelief. I was stunned and scared and frozen in place. Then without hesitation, I ran after him. My heart pounded against my chest, but my legs kept moving. He had already closed the distance between where I was and the tracks. I was terrified, but I couldn't let him do it alone. I knew Jake needed my strength, just as I always needed his willpower. As with all things, Jake and I were in it together.

CHAPTER THREE

JAKE PICKED UP SPEED THE SECOND HE HEARD THE NEXT TRAIN. HE had memorized the schedule so well he knew there would be little time in between trains for him to chicken out. As he ran along the tracks toward a spot farther down than we usually ventured, I sensed he had been out there alone, planning the escapade and assessing what location would give him his best advantage.

As I ran after him, I noticed he was heading toward a grassy area, just as he had suggested. He heard me behind him and yelled back over his shoulder, "No, Kat - this time it's just me." His hands were clutched, and his shoulders were set with stubborn determination.

By now I had caught up and was close at his heels. My face and hands were sweating, but I felt a sense of excitement unlike anything I had ever felt before. The train was looming closer, and then the whistle sounded. My backbone became rigid with both terror and exhilaration. We stood and watched as the engine passed and a number of freight cars zoomed by in tow.

For a brief second, I thought Jake had changed his mind, but then he turned in my direction and started running alongside the train. I had been behind him, so now he was coming at me full speed. His face was set, and his eyes were hard. I could tell he no longer even saw me. I had to turn and run in the same direction to avoid being trampled.

I heard Jake's steps behind me as we hit gravel. He was closing in on me, and we were both edging closer to the train. Within seconds, a freight car with an open door was at my shoulder. All rational thought abandoned me as I stretched up and caught the bar alongside the door, momentarily swinging in the wind. With the combined force of fear and euphoria, I pulled my legs up into my stomach and rolled into the car. I lay on the wooden car bed with my face pressed flat, hugging the splintered wood with relief. At the same time, I was flushed with unexpected excitement.

Within seconds, I was back on my feet and hanging out the door to see which car Jake had chosen. He would have had to wait for the next open freight car, and I was hoping he had caught one.

As I glanced down the length of the train, I was instantly stricken with horror. Jake was dangling from the handle bar of a freight car about ten cars back, and he couldn't seem to get his legs up onto the platform. He tried several times to swing his legs upward, but each time his effort was weakening. "Jake!" I screamed, just as he let go. Jake momentarily flailed in the wind as the train ejected him. Then he tumbled toward the hard and uneven ground below.

"Jake!" I screamed again as I leaped off the train. It was picking up speed, so the drop was a harsh one. I could feel my ankle give way as I hit the ground, causing me to lurch face-forward into the grass. It took me a few seconds to catch my breath and force the pain from my mind, and then I ran toward the location where Jake had fallen. Dragging my leg, I slowly covered the distance to where I thought I had last seen him. When I stepped over one of his shoes, I was stricken with another wave of panic. Once again, I desperately began to call out his name.

The tall field grasses swallowed my screams, but as I paused long enough to catch my breath, I heard a calm voice answer me, "Over here, Kat."

Jake had landed in a spot in the field where there was a hobo refuge, rife with debris and a collection of odd salvage. His body was atop a pile of broken bottles and strewn wood. As I approached, I could see blood from the cuts on Jake's bare arms, but they did not seem life-threatening. However, his leg was in a hideous position, as though someone had propped it up against his body.

"I think your friend is hurt real bad."

I turned abruptly to see an elderly homeless man behind me. I had seen him before by the hobo camp. He had a pronounced twitch, and he seemed quite confused.

Jake's body was trembling violently, so I knew we had to move fast. "You're going to be okay, Jake. Don't worry. We're going to get you some help."

I was frantic as I looked about. Finally, I spotted a large piece of plywood that had been discarded near the camping spot. I knew I couldn't manage Jake without the aid of the old man, who was staring at Jake with growing distress.

"Sir, can you help me get him onto that piece of plywood so we can carry him toward that house over there at the end of the field?" I tried hard not to cry as I became increasingly worried. "Please, sir?"

After a moment of hesitation, the old man set into action. We got the board as close to Jake as we could so we wouldn't have to move him much. As we slid him onto the board, I realized for the first time how truly small he was. He groaned in pain, but he insisted he was all right. He was trembling, but his face was resolute.

"I'm fine, Kat." Jake set his jaw and looked at me with unwavering determination. "And this gentleman's name is Pete. Right, Pete?"

"Yes, sir." Pete nodded at Jake as he hoisted his end of the board. It was only then that I noticed the old man had an atrophied hand. Pete caught my glance and increased his effort. "Don't worry, I can do it," he murmured.

When we started to walk, I almost fell. I had forgotten about my injured ankle until the searing pain gripped my leg again, causing me to moan loudly. "Set him down a minute, please, Pete."

Nearby on the ground was a filthy discarded shirt. I had to ignore the stench as I wrapped it around my ankle for stability. Once accomplished, we began our trek through the field to the home of Louise Schroeder, a girl I knew from school. I hoped the family would be accommodating.

When Mrs. Schroeder heard Pete banging on the door, she opened it up. "Hello, Pete." When she greeted him by name, I surmised that she had met him before when he was trading work for handouts.

Upon seeing Jake stretched out on the board between us, she looked startled, but after appraising the situation, few words were needed. Mrs. Schroeder called for an ambulance immediately before covering Jake with blankets and offering him a sip of water. She ripped the old shirt off my ankle and tossed it outside before reaching for the first aid kit in the kitchen cupboard. Her movements were rapid and precise. After pulling an ace bandage from the kit, she wrapped it securely around my ankle.

"Sit in that chair, Kat," Mrs. Schroeder directed while Jake was still lying on the floor on his plywood gurney. "Elevate your leg on the other chair. And Pete, you go help yourself to a glass of water and sit down. I'll make you one of my ham sandwiches that you like."

"No need, ma'am."

"Nonsense, Pete. Eating will take your thoughts off all the upset. I'll make us some coffee." Mrs. Schroeder's sense of command was reassuring to us all.

"Thank you, Mrs. Schroeder," I smiled weakly as she placed

an ice pack on my ankle. "Eisenhower could have used you at Normandy."

Jake smiled at me as though he understood that my feeble attempt at humor was for his sake. He was still shaking, but he seemed more alert. "I am so sorry, Kat. I thought I could do it. I really wanted to. Please don't be mad."

"Forget it, Jake. Let's just get your leg fixed. We will go back to safer pastimes, like counting cars and tossing bottles."

He dropped his head back down on the plywood with an expression of defeat.

As I looked down at his gaunt face, I realized I had not given him the reassurance he was looking for. He didn't want to return to our former antics and rituals. He wanted something more life-changing. Then it slowly dawned on me: Jake's ultimate intention was not to just hop a train - he intended to get on that train and not get off.

I was baffled. I knew he and Mr. Jackson had some sort of chasm between them, but not nearly as much as I had with my own father. I had always wanted to escape the confines of a small town with limited opportunity, but Jake's need to escape was driven by something much deeper. It wasn't long before I finally discovered what was driving Jake away from all of us.

CHAPTER FOUR

By THE TIME JAKE GOT OUT OF THE HOSPITAL, SCHOOL HAD STARTED again. That year passed slowly with Jake holed up in his room while he continued to recover. Whenever I could, I visited him at the hospital and then at home, bringing candy bars and library books. I read the books aloud in the animated fashion he loved, although he protested that my impersonation of Little Nell would "kill her off faster than Dickens did." However, our visits were strained because of unanswered questions neither of us wanted to bring up.

Jake had broken both his tibia and his femur, so he was in a cast for months. When the cast was eventually removed, he was left with a permanent limp. He joked about the limp just to make everyone else feel comfortable, and he often did pratfalls in order to entertain me. In spite of his ever-present humor, some-thing had changed. He was working harder than ever to act happy, but his growing depression followed him like a shadow.

I knew his parents sensed it too. They were constantly plan-ning activities to cheer him up. Sometimes George and Gladys had us all pile into the Ford to take it out for a spin. Mr. Jackson always put the top down, even if we had to bundle up. We drove through the scenic Indiana plains with miles of wheat fields laid out before us in an amber angora landscape. When the winds blew, the wheat all waved in one direction, as though urging us to keep moving on. And we did.

We crossed over covered bridges with clear waterfalls rushing beneath. In unison, we always yelled "hello-o-o-o" as we drove through the wood-arched bridges. Without fail, the hollow tunnels answered us back, each with its own unique voice. Most were adorned with hearts and initials that had been carved by lovers over many decades as a pledge of eternal fidelity.

Every bridge told a different story. Sometimes we made up tales about the names carved in the wooden slats, speculating about who got married and who betrayed the other. Jake always added a few colorful offerings, including prison breaks and Indiana's own John Dillinger. The more we laughed, the more ridiculous his contributions were. "That's the rock John Dillinger peed all over every time some fool uttered the name, 'J. Edgar Hoover.' Don't even ask about that brown rock."

Whenever we requested, Mr. Jackson would pull over so we could dangle our feet in the waterfalls. No matter how cold the temperature was, we loved it.

We visited many charming towns within driving distance of Wabash. Franklin was always a favorite, because there was usually an ice cream cone from Betty's involved just to top off the journey. Sometimes Gladys, Jake, and I sat in the car eating ice cream and playing word games while George ran into the Elks Club for a quick drink.

I always marveled at how Mr. Jackson could have just one drink and never take more. He was always mindful of the time and never got drunk or loud or behaved the way my father did. I wasn't old enough to understand my father's lack of control, although I eventually did learn to understand his pain.

The school year was almost over, and I had spent many nights sleeping on the extra bed in Jake's room. My dad was working the graveyard shift, so he never seemed to notice whether or not I came home. Jake and I went by the house once in a while just to make sure it was not in flames or the roof hadn't fallen in. Goodwin told us my dad was drinking even more than usual, so we always feared disaster.

We did hear of an incident where Sam Goodwin fatally shot Marie the rooster, who had developed a habit of sitting under Sam's window when loudly announcing daybreak. Ever since the chicken incident, Marie's inner clock was off schedule, so the confused rooster usually thought daybreak was around three o'clock in the morning. Rumor was that Sam, sleep-deprived and fed-up, was trying to scare the naked and befuddled creature when he "accidentally" grabbed his rifle instead of his BB gun. Although Sam swore it was an accident, the neighbors hailed him as a hero.

Word down at the Chop-n-Bleed was that when my dad discovered the rock-stiff rooster, he broke a window in Sam Goodwin's house and threw the reeking carnage into the kitchen. According to locals, Marie had a note attached with the message, "Best regards, Frank." Somehow, I took solace in hearing Dad was still acting like Dad.

Although I loved and missed my dad, staying at Jake's house was what I imagined staying in a hotel would be like. Growing up, I had always made my own meals. I existed on a diet of grilled cheese sandwiches, peanut butter, corn flakes, and anything that came in a can. Dad never ate with me - he would just heat up a can of soup when he felt like eating, which was very seldom. Alcohol was his main source of food. Therefore, at the "Jackson No-tell Motel," as we came to call it, breakfasts before school were the best part of the day.

Gladys made pancake breakfasts and packed a lunch for me every day. She sometimes even kissed me on the cheek before I left. I had never been kissed before (except by my old dog Roller, who unfortunately had lived up to his name by rolling under a moving John Deere tractor), so sometimes it was hard for me to accept the affection, although I craved it even more than her pancakes.

Our school was an old brick building just a few blocks away. Jake still wasn't attending class, so I rushed back to his home every day to teach him the lessons. Although he was a slow reader, he was a fast learner. We always finished in record time before I shared the daily local gossip.

I had discovered boys recently and had a terrible crush on a classmate named Ben Coleman. When I sensed Jake was a bit jealous about my desire to spend time with Ben, I described how Ben reminded me of him but was indeed a poor substitute. Jake seemed satisfied.

"I'll bet he can't paddle his oar like I can."

"No, Jake, and I heard he can't dock his boat either." We could carry on like that forever because we found double entendres to be endlessly entertaining.

Staring at the constellation of glow-in-the-dark stars Jake had glued to his ceiling (one of the constellations was in the conspicuous shape of a male appendage), Jake and I made a habit of talking and laughing late into the night.

In spite of our bond, I could sense that he was slowly disconnecting from me the way he had from his dad. I assumed it was supposed to be like that with families - periods of happiness and periods of troubles. But one night, as we were lying in our separate beds, Jake seemed especially distracted.

"You okay, Jake?"

"Yeah, I guess."

"What's up with you these days? You seem to be drifting away, and I hate that."

"Yeah ... maybe that's true. I'm sorry."

"Did I do something to make you angry?"

"No, it's not your fault. Really."

"Then why have you withdrawn? What's going on with you?"

"I've just been uncomfortable. I don't feel right about something. We have never had secrets and-"

"What secrets? We don't have secrets, do we?"

"Well, maybe but ... gee whiz, Kat, there are things I'm not supposed to mention around you and-" Jake hesitated while he tried to link together the words he needed to explain the silence that separated us. "This is eating me alive. I'm sure you'll find out sooner or later, and when you do, you'll never forgive us for not telling you." I noticed that Jake's voice had taken on an odd pitch I had never heard before.

I abruptly sat up in bed, a sense of dread washing over me. "Tell me what? Spit it out, dammit! Is it my dad? Is he sick?" I could barely get the words out of my mouth - and I was not prepared for his answer.

"No, Kat, it's your mom." Jake looked down and covered his face with his hands.

"My mom?" His words confused me. He had never known my mom, so I was shocked to hear him mention her. "What about her? What are trying to say?"

"Your mom didn't die of tuberculosis."

"Yes she did, Jake. I was two. You know that."

"No. I know that's what you were told - and believe. But the truth is ... she had a psychotic break."

I reeled back, stunned by his words. "Stop it! Just shut up, Jake. That isn't funny!"

"Kat, please. You wanted the truth. You're my best friend, and I owe it to you to tell you what I know. Your mom was mentally ill. She became violent, so she was institutionalized at Indiana Central State Hospital for the Insane." The information spilled out of him in a stunning blow to my chest.

"Shut up! Shut the hell up, Jake! You're a sadistic, rotten liar!"

"I'm so sorry. I'm so damn sorry."

I was so shocked all I could do was stare at him. Nausea washed over me as I studied his face. I could tell by his expression that he was telling me the truth - an unspeakable truth.

"Say something, Kat. Please say something."

I dropped onto the bed and tried to get my bearings. "Are you telling me my mother is mentally ill but still alive?"

33

"I don't know if she is alive. I suppose it's possible." Jake's face conveyed complete helplessness.

"How long have you known this?"

"Several months. I overhead George and Gladys talking, so I made them tell me. Don't hate them, please! They just wanted to protect you, Kat."

Jake's relief from the weight of secrecy was almost palpable, but in that moment, the burden and anger became mine to carry. "How could you keep that from me? I trusted you more than anyone in the world, but you were hiding a piece of my life that wasn't yours to hide! You participated in making my life a monstrous lie! How could you do that to me?"

My ability to trust was stolen from me that night, and without warning, I became ungrounded. My past had been manufactured, and I felt as though I no longer even knew who I was. What was most shocking was that the people I loved the most in my life had been the architects of that lie.

I punched Jake in his chest as hard as I could, and then I ran out the door and headed for the field. Jake tried to follow me, but he couldn't keep up. "Leave me alone," I screamed, "Leave me alone! I hate you!"

I know Jake was calling out my name, but the only words I could hear were those of the truth he had finally disclosed: My mother had not lost her life when I was two years old. She had lost her sanity.

CHAPTER FIVE

By the time I stopped running through the field, I had reached the hobo encampment. I dropped down beside a small group of travelers and stared ahead at the tracks. A few of them noticed I was crying and shaking, but no one interfered. They nodded and continued talking as though my presence was nothing unusual. In their lives, I suppose it wasn't.

That day passed into nighttime, and that night melded into days without direction in a suspension of time. I thought I was just catching my breath, but I stayed for weeks. The field comforted me. Jake and I had spent many nights sleeping in his back yard under the stars, so the outdoors was more of a home to me than almost anywhere. The open air gave me the freedom to stay or to run, but I had nowhere else to go. I couldn't go back to Jake's house, and I couldn't go home.

The encampment itself was as familiar to me as any other place in town, and the itinerant workers who passed through town had never frightened me. Many times, Jake and I had sat with the campers around their campfires, so I was somewhat familiar to them as well.

School had ended, so I had no place to be, and nowhere else I wanted to go. I needed time to organize my thoughts before confronting my father, who had lied to me about my mother's death. During that time, I ate and slept with the hobos near the tracks. I was too jumbled up inside to worry about safety or comfort.

It took time for the itinerant workers to accept me. At first they did not engage me, as I was more of a curiosity, but eventually I was just another fixture in their outdoor community.

I often washed in the creek like they did, and I accepted their handouts. Old Pete and his buddies would bring back buckets of water pilfered from hose bibs at the houses along the tracks. Others would contribute hamburger and hot dogs purchased with the change they had managed to panhandle. They would cook them over the open fire and insist I eat something. I did, but it was purely mechanical.

I sneaked home from time to time to get clean clothes or to clean up properly, and I always would bring back whatever sandwich fixings I could find. I was too adrift to sleep in my bed, and I did not want to see my father. I knew the Jacksons had been by my house to look for me, because there was fresh soup in the refrigerator, which I left for my dad. The house was more of a mess than usual, with cigarette butts in every ashtray and empty bottles lined up on the porch. I grabbed an unfinished bottle of whiskey to take back to the camp with me.

Although I was underage, I started drinking at night by the campfire. I welcomed the numbness, which helped me to understand the reasons my dad hid his emotions in a bottle. He had every right to try to stifle the pain. But he had no right to lie to me about my mother or to take away the one thing I believed would have made me whole - maybe I could have known my mother.

Every day, different train jumpers came and went from Wabash, leaping on and off the trains as though our little encampment was a depot. Some newcomers were surprised to see me, while others were indifferent, but most were respectful. I sensed an unspoken bond among the train riders - we were "us," while others were "them." We all shared something in common - the open air and lack of roots allowed for freedom from whatever each of us needed to leave behind.

There was a core group who frequented Wabash as their base. Many of them had led interesting lives before becoming homeless. Leland went to dental school before going to war, but after witnessing so much brutality, he could never reestablish his life in Scranton.

Leland once told me, "I just feel more comfortable with my rail mates. After the war, I tried to go back home, but I couldn't fit in. I even did a bit in jail for lifting food. One day I just hopped a train and took off. I doubt if anybody ever noticed I was missing. I've covered the rails for nigh some twenty years, but I like it here in these parts best. It's familiar."

"So you don't miss your old life at all?"

"Well, come to think about it, I sure miss my piano. I could play a mean honky-tonk melody or two." Doc moved his fingers as if playing a keyboard.

"I sure wish I could have heard you play." Leland fascinated me. He carried himself like an old country gentleman. His white hair and straight posture gave him an air of dignity. "Why do the others call you, 'Doc'?" I inquired.

"I had a little education, so these fellas treat me special. It may not be much, but every man has to have a bit of self-respect. This here is a good group of reg'lars. We get the occasional felon, but most are itinerant workers ridin' the rails looking for work. Wabash is a mighty good place to stay. The local cops and the railroad bulls who patrol the rails don't try to run us outta here like they do in other towns."

There were tales of great tragedy as well. Mary, a wiry and silent camper, had lost her husband and baby in a car accident according to Doc. Mary was now traveling the rails looking for seamstress work. I tried to talk to her, but she always politely indicated her preference to sit by herself. I could see she was terribly sad, so I didn't press her.

Sometimes I shared some food with Mary, and I was happy to accept one of her tea bags in return. One day I brought back a thimble I had found while walking in the field after dropping by to check on my dad. I saved it for her because it was the only pink thimble I had ever seen.

"It's a good'un," she nodded when I gave it to her, shooting me a rare smile.

The person I spent the most time with was young Joe, who had lost an arm in a combine accident. He couldn't find steady employment, and he couldn't deal with the way people reacted to him. His body seemed off-balance, but it didn't bother me at all. I think he appreciated my acceptance of his appearance, because he began to take an interest in me and to guide me to make sure I could take care of myself.

Charles was the saddest of all. His face was grossly disfigured as a result of devastating injuries from the Korean War. He was almost unbearable to look at, and he knew it. He had a mask he sometimes wore, but often he yanked it off in irritation and rubbed the mangled tissue that tentatively clung to the framework of his face. Sometimes I heard him moan during the night, which was sad and unsettling.

It was hard for Charles to talk, so he didn't say much, and he always sat by himself when he needed to eat. Once I saw Doc chopping carrots and green beans he had pilfered from a nearby farm. He minced them very fine, using his pen knife and the lid of a coffee can for a cutting surface. When he handed the mixture to Charles, I turned away and pretended not to notice.

On the few occasions when a new drifter joined our camp, Doc made sure no one commented about Charles's appearance. "He's a fine soldier and a good man," Doc pronounced.

The "Boxcar Willies," as they called themselves, seemed to have a language of their own, which I picked up quickly. Their encampment was its own society, and no one asked many questions about my circumstances. My solitude was simply accepted.

I was at the camp for more than a month before Jake and Mr.

Jackson spotted me one morning as I was returning from my house. Several times I had seen them driving slowly along the streets bordering the field, the bright yellow of Marilyn's paint standing out in contrast to the gray of my world. I knew they were looking for me, but I was not ready to confront them.

The day Jake finally saw me, he called out my name, but I headed straight back to the encampment. After that, Jake and Mr. Jackson came by fairly regularly to check up on me, but they kept their distance. Jake's limp was still bad, so I always noticed him coming across the field. Even though I was not ready to have any sort of conversation with Jake and Mr. Jackson, they always inquired of my welfare and left food and books for me with Pete and Doc.

Often Jake's packages included a note. Usually, his messages were full of remorse, but sometimes they were intended to cheer me. Once he included an amusing, hand-crafted necklace made of Cheerios and cotton balls with a crudely drawn price tag of $60. Another package contained a drawing of him swinging from a noose wearing only a Viking hat, which made me laugh out loud.

I missed Jake, but I needed time to find my direction. I knew it wouldn't be long before Mr. and Mrs. Jackson would call the authorities, but for the time being, they were giving me the space I needed to survive.

Every day I watched the trains go by, but I didn't have the motivation to throw bottles without Jake. During those nomadic days, Joe and I passed the time jumping on and off trains. Although Joe only had one arm, that arm was remarkably strong, so he could swing up with ease. He always went first, and I would board several cars behind. We liked to ride a short distance before hopping off as our unwitting iron and steel hostess slowed down to enter a bend. The thrill of the danger was the only emotion I wanted to feel. It was the only thing that made me feel alive.

Joe knew the route well. He taught me to get as close to the depots as possible for boarding and dismounting so the reduced train speeds would work in my favor. Once in a while, our timing would be off and a station master or a passenger waiting on the platform would spot us. There was nothing much they could do but shake their heads and continue with their business.

Joe took pride in being my mentor. "You never want to deck a car. It's crazy to try to climb to the top, and a fast train will throw you off her. You could lose your life that way, girl."

"Got it," I reassured him.

"And don't ride the blinds at the front of the baggage cars. Standin' on the couplers is real dicey - if there's a sharp jolt, you can easily fall between the cars. Just stick to what you know. You're good at hoisting yourself up, but don't go doing nothin' tricky."

I followed Joe's instructions carefully. I had a few narrow misses, but I became quite expert at hopping. Joe also taught me how to hit the ground properly - to lean forward and start rolling upon impact so the pressure of landing would not be centered in my feet. My ankle still hurt at times, so I tried to follow his technique precisely. At the end of each day, my muscles were always very sore. The adrenaline rush distracted me from my situation, and as foolish as it was, the constant danger helped me to ignore the anger brewing inside me.

Sometimes, I caught a glimpse of Jake standing quite a distance down the rails. Even in the distance, I noticed his posture bent by the weight of defeat. A burden too heavy to carry had been forced upon him, which I knew was unfair to him too. Had it been at my father's direction that the Jacksons never told me? Had it been Mr. Jackson's decision?

During my weeks at the encampment, I pieced together the life-long hints and clues to a puzzle I had not even known existed. All the years of furtive glances and conversations that abruptly fell to silence when I entered a room started to make sense.

In my mind, I replayed scenes I had dismissed at the time,

assuming the disapproving glances had something to do with my dad. Other times I concluded that the odd looks were a result of my wardrobe - masculine leftovers from Jake until I grew taller than he was, or old work clothes from my father after I sprouted up to his height.

Who else knew the truth? Did neighbors take pity? I remembered the day Louise Schroeder brought some dresses to school in a brown grocery bag, a gift from her and her family. Unfortunately, they were much too small because I had started developing breasts at an early age, but I kept the bag at the bottom of my closet like hidden treasure.

I accepted that I was different from other girls. I didn't have a mother to style my hair or teach me about boys or menstruation, but I did learn to hold my head high and withstand the glances because I thought I knew who I was. I *believed* in who I was. Now I didn't believe in anything.

At night I dreamed about my mother. I had created a mental image of her long ago. When you have never known your mom and have only one blurry photo, it's easy to imagine that mother as whatever you want her to be.

Because Jake and I were railroad fans, my mother became part of that world in my imagination. When we read that the Wabash line connected with the Southern Belle line in Kansas City, we were enthralled. He and I both thought "Southern Belle" was a magnificent name for a railroad. We even discovered there had been a Miss Southern Belle contest, and a woman named Margaret Landry from Baton Rouge, Louisiana, won the title. I saw her picture and thought she was beautiful, so I affixed her image to my mother – graceful and feminine (and no doubt having access to free train rides all over the United States, Jake surmised).

My self-created mother was a perfect mother. She wore flouncy dresses and taught me how to dance in a beautiful drawing room in some resplendent house nestled among the towering Louisiana oak trees draped in Spanish moss.

Jake and I even found a train poster of a woman in a ruffled dress standing on a balcony of an antebellum home waving her handkerchief at a passing train. To me, it was almost mystical. I often pictured myself with her on that balcony waving to the passersby.

The woman in the beautiful dress read stories to me at night, recounting tales of exciting train journeys. Together we ate in imperial dining cars and bunked in private sleeper cars. Those visions had kept me company through many lonely nights of my childhood. The mother I created was mentally sound and so lovely she floated through my mind like the scent of magnolias. Although I knew that mother was a fantasy, even that consoling fantasy had been taken from me, leaving nothing in its place.

CHAPTER SIX

ONE EARLY MORNING, I SAW THE YELLOW FORD AGAIN. NO MATTER how down I was, she always stirred my heart. Unexpectedly, I found myself walking to her as if drawn to the world of hope she had always represented - a hope I no longer had but desperately wanted to find again.

It was now late August, so the weather was cooperating, although the nights had been cooler. We slept "under cover of moon," as Joe described it. He gave me rolled up clothes from his bindle to use as a cushion for my head. I had snatched a blanket from home, and Leland taught me to cover myself with newspapers to protect against the late-night temperature drop.

The camp dwellers had created a makeshift lean-to out of several old tarps tied to a spindly tree with rope and bungee cords. The opposite ends were fastened to the remnants of an old chimney still standing upright in the field like a brick centurion - a reminder that a house once existed among the rows of corn. Although the tree and the chimney seemed strangely out of place in the field, the shelter was convenient during the occasional summer rains.

The transients collected blankets and even a clear shower curtain liner in order to make the area as comfortable as possible.

The ground was covered with bits of carpet pieces which, although shabby and worn, provided adequate protection from the elements. I was actually very impressed at what they had managed to piece together over time, noting how the clear shower curtain made the ground almost waterproof. I tried to do my part by adding an old plastic chair cover. The Furniture Assassin would have approved.

One afternoon, while helping to tighten the tarp, I glanced down and was astounded by what I saw. I started laughing so hard that I was in tears. I'm sure my companions were wondering what kind of person was living among them, but I couldn't believe what was beneath my feet. I had to look twice to make sure I wasn't imagining things. The tapestry of ground cover included a very old and tattered floor mat from a car. In the middle was a glue-like, indestructible glob of gum, long-ago hardened, yet still stubbornly clinging to its host. I knew the gum had to be Juicy Fruit. "Hello, Sunliner," I chuckled, "I'm glad you found a new home."

―――――

With nowhere to shower regularly and blankets full of ants and gnats, I was growing increasingly uncomfortable. During my stay at the campsite, I had to relieve myself in the field like everyone else.

Fall would soon be closing in, so I expected the nights to get harsher. To make matters worse, although my period had stopped when I first ran away, I had started to menstruate again. There was nothing convenient to use for toiletries, and my cramps were very bad. I knew it was time to leave. I still couldn't face my father, so there was only one place I could go.

Without forethought, I kept walking toward the edge of the field, where I spotted Mr. Jackson and Jake waiting in the Ford. I don't know how they knew I would return to them that day, but I suspected they had planned to sit there until I did. When I got into the car, there was no discussion expected. Jake silently placed one of Mrs. Jackson's hand-crocheted throws over my lap, and then he handed me a cheese and mustard sandwich he had carefully wrapped in wax paper.

Mr. Jackson started the car. He paused for a moment before he turned to me and quietly announced, "We're taking you home to clean up, dear. It's time."

I began to shake violently. "Yes, it's time," I nodded.

———

Gladys Jackson was waiting for our return. She threw her arms around me when I entered and rocked me against her.

"Kat! Oh, Kat, you're back! Oh God, I am so terribly sorry for everything, dear," she apologized.

Although I could see she had been crying, I offered nothing to relieve her guilt or shame. I did not have the capacity to look at the bigger picture. I stared at the floor, suddenly and irrationally longing to lie down on its cool tiles.

"Please forgive us. We tried to do what was right. But I know we failed you."

I gently pulled away from her, fighting the urge to flee again. "Does everyone know about my mother?" I couldn't bear the thought of others knowing my past, while I had believed a lie for so many years.

"No, no one knows the truth about what happened back then. Honey, your father demanded we not tell you."

"How could he do such a thing?"

"He didn't want you to fear it could happen to you. The illness, I mean. Her doctors told him it was best to keep the information from you. It was his request, and we felt helpless. We tried to honor his wishes-"

"But everyone was wrong!" Jake interjected. "I told you she needed to hear the truth!"

"Jake is right - I want the truth! Is my mother dead? Is she?"

As I demanded an answer, I was filled with grief. I had always loved my mother in the way that an inherent love for a missing parent lives inside all lonely and abandoned children.

Jake pulled out a chair for me just as my legs started to buckle. The months of tension were giving way to exhaustion.

Gladys looked at George before directing her gaze back at Jake and me. "We tried to get some information, Kat, but we were unable to get any confirmation if she is still alive."

"Then take me there." The room fell silent as everyone looked at each other in shock.

Mr. Jackson tried to put a hand on my shoulder. "But, Kat, Central State Hospital is not the kind of place-"

Depleted of energy as I was, I pulled myself back to a standing position and turned to leave. "Take me there or I'm leaving this town for good."

Although Indianapolis is only about eighty-five miles from Wabash, the drive seemed interminable. All four of us went, and Jake and I rode in the back in silence. Periodically Gladys reached back to squeeze my hand, but I was frozen in my seat. The roar of the V-8 engine seemed like the only thing that kept my heart beating.

As we turned onto West Vermont, there loomed ahead an imposing institutional building of dark red brick, an evil stain in the middle of the innocent blue Indiana sky. I immediately knew it was Central State Hospital for the Insane. The building was several stories tall, with towers jutting from the roof line at intervals. The building had a number of wings attached, and there were many narrow windows streaked with shadows – wary eyes staring back at me with equal abhorrence.

We drove slowly as we looked for a place to enter. When we passed one area, we spotted inmates roaming about a grassy yard. Many made almost inhuman noises as they called out to imaginary beings that existed only in their minds. Other lost creatures were wracked with involuntary, spasmodic movements. Orderlies mingled among them, sometimes struggling with confused inmates as they tried to disrobe. As we passed by, one orderly admonished a disoriented patient who was relieving himself in the yard.

We were astonished to witness a number of spectators lined up along the fence, gawking and taunting the inmates unmercifully. The more the inmates reacted, the more the spectators mimicked them as though they were monkeys in a zoo. One disturbed patient rubbed her privates continuously, while another rocked back and forth and occasionally slammed her head against a large oak tree that dominated the yard. At the edge of the yard closest to the fence, a woman picked at her skin and cackled back at the onlookers, who encouraged her with insults. It was a barbaric scene.

I wanted desperately to meet my mother if she was alive, but I couldn't help but wonder if my mother was among the insane lot who howled and called out for their lost sanity. I considered the fact that if she was alive, she could be an empty vessel diminished by medication and robbed of memory – a vacant being who would have no recognition of her daughter. I also knew it would break my heart if she didn't know me.

"Are you still breathing, Kat?" Jake spoke in hushed tones, as though his voice might shatter me.

All I could manage was a nod.

Gladys suddenly grabbed Mr. Jackson's arm. "Stop, George. Stop now!" As soon as he pulled to the curb, she jumped out and vomited in the grass. No one spoke because we all could feel the dread churning in our guts. Mr. Jackson reached into the glove compartment and handed Gladys some napkins. After she tidied herself up, she got back into the car and regained her composure. "Excuse me, everyone. Let's continue, please."

We parked by the entrance of an imposing building and knocked on the door for several minutes. While waiting on the sun-streaked stoop, we heard periodic screams as they briefly escaped their brick confines before falling back again into the hidden interior. Finally, a stern-faced attendant allowed us entrance into the building.

The front section of the building was designed like a private home, with a small foyer decorated with photos and stylish velvet curtains. It was a bizarre contrast to the sickness all around us. "We are here to check on a patient," Mr. Jackson, announced.

"You'll have to come back during visiting hours, sir," the attendant instructed as he nodded toward the door.

"No, I made an appointment with your administrator."

"I don't know where he is."

Reaching into his pocket, Mr. Jackson pulled out a wad of bills and shoved it into the attendant's hand. "This should help you locate him."

Within seconds, an elderly man descended the stairs. I sensed he had been waiting on the landing, listening to the commotion. "I am Dr. Alfred Strat," he stated as a way of introduction. "I am the director. How may I help you?"

"I'm George Jackson. We have an appointment. We're here to find out if a former patient is still alive."

"Oh, yes, of course. I didn't realize the time. I remember speaking with you. As I told you, we are not allowed to disclose information about patients via telephone."

"Well, we're here now. I need to know if Marie Caswell is still alive. She was admitted about fourteen years ago or so - maiden name Bryant. Here is her Social Security number." He pressed a piece of paper into the director's hand. "If she has passed, I would like to see her death certificate."

Dr. Strat eyed Mr. Jackson up and down, as if analyzing his motives. "Okay. Sit in the parlor there while I check the records. The younger members of your party will have to wait outside."

Jake, who had been almost silent our entire trip, finally spoke up. "We're not leaving. This is her daughter. She has a right to stay."

Strat eyed Jake curiously as if noting his determination. "Suit yourselves," he shrugged as he went to search his files.

The wait was longer than we anticipated. I was chewing on my knuckles when Jake grabbed my elbow and pulled me to my feet. "Com'on, Kat, let's walk a bit. It will ease your nerves." We attempted to exit the building, but the foyer door had been locked sometime after our entry. Noting my increasing panic, Jake abruptly turned me to face the opposite direction and led me down an adjacent hallway to a more clinical part of the edifice in his attempt to occupy me.

Ahead of us was a small, damp amphitheater. Under the dim lights, we could see tiered seating, each semi-circle level intended to give an unobstructed view of the central operating arena. A light was centered above to direct the attention of spectators toward whatever procedure might be taking place on any given day. I had heard reports of inhumane treatment at the hospital, so I struggled in vain to suppress images of sadistic experiments.

When Jake reached out to hold my hand, I didn't resist. "What if she is alive, Jake?" I was fearful that Strat might appear with a woman who had once been my mother – a woman who would see me as a stranger and didn't even know who she herself was. The thought terrified me.

"Kat, we need to go back to the parlor," Jake quietly urged. "This is too-"

"Wait!" I interrupted. From my vantage point, I could see into the adjacent room. Light from a high window reflected onto a table located next to the wall. An ominous machine, square in shape with dials on top, was alongside the table. A headset mounted on the wall connected to the box, while snake-like wires reached out from the mechanism as if seeking their prey.

Jake yanked me away from the door. "Electroshock therapy. This is horrible. Let's go back." I squeezed his hand harder.

"State of the art," I heard a voice utter.

I was startled to see Strat enter the amphitheater from a back stairway with a black leather-bound book tucked beneath his arm. He was alone.

"I think I found her," he announced, gesturing for us to follow him back to the parlor.

George and Gladys, who had come looking for us, met us near the curved wood staircase. "Come sit in my office," Strat directed.

We followed in silence to a room strewn with stacks of papers and books. The office was dim, but slices of the remaining sunlight entered through tall, heavily draped windows before falling upon the ornate carpet that was the only source of color. Strat lowered his hand as a sign for us to be seated.

"Yes, it seems Mrs. Caswell was here for a very long time. We have a lot of inmates, over twenty-five hundred total, with a disproportionate number in the women's building, but I remember her now. An extremely agitated type, she was. Schizophrenic."

As I stared at him, his mouth seemed to be moving in slow motion. "'Was'?"

"Yes. She has passed."

It was not until I heard his words that I realized how much I had convinced myself my mother might still be alive. Mr. and Mrs. Jackson had cautioned me, based on their long-ago conversations with my father, not to hold onto hope. But dreams of a mother, damaged or otherwise, were all I had held onto since learning of her fate.

I quickly thrust my head between my knees as dark spots rushed before my eyes like meteorites. Then I fell against Jake and buried my head in his chest. Upon witnessing my distress, Gladys came around behind my chair and pressed her body against my back to comfort me.

Strat closed his record book before looking up at us with an apathetic expression varnished over his face. "I'm the doctor who performed her lobotomy."

———

We were all shocked into silence. I had to hold the arms of the chair to keep from collapsing. I could picture my mother lying on an operating table, while curious onlookers blithely watched the doctor probe her brain.

After a moment, Strat filled the silence. "As I explained, she was highly agitated. After her intake, it took us some time to balance her medication. However, her rage was worse after each visit from her husband. We felt it was in her best interest not to allow visitors thereafter. Even him." He spoke of my parents as though there was no connection to the girl sitting in front of him - a child who had lost her mother and then watched her father lose all hope.

Strat continued his robotic recitation. "Lobotomy is a state-of-the-art procedure designed to control highly reactive personalities. Advanced medicine." He glanced down at his file before adding, "Hers was a procedure that was not a success. Most unfortunate."

His monotone was too emotionless, too callous, too finite for me to withstand. I sprang out of my chair, leaned across his desk, and screamed into his face, "You destroyed my mother's brain with a metal probe, and all you can say is, 'most unfortunate'? You robbed her of her mind!"

Strat's face was completely nonreactive. "Her mind was already gone, my dear. If you want to see her, I'll have the orderly escort you to our area of unmarked graves."

"Yes, thank you." Mr. Jackson snapped. He stood as a signal for us to leave before reaching out to assist Gladys, who was visibly trembling. Jake and I were already standing, each of us too overwhelmed to listen to the doctor any longer. "Let's all get some fresh air. Dr. Strat, I will need you to mail me the death certificate," Mr. Jackson demanded.

"Yes, of course. Incidentally, the lobotomy was not the cause of her death," Strat announced just as we were exiting.

We all turned back to him in confusion. Strat appeared satisfied to be delivering information which would absolve him of failure. "The procedure I executed was hailed by my colleagues as exemplary, but often a patient's condition is beyond the scope of medicine. Due to the ongoing schizophrenia with which Mrs. Caswell suffered, other aggressive treatments were required. Those procedures were also unsuccessful. She died while restricted."

I was momentarily confused by his words. "Restricted?"

"Yes. While confined in a jacket, she severed her own tongue."

This time I was the one who vomited.

———

For a long time, the four of us stood on the sidewalk outside the asylum, holding each other tightly as the sun dropped into the sky as if it had also surrendered to defeat. "Mr. Jackson, please can we go?" I whispered. "I don't want to see a grave that doesn't even acknowledge her existence."

There were people all around me, but I felt totally alone. Although I had finally learned the truth, I needed to hold on to the illusion of my mother a few minutes longer. I wanted to retreat into my imagination where I could see my mother once again, circling a dance floor in lavender organza, a bright smile lighting her face. As I stared up at the dark brick walls, my heart longed to see gay colors again. I found my refuge in the bright yellow Ford Crestline as she gently carried us back to Wabash.

CHAPTER SEVEN

IT TOOK ME WEEKS TO RECOVER FROM OUR VISIT TO CENTRAL STATE Hospital, and I still wasn't ready to confront my father, but at least my life was no longer a question mark. I wasn't religious, but I prayed for my tortured mother. I never went to church, so I really did not know how to pray. As with all things, I shared my concerns with Jake, who offered to help.

"I'm not the authority on anything godly, Kat. But I'll do some research."

A short time later, Jake returned from the library and promptly informed me that God did not care about technique. "According to my research, God's not a stickler for ceremony, Kat, as long as you don't pray while killing puppies."

Jake's mother heard his comment and told him it was inappropriate and inaccurate, so he should apologize.

"I'm sorry, Kat," he said contritely. "I guess God's okay with killing puppies."

Gladys was beside herself, but to me, Jake's droll humor was like a prayer.

Jake and I soon returned to our familiar routine of trainspotting, which Jake defined as a kind of medicine. Watching the Wabash Cannonball barrel down the tracks soothed the ache in my chest. As we lay in the field, I shared with Jake my fears of having a mental defect like my mother. He insisted I was perfectly normal, and if the "agitation" which led me to scream at Strat was abnormal behavior, then the authorities would have to institutionalize anyone within spitting-distance of such an exasperating man.

Over time, Jake had taken to calling Strat "Dr. Shat." We made stupid jokes about him in order to combat the ugly memories of the events of that day. Jake, in his best newscaster voice announced: "Dr. Shat is a master in his field. His self-administered lobotomy was a raging success and hailed by his colleagues as exemplary. He now jerks off daily and shits his pants on command. Hence the name 'Shat.'"

Mr. Jackson further alleviated some of my fears of inheriting insanity when he interrupted our conversation one day just as Jake was doing a rousing impression of Strat. When we looked up, he was standing in the doorway with Gladys at his side. They both looked tentative, but Mr. Jackson was straightforward. "Her death certificate says she had a brain tumor, Kat – a complete anomaly. It was discovered postmortem when they did an autopsy. You need not fear it will be inherited."

I had not discussed my fears with him or Gladys, but apparently, I wore my concerns on my face. The idea of someone cutting my dead mother's brain open for a specimen, rather than allowing her to finally find rest, roused my ire once again. However, the assurance of knowing I was not necessarily destined to end up in a hospital for the insane gave me some welcome relief.

———

After spring and summer finally passed and we had begun our senior year of high school, I was able to compartmentalize the memories of the mental hospital in a locked box in my brain. I made plans to go to Franklin College, so Jake immediately applied as well. "You're not going alone. You, Lone Ranger - me, Tonto."

"I think you mean 'Me, Trouble,' but that's great news!"

We loved the sleepy town of Franklin, and the school had a very good reputation. Almost immediately, I applied for a hardship scholarship, and my prospects looked good. (Poverty has its advantages.)

I knew my time in Wabash was limited, so I started going home every weekend to check on my father. He was always relieved to see me, but happy to be free of the responsibility of caring for me now that I was living with the Jacksons full-time.

One early fall afternoon when I was dropping off some soup Gladys had prepared, I finally got up the nerve to tell him I knew the truth and had tried to locate my mother at Central State Hospital for the Insane. His lower jaw went slack, and a flash of dark anger etched his face.

"I wish you had told me, Dad," I said. "How could you keep that information from me all these years?"

He was sitting at the table, and he didn't look at me. His fingers dug at the wood tabletop as if he were trying to leave fingerprints as some lasting proof of his existence. "I tried to help her – I really did."

"I know you did, Dad, but why didn't you tell me?"

"The doctors ... they said that it would be bad for you. You were just a little girl, Kat."

"But maybe I could have visited-"

"No," he said, cutting me off, "Don't even think like that! They wouldn't allow us to see her. She was violent and uncontrollable. We lost her ... and the bastards never even let me bring her home to rest."

"But you didn't lose *me*. You replaced me with whiskey." His head snapped back as my words struck him, and I immediately regretted my accusation.

"It wasn't intentional, Kat. It was all just too much to live with." As angry as I still was, the sadness in his face was painful to see.

"But we still could have been a family, you and me."

"A family of ghosts."

I did not answer, as I knew there was no response that could ever create a different outcome. My mother wasn't Miss Southern Belle. She was dead. And my dad's inner flame had burned out a long time ago. A lie had lived in our house for so long, there was an insurmountable wall between us. We each lived in our own worlds, and the only connection was a shared loss.

———

Now it was my turn to live. I decided to leave my past in the distance where it belonged. My goal was to graduate from college, and then Jake and I would take a train to California.

"This is a great plan," Jake declared as we mapped our route on the rails and memorized which trains we would catch and what cities we would visit along the way. "You'll see – with all that California sun and surf, our days will be full of *Life Magazine* moments."

I loved Jake's optimism. We decided that once we hit California, we would both get jobs and save our money to take a trip on the Orient Express to Paris. At that point in our planning, Jake hopped up and imitated the hunchback of Notre Dame, which had me in stitches.

I never became bored with his antics, and I knew he would be great to travel with. But Jake would never make it to California. And neither would I.

CHAPTER EIGHT

By the time Jake and I were finishing senior year of high school and planning for college, life had changed dramatically for me. I was in love. Ben Coleman, my crush since sophomore year, who still "didn't have an oar" according to Jake, had finally noticed me.

Gladys had been kind enough to sew new clothes for me and to teach me a little bit about hair and makeup. I still had an affinity for pants because I could do more activities when a skirt wasn't halfway up my fanny. The trousers Jake had outgrown - which were always my preference - were too short, so I suggested that Gladys turn them into Capri pants, which were all the fad.

Gladys was still unconvinced. "But they are still boy's pants, Kat. Tomboy clothing was fine when you were younger, but you are now a young lady."

I answered in my best husky-voice Mae West impression, "I may be young, but I ain't no lady."

Gladys smiled and agreed to remake the trousers, but she couldn't resist adding a few flower appliqués to the pockets. The compromise was a good one. I was still a tomboy, but at least I no longer *looked* so much like a boy. I didn't admit it to anyone, but I was starting to enjoy the change in my appearance.

My dark hair had grown out into shoulder length waves, which I often wore in a ponytail. I also had fully developed breasts - a "nice rack," according to Jake. I was taller than most girls my age, but still thin. My too-short short bangs had grown out, and I often wondered what aberrant brain cells had convinced me to cut them like Mamie Eisenhower's bangs when I was young. I eventually had to agree with Jake, who always told me, "Fashion challenged children should not be allowed to cut their own hair with garden shears and a rake."

Happily for me, Ben blended in with Jake and me like the third leg on a three-legged stool. Ben shared our love of railroads, which is all Jake needed to welcome him into our circle.

Ben's grandfather had been a train engineer, so he was full of great tales regarding rail travel. He could speak at length regarding hilarious anecdotes and shocking disasters. There were stories of boxcar weddings, robberies, wrecks, dead bodies, wild animals, and treasures left behind. He never ran out of material. We never questioned the veracity of his tales because we were bonded together by the romantic vision of the great railroads.

Ben liked to sport his grandpa's old chain watch, given to his grandfather upon retirement from the Monon Railroad Company. Although pocket watches were not in fashion (no one our age wore vests), Ben had fancied a way to attach the watch to his belt loop, which added to his roguish appearance. Sometimes in the middle of our activities, Ben would come to a sudden halt and place his hand over the watch to stop it from swinging. When he had everyone's attention, he would solemnly declare, "And time stood still." We referred to him as "Big Ben," and to the watch as "Little Ben."

Jake and I loved his sense of humor. He told us his father had left his mother for another woman, but the family had adjusted. We had just started talking about sexual topics, so he didn't hesitate to assert that his father had left to follow the "siren song of salacious sex."

"What makes you think his mistress had talent in those areas?" Jake prodded.

"Because she was a sword swallower in a circus," Ben replied with a straight face.

As if their moves were choreographed, Jake and Ben immediately began to choke and gag while rolling their eyes and moaning, all to my enthusiastic applause.

"It's all peaceful at home now," Ben assured us. "My mom married a nice guy. You know the postmaster? Nice, but a bit of a dud. A milquetoast."

"Oh," Jake nodded, "so he's a Milk Dud."

Ben loved Jake's comeback. No matter how sophomoric our jokes were, the days leading into our last summer in Wabash were filled with merriment.

"You've got the wrong name, Ben," Jake announced one day. "You should be named Andy. You have dark auburn hair and freckles. Guys like you should be called 'Andy,' not Benjamin."

"Why Andy?"

"It's just the way it is for redheads. You should meet the expectations of your following. It's a moral obligation."

"But 'Andy'?"

"Yes, ANDY! You know - like the red-haired, flat-faced Raggedy Andy doll."

"The stuffed monstrosity with the pants that come up to his armpits? Well, that's certainly an image to live up to."

"You owe it to your befuddled public."

"I suppose I could change my name to accommodate you and to avoid confusion, but it might be easier just to bleach my hair to a more Ben-like color. I can't do anything about the damn freckles – they are a mark of great distinction."

"I'll be happy to help you out there!" All of a sudden, Jake did a frog leap onto Ben, taking him to the ground. They rolled and wrestled as I stood by enjoying their usual antics. I knew

Ben could have tossed Jake off like a piece of lint, but he pretended to be held down as Jake pulled an ink pen from his pocket and connected Ben's freckles.

"At least now your freckles are disguised," he nodded with satisfaction. He drew a perfect big dipper with a North Star on Ben's forehead. I thought it was hilarious, and Ben was such a good sport he left the constellation on his face for two days until his mother made him wash almost all of it off. (He was able to keep the North Star hidden under a lock of hair. He assured us he needed it to help guide him home.)

Now that there were three of us to greet the Wabash Cannonball, Ben added a new challenge for us. It was called "Name the Parts of the Train." With due diligence, Jake poured over his Encyclopedia Britannica so he could come up with obscure names of train components to challenge Ben's knowledge, but Ben always seemed to know the answers.

One late afternoon we were walking along the tracks when Jake challenged Ben, "Okay, smart ass, tell me what an 'ashpan hopper' is."

Without hesitation, Ben came up with an answer. "An ashpan hopper is someone who hurls himself on top of ashes in pans to keep fires from spreading. It requires advanced firefighter training, and while at Ashpan Academy, the Italian hoppers are required to shave their asses for safety." His devilish grin cracked us up.

"Ah ha, I knew you were making shit up, you poser! Je t'accuse!"

"No, I'm not a poser, you Emile Zola wannabe," Ben said innocently. "And I can tell you what a 'dry pipe' is too. That's what *you* have from wringing out your johnson so much!" Ben playfully punched Jake in the arm, and the chase through the field back home began.

We would usually end our days at Jake's house for dinner, where Ben was always welcome.

The Jacksons thought Jake and I should have our own

privacy, so they set up separate quarters for Jake in a room over the garage. Jake loved it.

His relationship with his dad was cordial but still slightly strained, and they just didn't seem to have the ability to communicate. I sometimes noticed Mr. Jackson staring at his son as though looking for a way to reach him. Jake was eccentric, and eccentric can be confusing. Jake always feared he was a disappointment to his parents, but I assured him many times that he was simply a conundrum.

I was assigned Jake's old room. Although Gladys made it quite comfy for me, I felt bad for having usurped Jake's space, but Jake maintained that he preferred his private hideout over the garage. I understood why when I began to hear strange nocturnal sounds outside. When I asked him about secret visitors, he suggested I might be hearing squirrels in the attic.

"Uh ... *talking* squirrels?"

"We have very intelligent squirrels in this neck of the Hoosier woods, li'l lady," he drawled.

"Yeah, sure."

"If you don't tell on me, I won't tell on you," Jake bargained. "Ben is not exactly dainty when he's sneaking in and out your bedroom window. He might as well wear a cowbell." As humorous as the image was to me, I couldn't deny it.

Jake accompanied Ben and me most everywhere. A few times we tried to fix him up so we could go on double dates. I had overcome a lot of my shyness to forge a friendship with Louise Schroeder, whose mom had helped us the day Jake broke his leg. Louise was the only female friend I really had. She was nonjudgmental and cheerful, so I often wanted to include her in our activities. She confided in me that she thought Jake was cute, and she really didn't mind his limp, so I saw her interest as an opportunity to expand our group.

With enough prodding, Jake and Louise did accommodate us on several occasions. The four of us had a good time, but nothing ever came of my matchmaking, and Louise eventually developed a relationship with a guy who had graduated before us. Jake had no regrets - he claimed that he preferred to choose his own "talking squirrels."

That summer, we both had jobs serving ice cream treats and sandwiches at the soda fountain at Bradley Brothers Drug Store at the corner of Canal and Wabash. The place had enjoyed its moment of fame in 1942 when a circus elephant named Modoc got a whiff of the roasting peanuts in Bradley's and decided to help herself. She lumbered through the building, rolled a woman clad in a raccoon coat across the floor with her trunk, and then pushed out the back wall. Modoc rampaged through downtown Wabash for five days before they were able to lure her back to the circus. (Jake claimed that Modoc, who had left a pile of excrement during her break-in at Bradley's, left better tips than our high school peers.)

Ben worked at the Union Cigar Store nearby, which made it convenient for him to drop by for leftover snacks after work. Mr. Kessler, our manager, and a descendant of the woman Modoc had rolled across the floor during the great elephant escape, was so charmed by Ben that he stopped grousing about us sneaking him free food. After a period of time, Mr. Kessler even began to prepare sandwiches for Ben in anticipation of his arrival. Ben seemed to have a magical effect on people.

Everyone at Bradley's thought Jake and I were brother and sister, in spite of our different last names and dissimilar features. Occasionally, we would bicker like siblings, but we always looked out for each other.

During one lunch shift, a smarmy guy with the absurd name of Berve, grabbed my breast while I was serving him a sandwich. Jake noticed and stabbed Berve's hand with a fork, causing him to yell so loudly that the rest of the patrons stopped eating in mid-chew. (I was absolutely delighted.)

With a carving knife in hand, Mr. Kessler rushed out from behind the counter to inquire about the cause of the disturbance in the café area. "Berve's hand ran into my fork," Jake shrugged.

Mr. Kessler took one look at the exaggerated innocence on Jake's face and surmised what had happened. He turned to Berve and warned, "Berve, it looks like you're gonna need faster reflexes if your hands ever leave your sides in Bradley's again."

That summer was truly one of the best of my life. But as the season came to an end, I was filled with both anticipation and dread.

Jake and I were following through with our plan to go to Franklin College, and I had managed to get the scholarship I needed. The tough part was the knowledge that Ben would be leaving us. We had all become accustomed to being together, and I dreaded not seeing Ben on a daily basis. He was headed for Purdue, so we all feared that once studies began and we were separated by distance, there would be fewer leisure times. But we had no idea our good times would end so abruptly.

CHAPTER NINE

Franklin College, a small private school, is aptly named for the town in which it is located, as well as for Benjamin Franklin. There is an impressive statue of old Ben Franklin gracing the campus. Jake claimed they commissioned the statue so no idiot gets confused and thinks the institution of higher learning is named after Franklin Roosevelt, who of course was born in a different century. (Kudos to the college forefathers who had the forethought to take pity upon such moronic types.)

I managed to get an academic scholarship to supplement my financial aid, but accommodations were not covered. We figured out it was cheaper to rent a small apartment in town rather than to pay dorm fees, so we rented a one-bedroom apartment over The Koffee Kup, a restaurant near the Court House.

Jake decreed that I should take the bedroom and he would have the sleeper couch. When I mentioned that we should get an apartment where he also could have a proper bedroom, he convinced me there was nothing better than a place where we could conveniently grab coffee and donuts in the morning on the way to class. "This is our cheapest bet. Besides, you'll need your privacy if Ben comes wearing his farmland cowbell. And if I need some privacy, I'll kick you out to the curb. Fair deal?"

"Fair deal."

Autumn in Indiana is one of the most beautiful times of year. Jake and I walked to campus together with coffee in hand, breathing in the rich scent of autumn leaves. The colors were glorious as well. And the best part was our proximity to the railroad that traversed Franklin, so every day and evening we could hear trains as they passed close by the college. Even though we were newly adapting to unfamiliar living quarters and the challenges of academic life, the echoing whistles of the passing trains grounded us in something familiar.

I was a literature major, and classes were easy for me. I had read most of the books on the reading list already, so many of my courses were simply a review. Jake, who was a great writer and wanted to become a journalist, was required to take many of the same English courses I took. However, because of his slow reading speed, he had difficulty completing the assigned work, so we resorted to the effective method we had already developed during sophomore year in high school when he was laid up. I summarized my class notes, and then Jake read the summaries and remembered all the details. Sometimes he would write dates backwards, but I knew he was much smarter than almost anyone I knew.

All the enthusiasm and razzle-dazzle of college life was new to us. "These frenetic people must be training for the Rockettes!" Jake exclaimed while we were reviewing a list of events on the bulletin board that included an endless schedule of school dances. "I thought Baptist schools didn't allow dancing. These events must be for hell-destined heathens only. Our kind of folks."

"Yay – that's perfect for us!"

Louise Schroeder was accepted to Franklin also, so it was nice to have a friend from home. She often came over from the dorm to hang out in our little apartment, which we called 'The Squeeze.' Jake engaged more with Louise as he became increasingly self-assured in Franklin. Ben often came to visit me on the weekends, so the four of us attended a number of school events, including homecoming and several basketball games. (Basketball is a Hoosier tradition. You have to like the game, or they tar and feather you and dump your basketball-hating carcass in Kentucky.)

One weekend morning, Jake, Ben, and I were awakened by the soothing notes of a barbershop quartet. It was like being back at the Chop-n-Bleed. Jake peered out our second story window to determine their location. "There they are!" he yelled. "They're down by the courthouse. Get dressed – we're going down!"

Although Jake was small in stature, no one ever questioned his commands, because in spite of certain insecurities, he was always a master of determination. As we rushed out, we encountered Louise on the stairway that led to our attic apartment.

"Wrong direction, Louise," Jake stated matter-of-factly.

Without hesitation, she changed direction, trailing after us as we followed Jake in a duck parade down Jefferson Street to the town square where we all crammed onto one bench to listen to the barbershop quartet perform. When we had a chance to make requests, the first thing we asked for was "The Wabash Cannonball," which was closely followed by our request for their rendition of "On the Banks of the Wabash," and "Back Home Again in Indiana."

The four of us sat respectfully with all the other onlookers while we listened to the vocal harmony and gazed out at the picturesque brick buildings that lined the quaint streets. From our location near the old Johnson County Court House, we could see the ornate Artcraft Theatre on Main Street with its bright crescent-shape marquee announcing a Doris Day film, *The Pajama Game*.

Before every film at the Artcraft, the local crowd always stood to recite the "Pledge of Allegiance" and to sing "The Star-Spangled Banner." The four of us always joined in with exuberance, ending the song with rousing applause.

The Artcraft Theatre was known for its sprawling screen and

roomy seating. And unlike Wabash, where theatre crowds would sit quietly and politely, the Franklin theater patrons were always enthusiastic participants, cheering the heroes and booing the bad guys. Even seeing a flop at the theatre was an exciting event.

If the movie was a total bomb, we would hang out in the concession area with the popcorn lady, Irene Petro, who was known for her amazing popcorn, and who was a fixture at the theater for years. Using her own recipe and a Manley popper, Irene made hot batches of popcorn so delicious that people came in to buy her popcorn before taking it down the street to the other local theatre. Jake loved to get behind the counter to help Irene whenever she would allow. He often proposed marriage in exchange for a lifetime of hot corn, which always sent Irene into fits of giggles.

I was getting hungry thinking about popcorn just as the barbershop quartet was winding down, so I was about to suggest a matinee. However, Jake was too restless to sit for two hours … but because it was Saturday, he was also reluctant to end the fun. After we clapped and whistled for the quartet, Jake vaulted to his feet with a burst of energy and thrust his arm into the air like Tenzing Norgay guiding us to the summit of Mount Everest. "Onward!" he urged.

"Artcraft?" Louise asked.

"Grill!" Just one word was all Jake needed, because we knew what he meant - the old Grill Bar Tavern on East Jefferson near Water Street. We could grab a bite to eat there, and they always served Jake alcoholic drinks because he had managed to alter an ID card he had purchased from one of the soda jerks back at Bradley's.

It was a short walk to the tavern. We all enjoyed the place as much as Jake did because the warm atmosphere welcomed its patrons immediately upon entering. The old room-length bar was covered with initials that had been carved into the wood over the years, ours included. Steel stools with round vinyl seats, comfy booths, and a battered wood floor contributed to the comfortable ambiance. To save money, we usually shared one or two of their decadent fat burgers and ordered extra fries or onion rings.

Jake immediately ordered a Manhattan. When he saw me glance up at the clock, he yanked on my hair to tease me. "Lighten up, Susan B. Anthony. I'm merely practicing."

We all laughed at Jake's straight-faced delivery. "Practicing for what?" Louise prodded. She never missed a chance to set him up, even if unwittingly.

"I'll need to drink Manhattans when I'm a journalist. There are rules and regulations. I'm pretty sure it's required by most important news outlets."

"Oh, is that so?" Ben chuckled, tossing a fry his way.

"Absolutely. I'm sure I read it somewhere. I think it's written in the Book of Deuteronomy. Or maybe I heard on the *Huntley-Brinkley Report*. I cannot confirm at this time. Professional journalists are not allowed to reveal their sources." (We all groaned in unison.)

"Besides, I always let you guys eat the cherries."

"True," I nodded. "But to reiterate what the waitress told us last week when you ordered drinks, 'No, we do not sell keggers of Manhattans, lovey.' So don't badger her again today, Hemingway."

Jake flashed his signature cock-eyed grin, making it impossible to remain stern with him in spite of my misgivings.

———

After thinking a bit more about Jake's penchant for cocktails, I began to suspect I was overreacting. A few days later, I mentioned it to Ben, who assured me how common it is for students to drink more frequently once they enter college. "You don't have to look too hard to see some fool staggering down Jefferson Street almost every weekend night, Kat."

"True, and it's usually you and Jake waving your underwear

and yelling 'Go, Grizzlies'! You of all people, Ben Coleman – a Purdue Boilermaker!"

"Indeed, I am. At least we don't yell, 'Go Fighting Baptists'! That was what your team was once called, you know."

"How ironic - they could fight, but they weren't allowed to dance. They must have been terminally baffled."

"That's religion for you. Jake and I just like to cheer on your religiously confused team," he winked. "The alcohol is merely a warm-up."

I was still a bit concerned, but I didn't bring up the drinking topic again because Jake had backed off the alcohol a bit. After he started going on a few dates with Louise, his mood seemed lighter. He obviously enjoyed having her around.

Jake, the master of nicknames, had gone from calling her "Wrong-way Louise" to dubbing her "Lulu," which morphed into "Looney," then "Lunatic," "Ludicrous," and even "Luftwaffe." But he came up with his best appellation for her the day we were all crawling around in the leaves looking for the crown she had lost from her tooth. After an extensive search, Jake, full of triumph, popped up and yelled, "Lutitidinous, I found your fang!" We didn't know if "Lutitidinous" was a real word and we didn't care. It became part of our everyday vocabulary, and we used it for every possible speech part, such as, "Pass the lutitidinous, please," or, as in Ben's clever contribution, "Your lutitidinous is hanging out."

In addition to lutitidinous Louise, we had a fifth companion – the wandering dog who belonged to the owner of the café below us. The dog was a small black and cream mutt who Jake promptly renamed "Latte" instead of "Java" because of his coloring, which was highlighted by a white muzzle.

"You'll confuse him with the names. He's cute, but he's a little dim," I observed.

"No way. Watch this, Kat - he always comes whenever I call." Jake whistled and tossed a piece of hot dog out the window to the street below.

"That's because you lure the little beggar with wieners and Pez candies from Nick's Candy Kitchen! That fat little hound sits down there on the sidewalk waiting for treats to drop out of the sky."

"True. But look at him, Kat - it's like dropping chocolate bars over France." Jake clapped as Latte spun about with excitement.

"How do you always know when he's down there?"

"Because he calls out to me, 'Stella ... Stella!'" Jake's impersonation of Marlon Brando in *A Streetcar Named Desire* was award-winning.

Everybody loved Jake, who had become quite well known among the local proprietors. One day he showed up at our apartment wearing an old black beret he found in the thrift store. He loved his new rakish look, so he began to wear it constantly. "Don't I look like one of the Beats, Kat?"

"I'd say more 'beaten-up' than Beat. That thing looks like a battered hubcap."

He dismissed my snide remark and cocked the beret further over one eye. "Let's go see what's new at the bookstore, and afterward, we can splurge on that Sam Cooke record you want at Betty's Record Shop. I want to show off my new look." He pranced down Jefferson Street, tipping his hat to anyone we passed, including Latte, who joined our procession.

Although Jake was so congenial, he was usually greeted more enthusiastically at the Grill Bar Tavern than at the bookstore on Court Street, managed by Leo Fry. Jake drove Mr. Fry a bit nutty, but I knew their banter was exaggerated, because it was obvious Mr. Fry really liked Jake.

As we walked in, Mr. Fry looked up at the sound of the door chime. When he saw Jake, he rolled his eyes dramatically. "Oh, no," he moaned, "not today. You are such a load." (I was highly amused.)

"What do you mean? I'm your best customer!" Jake protested.

"Customer? Boarder, you mean. I should set up a cot for you.

You handle our books and read for hours, but you never buy. You leave fingerprints!"

"A cot would be useful, thank you kindly. And just so you know, you underestimate my value. My prints would be of great interest to the FBI hacks who consider me a person of interest for a string of bookstore robberies across the Midwest ... for which there is a handsome award, I might add."

"It can't be you - you don't need to steal books. You *live* in my store. And you sleep in the fiction aisle!"

"Only the Jane Austen section. But I bring you customers, Mr. Fry. You know my devastatingly handsome face draws crowds."

"All you draw is flies! Aw, just go home," Mr. Fry groused while trying – and failing - to suppress a smile. "And take that mangy dog with you."

On occasion, we would spend the afternoon at the home of a kind and interesting local resident, Elwood Neff. Jake had met Mr. Neff one day at the bookstore, and Jake, always one to engage in conversation, learned that Mr. Neff had created an elaborate train setup that encompassed his entire garage. When he invited Jake to come to his home, Jake jumped at the chance, insisting that I accompany him of course.

Mr. Neff's train town was extraordinary. The trains ran through a miniature village he had crafted by hand. We were fascinated as the trains wound their way over bridges and through foliage-covered tunnels while passing pleasant little depots along the way. There was not only a town, but also little people, luggage, cargo, and even well-stocked grocery stands full of tiny fruits and vegetables.

The setup was electrified, with signal lights and warning lanterns, and crossing gates that would rise up or lower as the trains passed through. Amiable Mr. Neff would even join in with us as we spun tales about the different little people waiting on the platforms. It was always a great way to spend a Saturday afternoon, especially as the cold Indiana months set in.

That winter in Indiana was brutal. All we had in our apartment was a small space heater, so we were never really warm. Jake swore our refrigerator was warmer than our room. "We should sleep in the refrigerator and keep our milk on the sofa," he suggested.

———

On Saturday nights when we couldn't afford a movie or the Grill Bar Tavern, we gathered in The Squeeze to play cards and to listen to Elvis Presley or Rick Nelson. (Ben and Jake found an old but perfectly good record player at the local thrift shop.) When we weren't playing records, we could just lie on the floor and listen to the ragtime music, accompanied by whoops and hollers, from the Sassy Seniors Dance Club two doors down. "There are no Baptists in that crowd," Jake chortled.

Our Saturday night activities became more exciting the night Louise rushed in with a book in hand and gushed, "You guys have to hear this - it's forbidden fruit." The book, *Peyton Place*, was a racy book full of lust and tales of adultery in a small town.

"Read aloud, Lutitidinous," Jake directed as we all plopped down on the floor. Of course, we encouraged her to read the salacious parts, but she insisted on reading the entire book to us "for background color."

After a few beers, Ben and Jake would act out the scenes, which, more often than not, resulted in additional beer consumption followed by even more cacophony caused by the next-door neighbor yelling "Shut up, you imbecilic weirdos," thereby sending us into fits of laughter.

Ben slept in my bed whenever he was in town. We fooled around a lot, and although I was always aroused, we didn't have sex, because "good girls" were supposed to wait until they were married ... and pregnancy was always a great fear. A few girls in my high school had disappeared for nine months at a time - supposedly on vacation with some mysterious aunt - but I didn't have anybody I could vanish with, so we restrained ourselves "like God-fearing Puritans," as Ben described it. It was a challenge with very little reward.

We did, however, suspect that Jake and Louise had taken things much farther. At night, Louise would usually go back to her dorm, but one evening Ben and I were in the bedroom when we heard moaning accompanied by loud thumping. After the noise became embarrassingly loud, Ben decided it was time for Jake to use a little propriety.

When Ben went into the living room, he discovered there was no one in the room other than Jake, who was pounding on the wall and making panting sounds. Jake continued his antics when he saw Ben's perplexed face. "Oh Lutitidinous," he moaned into a pillow, "you naughty little vixen!"

Ben playfully lunged at Jake - a move which resulted in a prolonged wrestling event that should have been televised - and much to my delight, the high jinks continued well into the night. I was finally happy again, and I wanted those nights to go on forever.

———

As Christmas approached, the courthouse was strung with hundreds of lights to form a giant Christmas tree. We all gathered on Main Street to cheer the official lighting ceremony in early December, just before Jake and I returned to Wabash for a few days.

While in Wabash, we spent our time at Jake's house, which was decorated with almost as many lights as the Franklin Courthouse. Gladys had prepared a feast of delicious treats in anticipation of our visit, which we scarfed down with relish. Even Marilyn was prepped for Christmas, with tinsel hanging over the rear view mirror and a wreath affixed to her front grill.

On the several occasions we stopped by to see my father, Jake and I agreed my dad looked thin and gaunt. As was our habit, Dad and I sat in silence, but I was oddly content just to be near him. He gave me a mug with a rooster on it as an early Christmas gift. I loved it. I wrapped a framed photo of me standing by the statue of Ben Franklin and left it on the table before I returned to Franklin.

Jake and I spent the rest of Christmas break in Franklin, taking in the Artcraft's run of Christmas movie greats. Local pubs were serving grog, a delicious wine drink I had never sampled. Candy canes and Santa hats were in abundance, and the town remained festive throughout the holiday.

Jake and I agreed not to exchange gifts due to our limited funds, but I found a half-eaten Hershey bar hidden under my pillow on Christmas morning. "Those damn capricious elves," he shrugged innocently. I bought him a package of wieners with Latte's name on the label. It was a great Christmas.

We had settled into 1958 after the best year we had had since our unforgettable summer when the bright yellow Sunliner first entered our lives.

In January, the U.S. launched the Explorer 1 satellite. There was general euphoria because the Americans finally caught up with the Russians, who had launched the Sputnik 1 the preceding year. It had been such a milestone that there were gumballs named Sputnik being sold in penny candy stores.

"Up yours, Russia!" Jake and Ben yelled with excitement when we heard the news. The year was off to a great start, even as the usual Midwest January doldrums set in.

On gray days, Jake, with Latte at his heels as always, forced me out of the apartment so we could go down to the train depot at the east end of Martin Place. The station was not far from our apartment, so even on cold days, we liked to sit by the tracks and watch the trains go by.

"Right on time." Jake checked his watch and pointed to the first train that went by, before directing my focus to a face in the window of the passing train. "Ruthless kidnapper!" The face belonged to a young boy, so I knew Jake was testing me.

"I don't feel like it today, Jake, even if the kid is holding Amelia Earhart for ransom. I just don't have the energy."

"Aw, Kata-clysmic, how can I cheer you up? A lutitidinous movie at the Artcraft perhaps? Chocolate milkshake at Nick's? A Citizen's arrest for public moroseness?"

"No thanks. It's just Ben. You know how he's staying at Purdue more often these days. I know he has a lot of work to do, but I feel like he may be losing interest. I really care about him, and I thought we had a nice romance going."

I thought it odd when Jake did not argue or try to convince me I was mistaken. He just listened without comment. I knew when not to prod Jake, so I let my remark linger in the frosty air as we watched a train leave the station.

The Franklin train was not as dear to us as the Wabash Cannonball, but she was still a beauty. The line, originally a combination of the Cleveland, Cincinnati, Chicago, and St. Louis railways, was known as the "Big Four Railroad." Her steam whistle was higher in pitch than the whistle of the Wabash Cannonball, but nevertheless, her music provided the solace I needed that winter and through the long-awaited spring.

As the spring semester was drawing to a close, Jake and I were sitting atop a low wall on campus, not far from the revered Ben Franklin statue. As usual, revelers from the night before had adorned him with underwear and other discarded garments of clothing in the blue and gold team colors, but Mr. Franklin remained stoic.

Jake tossed treats to Latte, who followed Jake everywhere. Although Jake always enjoyed the playful dog, he appeared to be in a nostalgic mood, and somewhat distant. "What are you thinking about, Hemingway?" I asked.

"I like the green leaves, but I miss all the colors of fall, Kat. Remember how every autumn we used to rake leaves into a huge heap and then jump into the piles?"

"Yeah, that was a lot of fun, and a good way to make money. Maybe we should consider raking leaves again next fall for extra cash."

"Oh God help us all. Kat wants to start a business!"

"Com'on - it's a great idea. We can call our enterprise 'Leaf It to Us.'"

"Ha! You're as clever as a paper raincoat. The only business I want to start involves selling my own writing."

"So how come you never let me read your stuff?"

"It's not polished yet, but believe it or not, I wrote a lot while you were in class this year and I was studying at The Grill."

"Studying?"

"There's a lot to learn in a tavern. Right now, I'm working on a story about the Lake County Jail that John Dillinger escaped from in 1934."

"I've heard about it."

"Yeah, it's great. We've got to a find a way to get up to northern Indiana to Crown Point to visit the place. I figure it will be useful to learn how Dillinger and Youngblood broke free from an escape-proof jail."

"That knowledge will come in handy when you inevitably will need to break out of jail someday."

"I can't argue with that. But to tell you the truth, I'm getting restless. This is a real nice place, but I've seen enough Victorian houses and quaint buildings to last me a long while. It's all idyllic, but I'm antsy - I need something new to stimulate me."

"Maybe we should get involved in more college activities."

"Are you kidding me, Kat? The last activity included pumpkin carving, and I nearly lost my thumb. I had more fun when my hemorrhoid exploded."

"That's undeniably gross. So what if we go to a few more basketball games?"

"No more games, please! I just can't get hyper enthusiastic like the others do at basketball games. Good God - all that Hoosier Hysteria!"

"Oh com'on – you know Franklin won the Indiana State Basketball Championship three consecutive years in a row, and now we have players like Roger Schroder and Gene White starting for the Grizzlies. They played for Milan High School. You've heard of Milan. Remember the Milan Miracle of 1954?"

"I may not be into sports, but everyone in Indiana remembers that – even Latte has mentioned it a few times."

"But you have to admit, it's pretty exciting. That was the smallest school to ever win the state basketball title."

"Yes, I know. The school had 161 students. Two of them were cows."

"Very funny. Basketball is air to Hoosiers, even non-athletes, and you know you had fun at those games we attended."

"I only went with you and Benjamin a few times in hopes a bloody brawl would break out, but Hoosiers are too damn polite - I didn't even get to witness a compound fracture."

"You should be thankful. When we gave blood to the Red Cross, you fainted, remember?"

"I was doing my impersonation of Marilyn Monroe in *Niagara* just for you. A brilliant performance, I'd say."

"It definitely was a crowd pleaser – to this crowd of one. Anyway, I love this town. I know it can be quiet here, but that's what makes it so ideal."

"Quiet to you is moribund to me. The most exciting thing to happen all semester was when Latte dragged that old sock into the Koffee Kup and everybody ran out like hysterical ninnies."

"That's because somebody – and that somebody might have been you - yelled, 'It's rabid!'"

"See what I mean - even the local dogs are trying to stir up some excitement."

"He did an admirable job of it. It was very entertaining to watch the usually sluggish morning customers streaming out of there like it was an air raid. But I'm not so sure your decision to hurl pieces of hot dog at them was well-received by the café crowd."

"Oh, you know you loved it! Besides, I think I only hit a few laggards. Latte loved it, too. He deserved a reward for his effort."

"Agreed. So, let's tell the landlord we will rent our apartment again so he doesn't lease it to two other suckers."

"Kat, don't get upset, but I think I'm done here. I'm more than restless - I have a strong urge to move on."

I was completely taken aback. "What are you talking about?" I asked. "Where will you go? What will you do? Do your parents know this?" I was firing so many questions at him he started to laugh.

"Slow your jets, Chuck Yeager! I never can keep up with you!"

"I'm serious, Jake. Don't try to humor me! What in the hell are you talking about?"

"I don't really fit in here. This doesn't line up with my future. I'm thinking if I want to be a serious journalist I should go to Chicago. I just want to get out of Franklin, and I have made up my mind that I am not going back to Wabash either."

"Why? What's wrong with you? Something has been eating at you, I can tell. You're drinking way too much ... and I never see Louise anymore. Did you break up with her - is that what has you down?"

"Kat, you never come up for air. No, I didn't break up with Lutitidinous - she broke up with me. She informed me that I'm not boyfriend material, whatever that is."

"'Boyfriend material'?"

"Yeah – material. Like wool, I guess. Apparently, I'm not wooly enough for her."

"That's ridiculous."

"No, she is right. But there was really nothing to break up. We were just good friends."

"But I know she liked you and-"

"Kat, she wasn't my type. She's a real sweet girl, and I wanted us to be a foursome, just like you did. That way I could always hang out with you and Ben. But it's time for me to grow up and separate myself from you and everyone else in my life. I need some independence. I'm not like you."

"What's that supposed to mean?"

"I'm talking about the fact that you're ... you're *solid*. I know I'm different."

"Who cares? Your differences are what everyone loves about you. You're smart and weird and funny and eccentric. And you have a slow tooth. That makes you *interesting*, you idiot. You are so exasperating sometimes! Don't you get it?"

"I don't want to be *interesting*. I want to be *normal*. I want to find a place where I truly feel at home like I did when we had the Cannonball and the rails that led to all those exotic places we read about. And we had the field where we could hide out. Being down by the tracks was the only place I felt calm."

"Jake, we were kids then."

Jake held up his hand and nodded. "I know, and I also know I can't relive those times, but I think I can find some peace and maybe find a way to quiet my insides a bit if I make a clean break."

"From me?"

"No, not from you, funny face. Never. From me."

Jake turned away and reached down to pet Latte to further avoid my gaze. He seemed sad and lost, but I didn't know what to say to reach him. As we sat in silence, I feared I was losing him.

———

That night back at the apartment, I had difficulty falling asleep, even though I was emotionally depleted. I had been close to Jake my whole life, but now he was talking about leaving. I was only safe when he was in my world. He was my best friend and my brother. The absence of a mother had created a hole in me, but at a very young age, I had become accustomed to the longing. It was different with Jake, I knew if he left, the loss would be even greater. He was my core, and without him, I would lose the center of my being.

After I finally succumbed to exhaustion, I was sleeping fitfully when I felt a crushing pressure on my body. I absorbed the pressure into my dream state - I was under water, and the pressure of the water was compressing my lungs. I began to gasp for breath. I knew I was suffocating, and I became more and more desperate for oxygen. I flailed, but the pressure increased, so I screamed out for help.

In the moment I woke from my nightmare, I was overcome with confusion. I could feel Jake's breath as he pressed his mouth against my lips and ground his body into mine. My muddled mind thought it was part of my nightmare. As I tried to come to my senses, the reality of the situation became clearer - Jake was on top of me. I screamed and tried to shove him off, but he persisted. He reeked of alcohol, and his mouth tasted foul.

"Help me. Help me be a man." Jake's speech was slurred, and his arms flailed about as he awkwardly attempted to kiss me again.

I was overcome with nausea and horror. I managed to kick him in his bad leg, which made him cry out in pain. In that moment, he seemed to have unusual strength, but his reaction to the pain allowed me to shove him off onto the floor. When he landed with a violent thud, his head bounced on the tiles with a sickening sound.

I knew I was screaming, but I didn't care. "What are you doing, Jake? What is wrong with you? How could you do such a horrible thing, you sick son-of-a-bitch!"

Jake rolled over onto the floor face down, shaking and sobbing. I was above him now, peering down at an injured animal. I screamed again and kicked him several times with my bare foot. Finally, he stopped moving, and the room became deathly quiet. I was so overwrought that I kicked him again. "Get out of here, you pig. And don't come back!"

Jake stumbled to his feet and stared at me as though he

barely recognized me. A look of profound sadness spread across his face. "I am so sorry. I'm sick. I can't feel what normal men feel." He was so unsteady that he had to hold onto the door frame to remain upright.

"I don't give a damn what you feel. You're drunk out of your mind. Get out!"

"You, and Louise, and all the others – no one understands. I can't help that I have this, this bad thing inside me. It's not what I want. I didn't want to love him."

"Love who?"

"Ben."

"Ben? What are you saying?"

"Kat, I'm in love with Ben. I'm trying to make it go away. Please help me!"

The jolt of his words was so intense, I collapsed on the bed, too weak to stand any longer.

"I'm an aberration."

"Just stop talking, Jake. Please stop talking. Let me get my bearings."

"I called Dr. Strat. He thinks shock treatments might-"

"Strat? Shock treatments? Stop this insanity! I don't want to hear that man's name! I forbid you to ever speak to him, and I won't listen to this any longer!"

"Kat-"

"Shut up, Jake! I have to think! None of this makes sense. If you love Ben, what were you doing just now? Were you trying to punish me because Ben loves me?"

"NO, NO! You're the only one I can trust." Jake lost his footing and fell against the wall before pushing himself upright again. "I thought maybe you could ... make me like, like normal." Jake wiped away tears as he grasped for words. "I'm so confused! I wanted someone to just help me a little - like an experiment. Just to get me started, to help me find-"

"You are delusional! I don't give a damn who you love - you

can love whoever you want - but you and I are like brother and sister!"

"I know! I know! Please, please. I don't feel safe with anyone but you. I just wanted to look at you. To see if ..." Jake began pulling violently at his hair as if trying to localize his pain. "In my mind, you weren't *you*, you were, you were ... I wasn't going to do what you thought I was-"

"But it *is* me – and I want you to get out! Get out now!" I quaked and shuddered with the disgust of what Jake had done. I could not control my crying and moaning because I knew what had happened would separate us and change our relationship forever. I sensed that Jake, as drunk as he was, knew it too. My throat was the only escape route for my shock and pain.

"I'm going. I'm going. I'm so sorry, Kat. But don't go back to Ben. Please. He hides it, but he's just like me. We're not normal. Neither one of us deserves to live."

"Don't say that! Did that sick bastard Strat tell you that bull-shit? Jake, answer me!"

Without responding, Jake stumbled out the door. I heard him fall on the stairway, but he got up and kept running. When I looked out the window, I could see him under the glow of the streetlights. He was tearing East on Jefferson Street, his bad leg always one beat behind the other. Latte had appeared out of nowhere and was at Jake's heels, but Jake did not seem to notice. He tripped and fell again, but once he managed to upright himself, he kept going, taking a piece of me with him.

When Jake turned south on Water Street, I knew if he turned left again at Monroe, he'd be heading in the direction of the tracks at the Monroe Street crossing that we passed daily on the way to classes. That's when the realization hit me. Jake had wanted to run away for so long ... now he was finally going to hop a train and leave forever.

As angry and confused as I was, I feared for him, and I couldn't let him go. I shoved my feet into my shoes and took off after him. "Don't go, Jake," I pleaded aloud as I ran toward the tracks. When I got closer to the crossing, I heard the whistle of the approaching train. The train rounded the bend, its beacon of light outlining every object near its path. Then I saw Jake.

The warning lights bathed Jake in grotesque colors as he stood near the crossing, his hands clutching a light pole not far from the slope that led up to the tracks. Jake inched around the pole, unsteady on his feet. Finally, he let go and stumbled closer to the rails.

"Don't leave me behind, Jake," I begged. "I'll come with you. Let's talk it out!" I called out his name over and over, but I knew he couldn't hear me.

Jake moved closer to the tracks. He was waving his hands wildly when, in a moment of horror, Latte ran toward Jake. "Jake," I screamed, "Latte is behind you! Oh, God, no!"

Jake couldn't hear me over the noise of the train's engine and the whistles of warning. But after a heart-stopping moment, Jake spotted Latte, who was now close at his side. He reached into his pocket for a treat, and then he threw it far from the tracks so Latte would head in the opposite direction.

Jake abruptly turned, as if he somehow knew I was there. When he saw me, he smiled sadly. Just as I smiled back, Jake lifted his hand in a slight wave. A second later, he turned back around and stepped in front of the oncoming train.

Time was suspended as my knees buckled, and my head hit the pavement. I descended into darkness.

———

Five days later, Jake's parents arrived in Franklin to take me back for the funeral. No one was able to speak on the return trip. Even the yellow of the Sunliner had retreated into silence. The beautiful Indiana countryside was now funereal as the pale wheat bowed at our passing.

Gladys cried the entire way, and Mr. Jackson subtly wiped his eyes and nose many times during the trip back. When they had first arrived in Franklin to pick me up, they tentatively asked about Jake's death, but I sensed they really did not want to know more than what the police had already told them. They believed he had fallen in front of the train, and I did not provide any other information as we made our way to Wabash to bury Jake.

I sat frozen in the back seat, fearful that any movement would cause my body to fall apart. The damaged pieces of me were tenuously connected, held together only by relentless pain. The shock and gruesomeness was too raw, and my confusion about that night was even greater.

Since Jake's death, I had spent every moment trying to keep the memories of that night at bay, but it was a futile struggle. The images tortured me, as over and over again the train lifted Jake into the air. The desperate, warning train whistle, the grinding brakes, the squeal of metal against metal, the screams of the onlookers – all the horror grew louder with each passing day.

I was also overwhelmed with shame for hiding the truth. After I regained consciousness on the night Jake died, I told police that Jake had been running near the train when he tripped and fell in front of it. I couldn't find the words needed to describe what I saw happen. I was barely able to speak, so I buried the truth about Jake.

After the police questioned me, they spoke with the engineer, who thought he saw Jake step in front of the train, but he wasn't sure because that point on the tracks was streaked with shadows. My version of events became the official report. I feared if George and Gladys knew the truth, they would blame themselves for something they understood even less than I did.

I was wrong to hide the truth from them, but I believed I could bear the burden better than they could. Or maybe I just wanted to help carry it *for* them. No matter what my instinct, when I was questioned, I lied, and I would forever have to live with that lie. A piece of my soul died with Jake that night.

———

Immediately after we arrived at Jake's house, I packed some of the possessions I had left in my room. I stuffed mostly necessary items into a satchel, avoiding one zippered pocket on my bag. It contained Jake's beret, which he had left at our apartment the night he ran out. I ran my fingers along the outside of the pocket before I pulled my hand away and methodically finished packing. I couldn't bear to look in the pocket, but I needed to keep Jake with me.

Gladys and George Jackson were dressing for the funeral when I went to the kitchen. As I looked around, I noticed how drab everything seemed. There weren't any homemade baked goods on the counter, and the fruit in the Fiestaware bowl was brown. Even the paint on the walls had lost its luster. There was no longer any life in the once cheerful room where we had so often gathered.

I remained at the table a moment before I propped up a letter I had written to them. Inside the envelope with the letter was a photo Ben had taken of Jake and me. In the photo, we were sitting on the landing of the Franklin Big Four Railroad Depot, drinking root beer.

I looked around the room one more time. After lingering to breathe in the scent of the only real home I had known, I turned and walked out the back door.

With my backpack in hand, I headed for the tracks. Jake and I always loved and honored locomotives, and yet a menacing steel beast had ripped Jake from me. I knew my one way to live with such bitter irony was to somehow change the meaning of his death. I wanted, in my own way, to follow Jake.

The train was approaching, but her rumbling sound was different than the frightening hiss and the warning whistle that screamed at Jake on the night he killed himself. As I turned toward the whistle, I heard a voice of greeting, not threat, and it was the only voice I could bear. She was *our* train, and she would be my escape from the horror of Jake's death.

When I saw her coming around the bend, I waited for my

opportunity, and then I ran. My focus was unwavering as I tried to flee from the nightmare that shadowed me. With each step, my feet held onto the steep slope along the tracks. The ground shook as the train roared by, her speed increasing as she passed. I ran faster.

There was no turning back. I jumped aboard the first open freight car when it passed alongside me. Death had fastened its claws to the walls of my chest, and I had become so weak I barely had enough strength to hoist myself onto the train car. As I lifted myself up, I struggled against my own dead weight, but my legs finally followed, and I surrendered to the single thing in my world that was still solid – the floor of a boxcar on the Wabash Cannonball. I didn't know where I was going. All I knew was where I could no longer be.

BOOK II

THE RAILS

CHAPTER TEN

I NESTLED BACK INTO THE CORNER OF THE FREIGHT CAR AND allowed the rocking to soothe me. The rhythmic clackety-clack of the wheels on the rails numbed me into a deep sleep - the first time I slept in days. The right side of my face had an angry bruise from falling on the sidewalk the night of Jake's death, so I had to lean to my left, propping up my head with discarded newspaper.

The smell of urine mixed with straw was an indication that a rider had been there not long before me. Many of the jumpers honored the trains by not relieving themselves while aboard, but those of unsound mind or under the influence of alcohol or other substances relieved themselves where they slept. Doc had always referred to them as the "Boxcar Crashers." As an uninvited guest on the Cannonball Express, the irony was not lost on me. Eventually, the unpleasant odor of the boxcar receded into the background ... and I was too tired to care anymore.

As I stared at the hobo graffiti on the boxcar walls, I was able to decipher most of the messages. The hobo language had been taught to me by Doc and Joe, and the familiar symbols briefly distracted me from the persistent, tormenting memories of my last night with Jake. The agony of losing him clung to every cell of my being.

I had seen Jake drunk before, but that night was different. He was so tortured and confused, his secrets were too dark to share even with me, and those secrets made him choose death over life. I didn't totally understand what he had called his "aberration," but although I was still quite inexperienced, I did know he would not be accepted the way he was if anyone were to discover his secret - not in a rural Midwest town in 1958. The unyielding shame had become too agonizing for him to bear.

I was even more confused about his comments about Ben. *Talk to me, Jake. Make me understand.* There was never an answer to my silent pleas, but in the end, it didn't matter. I was leaving my past behind – all of it, including Ben. I knew it was the only way I could survive.

In the letter I had left for Gladys and George, I assured them I just needed time away and would be back someday, but in my heart, I didn't believe my own promise. I also felt there was no need to explain what had happened between Jake and me that night to make him step in front of a speeding train. In hindsight I realized that Mr. Jackson, deep within him, must have known of Jake's struggle, but he had not known how to close the chasm between him and his beloved son. *He would never have stopped loving you, Jake.*

I closed my eyes again and tried to focus on where I was going, rather than where I came from. One direction was frightening, while the other choice was too painful to think about.

I had never been as skilled as Jake at memorizing the stops along the Wabash Railroad. Nevertheless, I was quite sure the train I was on would take me as far as Kansas City - as long as the railway cops, called "bulls" by the other jumpers, did not catch me. Before leaving Jake's house, I had packed a loaf of bread and a package of cheese for enough sandwiches to get me to Kansas City. I had also grabbed Jake's camping canteen with a supply of water. As I held the canteen in my lap, I rubbed my hand over its canvas exterior, trying in some way to touch Jake.

The sway of the train was lulling me back to sleep when suddenly a noise awakened me. "Dang, you're a girl," the husky voice announced.

I was startled. My temples were pounding, and I had a hard time shaking off the heaviness of sleep, but gradually I realized that a tall, thin young man was standing over me. His gruffness belied his stature and made him sound far older and sturdier of frame.

Unexpectedly, he leaned down to reach for my canteen. Out of instinct, I kicked out my right foot and swept it hard against his legs, knocking him to the floor of the train car. He looked at me in shock before letting out a sharp whistle of admiration. "Damn, girl, that was good!"

"Don't be rude. If you're thirsty, I'll give you a sip, but you need to ask first."

"Okay, Sergeant. Please may I have a drink?" He nodded contritely and rubbed his leg as he accepted the canteen.

"Not too much. It has to last to Kansas City."

"That's where I'm going too. 'Name is Davey. I'm a cattle stiff – bull rider. I have to get to Kansas City in time for the rodeo. You do this route a lot?"

His question was odd to me - as if it were perfectly normal for a young woman to be traveling in a boxcar.

"No, but I know what I'm doing, so don't think you can mess with me."

"Whoa! Relax, sugar tits. I'm just making conversation. It looks like we're going to be together for quite a few hours. We might as well be friends."

"I don't need friends, thank you. I need to sleep."

Davey gave me a long look, as if sizing me up. Then he abruptly reached behind his back and yanked a gun from his waistband. I screamed and automatically raised my hands to shield my face.

When I screamed again, he threw his body on top of mine and clamped a strong hand over my mouth so I couldn't call out. The splinters of the rough boards beneath me dug into my legs as I kicked him hard and clawed his arms to force him off me.

"Shh, stop fighting." As he uttered the warning, I could feel his hot breath on my ear.

Several times I tried to bite his hand, but I could not get my teeth into him. Although I fought desperately to thrust him off, after a long struggle, my body finally surrendered. With no more strength or energy to fight, my body yielded to his weight.

He pushed in closer, shoving his face up against mine. "Jesus Christ, sugar tits," Davey said under his breath, "don't scream again! I'm just trying to keep you quiet. Someone is right outside the train. They're gonna hear us and throw us off the dang train – maybe even toss us in the clinker."

All of a sudden, I realized the train had pulled to a stop. When Davey turned his head to look at the freight car door, I saw an opportunity. I bit his hand simultaneously as I slammed my knee into his groin.

He rolled off me, clutching his groin in pain. "Damn it to hell, woman!" he moaned. "I was tryin' to protect you. That's why I showed you my pistol. But you don't need no protecting. You're dangerous as hell!"

"You better believe it," I snapped at him. "And don't ever touch me again."

"I ain't gonna touch you. But I kinda wish I done shot you."

"What kind of a fool pulls a gun out without warning someone?"

The countenance of Davey's face immediately changed from bravado to remorseful. "Maybe I was just trying to impress you - didya ever think of that?"

I didn't answer. There were rustling sounds outside the car, and I was sure we were going to get busted. I held up a finger to my lips. "Hush, I hear something! And remember, no matter what happens, I don't need you to protect me."

"Well, hell's bells, maybe I need *you* to protect *me*!"

I smiled in spite of my irritation. "Shh, listen up." As the moments passed, I grew increasingly nervous. The conversation outside the train moved closer, and I could hear heavy, determined footsteps grinding into the gravel alongside the tracks. My heart began to beat even harder when the footsteps stopped directly in front of our boxcar. Davey and I looked at each other, both of us barely breathing.

"Check this car out," a hoarse voice commanded.

Davey nodded to me silently. Without a sound, we both grabbed our bindles and slung them over our shoulders. Within seconds, the door screeched open, and daylight streamed into the boxcar.

"Vagrants!" the railroad cop yelled into the blinding light.

That was our cue. Davey and I both leaped off the train right in front of two railway bulls. A strong arm grabbed the canteen that was slung over my shoulder and pulled me back as I tried to escape. Within an instant, Davey was on top of the guy, and with a downward motion of his arm, he forced the cop to release his grip. "Run, girl!" he yelled.

To our luck, we were near another one of the many cornfields that blanketed the Midwest. Running as fast as I could, I made a beeline through the field. I wasn't afraid of jumping off trains, but I was terrified of being arrested by the Railway Police. I had heard a lot of stories about how hobos were treated in jails, and I knew I would be treated just as badly. Train hopping was trespassing, so the bulls had no mercy.

I continued to run as fast as I could, zigzagging between the rows of corn. When I heard the sound of footsteps close at my heels, I forced myself to run faster, but the steps closed in on me.

"Dadgummit! Slow down, sugar tits!"

"Davey!" I was overwhelmed with relief.

After stopping in a clearing deep within the corn field, we both gasped and panted while trying to catch our breath. "I'm pretty sure we ditched them," Davey wheezed.

"Great." I reached for my canteen and took a long swig of water before passing the canteen to Davey. "You need to carry water. And stop calling me sugar tits. It's disrespectful!"

"Did ya consider that if you were polite enough to tell me your damn name, then maybe I wouldn't have to call ya that?"

"It's Kat with a 'K.' Please hush up while I think."

Davey surveyed our surroundings. "I know this route. We've already crossed the border into Illinois. There will be another train we can jump in the morning - just after dawn."

"No, thanks. I think I'll go it by hand."

"Hitchhike? That's dangerous for a girl to do. Didn't your parents teach you anything?"

"I don't have parents … not that it's any of your business." With Davey close behind, I continued trekking through the field toward the nearest road, but I slowed my step. I had never hitch-hiked before, and I knew I would feel safer on a train. I didn't know why I had chosen Kansas City as a stop-off – maybe because Jake always wanted us to go there – and because it was anywhere other than the painful places I had been. It was my sole destination until I could find my direction, and I knew the Wabash Railroad would get me there.

After I plopped down in the field with resignation, Davey caught up with me and dropped his bindle. He spread out a blanket for us to lie upon and made pillows using our bags. "We'll spend the night here," he announced.

"You gonna try any funny business?"

"No ma'am. Here, you can have my gun. If I get out of line you can shoot me."

"That's the best offer I've had in years. I may shoot you just on principle." I took in a deep breath as I lay back on the blanket and closed my eyes.

Davey stretched his long limbs before he settled in. "Just so you know, Annie Oakley, I did have me some water, but I lost my satchel on my last ride due to another run-in with the cops."

"Great, you're a walking good luck charm. Now please stop talking."

The sun was going down, and the air was cool and sweet. I could feel the curve of Davey's back as he arranged himself on the blanket next to me. I liked his warmth and his masculine scent. It was nice to feel that part of me awaken again.

"By the way, 'Kat with a K,' that's a nice bruise on your face. No doubt you were in a barroom brawl. And probably won."

I elbowed him in his back just before I closed my eyes and allowed the sound of his breathing and the crooning of the crickets to lull me into a welcome sleep.

CHAPTER ELEVEN

THERE WAS NO CHANCE OF OVER-SLEEPING THE MORNING TRAIN. Due to the humming of a John Deere tractor and the cacophonous crowing of roosters announcing the light of day, we both were awake and alert at dawn. I noticed Davey rifling through his backpack as I stretched my legs. I let him suffer awhile before I spoke.

"If you're looking for your gun, I have it. I still don't trust you."

"You damn well oughta, girl! I'm the best thing you've got." He took a spoon out of his backpack and dipped it into a jar of peanut butter before offering it to me.

"Is that spoon clean?"

"Of course. I just use it to scrape cow patties off my boots. Where are you from, Miss Cynical with a 'C'?"

"Wabash, Indiana. How about you?"

"Austin - great state of Texas," he proudly announced.

"But you jumped on in Indiana. Are you on the lam or did you lose your sense of direction?"

"Very funny. I was able to get me some work at a farm in Ohio my uncle done heard of. Pretty good money, but I follow the rodeo circuit and it was time for me to keep movin' on."

"You always use the rails, cowboy?"

"Nah. I had me a Chevy truck, but it gave out on me a few months back. What's your story?"

"First trip. My life took a turn, so it was time for me to leave Indiana."

"Hmmm ... my guess is you're on the FBI's Most Wanted List for groin assault. Well, you better be careful. Not everyone on the trains is as nice as I am. Where are you going?"

"Not sure. Just away."

"I get it. No questions. But you should visit Austin sometime. It's real beautiful there. Or better yet - New Orleans. I used to live there, too. It's another real exciting place. It's easy to lose yourself in New Orleans, if that's what you're fixin' to do."

"I'll keep that in mind."

"Pack up, missy. It won't be long now before our next ride comes through."

I tossed him his gun and started heading toward the tracks just as we heard the next train coming down the line.

———

Davey and I were together almost two days. The actual train time to Kansas City is much shorter, but we had to make very short jumps. We kept disembarking just to make sure we were not discovered when the boxcars were loaded and unloaded.

Oftentimes, the railroad bulls were lurking about, forcing us to wait for hours to catch the next train. During our breaks in travel, we would walk around small towns just to see the sights. Cowpoke Davey loved to look at horses, which we often saw because we preferred to stay on the outskirts of town unless we needed a bite to eat.

I found Davey to be good company, and he was generous - always sharing his food. I appreciated his kindness because I was running out of the money I had saved from my days working at Bradley Brothers. My plan for survival was not well thought out, but I had faith that I could get a waitress job wherever I ended up.

We had to hop off and back on again in St. Louis, and I regretted not having time to see the city. To entertain me, Davey surprised me by pulling out a harmonica. He did an exciting rendition of the old tune, "Meet me in St. Louis." Jake would have loved it.

For the most part, we had good rides as long as no one hassled us. The short rides were usually uneventful enough for us to take naps. At every stop, if not disembarking, we remained alert, listening for any signs of threat, but we were always able to go back to sleep as soon as the train left the station.

I liked being with Davey, and I often moved closer to him when we were napping. I told myself it was because he made me feel safe, but I also loved the tingling feeling in my stomach when he touched me.

Davey had a pack of cards in his backpack, so we spent some time playing poker, a game Jake had taught me when we were in Franklin. I never won a hand, but I just assumed it was because I was still somewhat new at the game. After a number of hands, however, I sensed something fishy was going on with Davey.

One day I threw down my cards and looked Davey straight in the eye. "You're a goddarn card sharp, aren't you?"

Davey let out a big belly laugh. "Damn girl! I was wondering how long it would take you to figure it out. I'm a rounder. I find me games wherever I go. That's how I make extra dough."

I kicked him in the leg before retrieving my cards. "You're slicker than a wet donkey turd," I snarled playfully, emphasizing one word at a time while flicking each card at his head as he ducked and fended off my assault.

I grew very fond of Davey in the short time we were together. He had an easy spirit about him. At twenty-three years old, he was only slightly older, but he had seen a lot more of the world than I had. I told him about Jake, although not much. Jake was buried deep within me, and it was still too hard to find the words to do Jake justice.

I allowed Davey to believe Jake's death was an accident, and he never asked for more information than I was ready to give. He was respectful that way. He just nodded and listened. "I'm sorry, Kat. Good friends who are like brothers are real hard to come by. You gotta keep 'em right here." I was touched when Davey placed a fist to his heart.

Davey recounted wonderful stories about learning to bust broncos from the time he was a "knee-high to a June bug." His dad had been on the rodeo circuit also, so rodeo performing came naturally to him. He told me he was most comfortable on a horse. "Finest critters on earth," he mused. "Them and dogs – both are as devoted as the day is long. They've always got your back."

"Like Jake did."

"Yes, like Jake. I'll tell you what - seeing as how you don't have a particular plan in mind, why don't you come with me and watch me ride in the rodeo in Kansas City? I usually make myself a little money, and I have lots of connections for jobs and all sorts of things everywhere I go – legal and illegal, just in case you need a new ID or somethin' similar."

"Ha! You're a man of many talents."

"You bet I am. And afterward I'll take you out for a bigass Kansas steak dinner like you told me Jake always talked about. We can even order up an extra steak and another place setting for Jake. It will be symbolic … a way to pay respect. My buddy has some bunkhouses at his ranch where you can bunk up before you move on and I head back to Austin. How would that suit you?"

"I think I'd like that a lot."

We were relaxing in silence when we felt the train braking slightly. Davey slid the box car door open just long enough to look out at the station ahead. "Salisbury, Missouri. Small town. It won't take us long to find a store and buy us some soft drinks before moving on."

He reached out to help me to my feet. When I grasped his hand, I could feel the warm roughness of his skin and wanted to hold on longer. His hands were strong and comforting. I had a strong urge to touch his chest and to bury my face in his neck.

"Davey, I-"

All at once the train lurched as it began to brake. "Hold that thought, Kat. We have to get ready fast."

I pushed my thoughts to the back of my mind and prepared for the jump. Just before we got to the Salisbury station, we both leaped to the ground. It was an easy dismount because the train was at a crawl. Davey signaled me to follow him as we ran behind the depot, assuming no one had seen us. The hobo symbols that had been crudely drawn on the side of the building indicated that it was a safe and friendly stopover.

We thought we were clear when, out of nowhere, a burly rail cop descended upon us from the opposite side of the depot. The station master was behind him, pointing in our direction. We were both shocked, because the smaller depots were not known to have the aggressive rail security that train jumpers had to avoid at larger stations.

"You two are under arrest," the cop yelled. "Stop right now!"

The train was just pulling out again when the cop caught hold of Davey's arm. As he tried to wrest himself from the cop's grip, Davey screamed at me to jump aboard the moving train. "Go," he yelled, "run, Kat!"

I turned to my right and started running back toward the tracks. When I glanced over my shoulder, I could see Davey struggling to free himself, but the cop was hanging on his back.

"Go on! Jump, Kat!" Davey screamed as I got close to the rails.

With one hand, I grabbed a bar and pulled myself onto the side of a closed boxcar. I looked back at Davey just as he managed to throw the cop off his back. He started to run toward the train.

The train was picking up speed rapidly, but Davey kept on coming. There was nothing ahead but straightaway, so I knew we would continue to build speed. I also knew Davey wasn't going to make it. "Don't do it!" I screamed. "Don't do it, Davey!"

He did not hear my warning. His timing was off, and the train was moving too fast. Davey reached up as another boxcar zoomed past. He almost got a grip, but then he lost his footing on the loose gravel beneath him. As he stumbled, he fell backwards along the edge of the tracks. I gasped in horror when I saw his body twist awkwardly as he landed, forcing his legs toward the speeding train. As he tried to roll away from the track, one foot caught on the rail.

Davey's mouth looked grotesque as it formed a scream that was drowned out by the sound of the train. Blood gushed from his boot. He rolled onto his side and grasped the remaining part of his severed foot.

In the last glimpse I had of Davey, he raised one bloody hand to signal me onward.

Shocked and horrified, I continued to cling to the grip on the end of a boxcar. There was no place to safely stand as the train hurtled toward its next destination. I knew I would have to step on the couplings for support, something One Arm Joe had warned me never to do. I was shaking and losing my nerve, but the train was going too fast for me to leap back off.

Fighting my terror, I inched around the corner of the boxcar with my pack slung over my back. One foot at a time, I shifted onto the couplings where I could stand. As I clutched the ladder on the back of the car, the two adjoined train cars pushed and pulled against each other. The tracks raced beneath me, and I couldn't look down without getting dizzy. I was petrified I would fall through the opening between the cars and be crushed on the rails below. Images of Jake being ripped apart the night he died flashed through my mind at a punishing speed. My knuckles ached from the tight grip I had on the ladder.

Somehow, I managed to hang on until the next station, where I jumped off the second the train slowed. I ran to the depot without looking around to see if there were any railroad security officers about. I didn't care anymore. I threw myself onto a bench on the platform and started sobbing until numbness came over me again.

———

The sun was just peering over the top of the train depot when I awakened, still face-down on the bench on the empty platform. I was tired, hungry, and defeated, and I wondered how long I could keep on running. As I pressed my face against the smooth wood slats of the bench, I was startled to see boot-clad feet standing next to me. Fueled by adrenaline, I bolted upward, ready to run.

"It's okay honey. Nobody around here is going to bother you."

I was looking into the round and cheerful face of a woman clad in overalls and rubber boots. Atop her head was a tattered canvas fishing hat, chockablock with colorful lures. It was fascinating. Whispers of white hair sprouted from under the hat as though reaching for the bright red kerchief wrapped around her neck. I concluded from her demeanor that she was in her late seventies, but her face was relatively unlined.

"I'm Margo," she said by way of introduction. "You look like you could use a bath and some food. I can offer you a little something in exchange for some work."

"Really? What kind of work?"

Margo chuckled and crossed her arms. "Probably not the kind you're suspicious of. Just ask the station master 'bout me. I live right over there." She pointed to a lone white farmhouse about a quarter of a mile from the station. "He'll tell you how I often give work to train jumpers."

"I don't jump trains," I lied.

Margo suppressed a smile. "Yeah, and I don't wish I was married to Gary Cooper!"

"So, you're looking for help?"

"Yep. I don't hire much help from in town. They always try to gouge me. Itinerant workers expect fair pay and work harder. Can you paint?"

"Yes, I can paint."

"Good. I'd rather hire a strange girl than a strange man. Come on honey, let's go." Margo didn't wait for me to agree. She picked up my bag and started walking across the field, expecting me to follow.

"Hey!" I yelled.

She turned to look at me with a sigh of exasperation. "You better keep up if you want to work. Would you like to get a couple of nights' sleep in my guest room and put some home cooked food in your belly … or do you just wanna sit on a bench waiting for trouble to land in your lap?"

After a beat, I followed. As we approached the old farm-house, I noticed buckets of paint and a few brushes on the side-walk that led to the porch. Although the paint was peeling off the clapboard, the house was very inviting. The veranda was lined with potted flowers, and a bright red bird feeder was hanging in front of the large picture window. Positioned at one end of the veranda, an old porch swing with well-worn striped cushions rocked in the breeze.

"There's a small bunk house back there past the rose trellis. You take your stuff and plant yourself there. Don't worry, you'll be safe. No one will bother you. After you've showered, you come and knock on my door, and then I'll rustle us up some breakfast."

"All right. Thank you, ma'am."

"No need to thank me. You'll do some work in exchange. But you'll eat first. A young woman like you shouldn't be out there travelin' on your own."

A young woman, I thought. Was I? I was about to turn nineteen, but I had no illusions of womanhood. My period had stopped again, and my body was merely a weed clinging to whatever insured my survival. How odd that she saw me as even vaguely feminine.

"Go," Margo ordered. Her voice was stern, but her smile was soft. Her body appeared soft too - the kind of body that a person needing solace could fall into and feel safe.

The back house was nothing fancy, but it was comfortable. The bed was covered with a colorful quilt, and a knit afghan was strewn across the footboard. There was a small table, a reading lamp, and a white wicker rocking chair. I rocked in the chair for a moment before I took a hot shower, grateful to feel clean again.

I didn't need to knock on Margo's front door. She was holding it open as I stepped up onto the porch. She ushered me in with decorum, as though presenting me at court. I couldn't fight my feelings of suspicion. Why was this woman being so nice to me? I was ready to move on at any moment, but the smell of bacon was a definite sign I should at least eat something first.

I hadn't had such good food since my days staying with the Jacksons. There were pancakes with eggs, bacon, and coffee. "I should pay you for the food," I offered.

"What, you're a Rockefeller? You just eat. I'll be right back."

As I sat at the large oval table, I inspected the black and white checked linoleum floor which was spotless. Tall, cream-colored cabinets were ceiling high, and a large bowl of fruit brightened the pale blue counters. On the shelf above the stove were two fresh pies and a collection of salt and pepper shakers.

I was staring at a set of shakers shaped like cows when Margo returned with a pile of clothing and a duffel bag. "Here - my daughter left these with a bunch of other things she didn't want. She's all grown up now - good girl, that one. She moved with her accountant husband to Jackson, Mississippi. I get to see her and my adorable, smart-ass little grandson every Christmas."

"I don't know if I should-"

"Nonsense," she protested, cutting me off. "You'll take these. She's about your size. You're awfully thin though, so they may be a little loose. You should get rid of that dirty bag of yours and use this here duffel bag instead. You can strap it on your back so as not to get hurt when hoppin' trains."

"But I don't-"

"I know - and William Holden ain't dreamy," she responded, cutting off my feeble attempt at denial.

"Thank you, ma'am." I noticed she was still wearing her hat indoors, which was odd, but not any stranger than a lot of things I had seen in my life. It seemed the polite thing to do would be to acknowledge her unique choice of headgear. "I like your hat. You sure must love fishing."

"Oh honey, I wouldn't hurt a fish. This belonged to my useless husband. I kicked him out, but I kept the hat - refused to give it back. I figured he was out fishin' for women, so he had no need to be fishin' for bass." Margo's low, rumbling laugh filled the kitchen.

"It's a great hat, and it looks real nice on you."

"Thank you, darlin' child. So now, are you gonna tell me your name? Or are you gonna make me guess?"

"It's Kat."

"Kat, huh? That resonates. It's got intrigue."

Intrigue. I liked that.

As I was finishing up my pancakes, I felt Margo's presence behind me. "Let this ol' granny take a whack at this mess for you," she said. I was startled when she began to brush my hair. When I tried to rise from my chair, she gently eased me back down. "Relax, dear - 'not being personal here - just doin' what a hairdresser would do with this mess. Although by the looks of my hair, a body would think I never met a beautician in my life." She laughed again, and I could feel my shoulders relax.

"You've got yourself some beautiful long dark hair here, but I can tell you haven't brushed it in a coon's age. Let's get it smoothed out. It would be best to tie it back, so that way it won't get in the paint. I don't need no hairs stuck to my siding."

No one had ever brushed my hair before. It took me a while to relax and allow her to work through the snarls. After the brush slipped through my hair freely, she continued to brush. Her touch was rhythmic and gentle. I was confused when tears welled up in my eyes and my throat tightened. Without waiting for her to stop, I pulled away and shoved my plate aside. "Thank you very much for the food. I'm ready to work now."

Margo tapped me on the shoulder. "Breathe, sweetheart," she smiled, "sometimes you gotta exhale the bad before the good can come in."

———

I stayed with Margo for a week. The painting was hard work, but I enjoyed it. It felt good to make the house clean and tidy. Margo told me I had a natural flare. When we finished the areas on the house that needed painting, we even touched up the back house.

We talked a lot over those days, and I grew very fond of her. She was full of energy and had a great sense of humor. "I'm seventy-five years old," she announced one day as she swayed to a jazzy tune by Duke Ellington coming from the radio, "and look at me - I'm still sexier than a red Corvette."

She told me she had made a good living as a seamstress. I was shocked when she recalled meeting an itinerant worker named Mary who was also a seamstress. I knew she must have been speaking of the same woman I had spent time with at the hobo camp back in Wabash. Margo had helped find Mary some piece work, which I was pleased to hear. I didn't mention I had met Mary too, because I didn't want to answer any questions.

"When you live near a train depot, you see a lot of people

coming and going. I like to wander over there when the field is dry. I've been doing it more since my dog died 'cause I need the company. I suspect the station master thinks I'm just not an old lady who has lost her marbles, but it's my way of meeting real interesting people like yourself. 'Keeps me from getting lonely."

Most of the time, our evenings were spent on the porch swing where we could enjoy the night air and watch the trains go by in the distance. One evening she nodded in the direction of a passing train just as it blew its melancholy whistle. "You know, over the years, I've seen a lot of travelers who jump trains, even though I know you have never done that sort of thing ..."

"Hmm ... then I guess you might have seen me from here, huh?"

"Sure-as-shootin', honey. I went over to the depot to check up on you several times during the night while you were sleeping on that bench. I didn't want to disturb you, although all your tossing and mumbling gave me the idea you weren't having a good rest."

"I just have a lot on my mind."

"Most folks who pass through here have a story. If you don't object to my askin' - what's yours?"

"Not much to tell, Margo. No family to speak of. I went to college for a short time. My best friend died unexpectedly, so I left. And to tell you the truth, I'm not sure where I'm going."

"Hmmm, that's a tough one." She didn't press me for details, but as we sat in silence, I began to feel comfortable enough to share a great deal about my past. She enjoyed my recollections of many of Jake's antics, but I was careful to avoid any discussion of his death. I did, however, tell her about his confusion and his fear of being in some way different from other men. She nodded knowingly and patted my knee.

"Those who are different are often the most special. God made us all from different recipes. It makes me real sad to know that unique folks like your friend Jake aren't always appreciated and accepted. That causes a lot of needless pain in this world. I'd like to say your mom and Jake are in a better place, but I don't really believe that. I do hope they are at peace though."

"You don't believe in heaven?"

"Oh yes, sweetheart, I do. But after we die? I'm not so sure about the timing on that one. It's the where-what-and-when of the whole concept that stumps me. I think maybe heaven is ours to find right here on earth."

"With all due respect, I can tell you for a fact, heaven is not here on earth as far as I can tell."

"Ah, you're young, Kat. And you've been through a lot, it's true. But maybe you need to look a little harder. It sounds to me like you had a lot of moments of heaven with, Jake. Maybe that's heaven – perfect moments."

"Yes, I do see your point. I need to remember that." I went on to tell her about Ben and the Jacksons and Davey.

"Davey sounds like a real good guy. Honest folk, that type. I sure hope he can ride bulls again. Terrible accident. That's why I don't like the idea of you throwing yourself onto moving trains … if you were ever of a mind to do such a dangerous and crazy thing, that is."

"Never!" I grinned "But thank you so much for caring. I always enjoy our talks, Margo, and I sure appreciate your hospitality, but now that the painting is done and the place is tidied up, I think it's time for me to move on." I didn't really want to leave Margo, but the darkness was hovering again. My instinct was to get as far away from my past as possible, and I hoped the next train would take me even farther. In spite of Davey's horrible accident, the danger of train hopping did not deter me. It kept a much deeper pain at bay.

"There's always more work to be done here, you know, dear. But I understand how sometimes people need to keep going until they find themselves. I'll be sad to see you leave - probably even going to miss you."

"I'll miss you too, Margo. It's been real nice here. I think you even fattened up my scrawny figure a bit."

She smiled. "You still got some eatin' to do if you want to be voluptuous like me, doll. Where are you heading?"

"I don't know. I'll figure it out when I get to Kansas City."

"You know, Kansas City is a mighty big city for a girl who doesn't know her way around."

"I have to go there, Margo. As I mentioned, it's where Jake always wanted to go. I need to do that for him - to honor him, you know? Maybe I can find a place for a Kansas City steak like we planned. He always talked about that. After that, I'll probably move on. I just don't know where yet."

"K.C. is just down the road a piece. You stopped just short of there, darlin'. I'll drive you to the station in the morning. That way someday you'll remember how to get back to my house from the street side also, by golly. But right now, you're going to go inside and call the Jacksons on my phone just to let them know you're safe. You don't have to say much more. They'll understand. Just do it. After you give them some peace of mind, you come on out to the table, because I'm making a special dinner."

———

The Jacksons were not at home, and I was relieved. I did, however, reach Louise's mom. Although I knew Mrs. Schroeder wanted to have a conversation, I kept it very brief. After I made sure my dad and Louise were well, I asked her to leave George and Gladys a message to assure them I was safe and would be in touch again. I also asked her to tell them to please forgive me for avoiding the funeral. In my heart, I knew they would understand that I could never say good-bye to Jake.

By the time I returned to the kitchen, I felt a sense of relief. As I sat down, Margo placed a dinner plate in front of me. On the plate was a huge steak. She smiled and announced, "Kansas City's finest cooked to perfection right here in Birmingham,

Missouri, just in case you decide it's best to hold onto your money once you hit the big city."

"My money is close to gone anyway, Margo," I chuckled.

"Nope, here you go." Margo shoved a pile of bills in front of me.

"Oh no! The food, the clothes, a bed – all that cost more than the work I did."

"You hush now! I'm the one who sets the wages around here, Kat. Now go on and eat your steak 'cause it ain't gonna attach itself back onto the cow."

I had never even tasted steak, but that piece of meat was the most delicious thing I ever ate. Margo was thrilled when I oo'ed and ah'ed with every bite. As soon as she was done with her meal, she got up and brought another platter of steak over to the table.

"Oh, no," I protested. "I can't eat another bite unless you have a desire to clean masticated steak off your floor!"

"Sounds delightful," she smiled, "but it's not exactly for you. I liked what Davey told you. He was right - some things are symbolic. This one's for Jake."

For a moment, I remained motionless, and then all my walls fell down. I was so overwhelmed by her kindness, my body trembled, and then I began to sob as the conflicting emotions crashed and tumbled within me. I could feel Jake's presence, and he was smiling. Margo silently held my hand and stroked my back until I fell into her arms for comfort. Although I was still harboring the sorrow I had lived with so long, in that moment, a little piece of heaven slowly crept in.

———

The next morning, I packed the cold steak and clothing into the duffel and rode with Margo to the Kansas City train station. We were both sad when I waved goodbye, but I promised her I would always remember where she lived and would one day return. In the last glimpse I had of Margo, she was flapping her fishing hat out the car window as she drove away.

My loose plan was to see a little bit of Kansas City because that was Jake's dream. I also wanted to locate the rodeo so I could ask around to see if Davey ever made it.

However, as I stood in the middle of the terminal, I was overwhelmed. The station was bigger than any depot I had ever seen - vast, exciting, and intimidating.

I stared at the overhead slip-flap schedule board that changed rapidly with the ever-changing information about incoming and outbound trains. Each clack-clack-clack sound introduced a dizzying display of connections to exotic places as far away as California. I was lost and confused until the board stopped long enough to announce a departing train with a destination I didn't even know I was looking for:

10:15 AM: Kansas City to New Orleans. Train: Southern Belle.

The Southern Belle.

I found my direction.

CHAPTER TWELVE

FIGHTING MY WAY THROUGH GROUPS OF ARRIVING PASSENGERS AND porters laden with luggage, I descended to the station platform where the trains were lined up in a beautiful display of strength and might. There she was in all her glory - the Southern Belle. She had lived in my imagination for so long I had begun to doubt her actual existence. Standing on the platform, I was overwhelmed as I appraised her streamlined red and yellow aluminum alloy cab and beautiful illuminated insignia with the Kansas City-Louisiana-Arkansas letters proudly displayed. She was the pride of the Kansas City Southern Railway Company.

I could identify every car and knew the purpose of each. I walked slowly along the platform until I saw the regal observation car. As I peered around the back end of the car, I gasped. The face of Miss Southern Belle was smiling at me, and she was as beautiful as I imagined. The Southern Belle was the only train to carry a face on its emblem, and I had long ago memorized every detail of that face.

My body was shaking with excitement. In my mind, I was aboard the train, savoring every aspect of her glorious design. My eyes moved along her mighty structure, scanning the dining car where I had long ago imagined I would eat before experiencing a night in the Pullman sleeper car. I was overjoyed as I mentally experienced every luxury she offered.

She was calling to me, and her force was driving me to some unknown destination. She was my past, my future, my mother, and Jake all wrapped into one. I longed to ride her, and I trusted her.

There were enough bills in my pocket to buy a passenger ticket, but I would be left with almost nothing. As foolish and impulsive as it may have been, I turned and walked back into Union Station to the ticket counter. My chest was heaving as I suppressed an urge to whoop with joy. This time I would ride in style.

———

Overwhelmed with anticipation, I stepped up onto the car platform and handed a friendly conductor my ticket. He was dressed in a uniform as regal as the Belle herself.

I had a hard time containing my unabashed excitement as I entered the magnificent passenger car. The scene in front of me was like a salon in an elegant hotel. Curved booths and comfortable chairs were arranged around circular tables with small lamps, all accented by interesting photo murals on the pale green walls.

True to the photos Jake and I had studied, the crisp celery green finishes heightened the deep wine color of the carpet, which seemed almost too luxurious to walk on. I skirted around a Negro man in a white coat and gloves who expertly balanced a tray of beverages while he served refreshments and assiduously tended to the passengers' requests. The passengers were in good spirits, evoking a mirthful chuckle from the waiter that sounded as if it had surfaced from the bottom of a deep well. The atmosphere was one of warm Southern hospitality.

After I placed my duffel bag in the rack above me, I dropped into the cushy seat, which was like an easy chair that could rotate or recline. I smiled to myself, knowing that Jake would have compared the seat to a dentist's chair. My days with Margo and Davey had taught me that it was impossible to force Jake from my mind – it was easier to keep him with me. *You should be here, Jake. You'd love this.* I spoke to him often. The conversations protected me from moments too painful to remember.

I studied the other passengers, who were all nicely dressed. The air of anticipation was infectious. I was grateful I had washed my hair and was wearing the clothes and leather boots Margo had given me, but my new look felt dishonest. I was an interloper - a jumper riding in a passenger car. I felt guilty for having such privilege after stealing aboard trains so many times in the past, but I was determined to freeze each moment in my memory.

To go from sleeping on the rough, dirty boards of a boxcar to experiencing such luxury in an air-conditioned train car was a momentous experience. *How am I so lucky to have this happen to me?* I thought. A grin lifted the corners of my mouth as the answer finally dawned on me: Margo had given me the money in hopes I would buy a ticket. She wanted me to realize my dream, and I believe she knew I would choose the Southern Belle. I was filled with emotion at the thought of her kindness.

When the train rocked forward and the gears slid into action, I knew we were about to pull out of the station. The thrill was irrepressible. *Thank you, Margo,* I said to myself as I instinctively reached into my pocket to touch the hand-written note she had included with the bills. *Safe journey until you return. Happy 19th birthday, Kat.*

CHAPTER THIRTEEN

THE TRAIN ROCKED SLOWLY, THE SOFT, UPHOLSTERED CHAIR cradling me as I rested my hands on its arms. I slowly rotated to get different views of the passing scenery. I wanted to remember every single detail of the experience.

"Excuse me, miss, would you mind if I sit here, please?"

I turned my chair and looked up at a tall, thin elderly man. His hair was like silver thread, which set off the blue in his eyes. He was very old - even older than Margo, I was sure - but he was spry and alert, with impressively straight posture.

"Please do, sir," I nodded as I gestured to the seat next to mine. He placed a brown and yellow straw suitcase in the rack above us before lowering himself into his seat.

"Wow, you're tall," I couldn't help but remark.

"Yes, ma'am, six foot five. My mother called me a tall drink of water, my father called me a string bean, and my departed wife just called me to dinner."

I knew he had used that line before, but I couldn't help but laugh - he was just so very congenial.

"Where are you off to?" he asked. His manner of speaking was much stronger than any man of his age I had ever spoken with.

"I think I'm going all the way to the end of the line."

"Fine choice. Fine choice," he repeated with a nod. "I'm getting off in Shreveport, which is where I live. A few days after that, I'll be back aboard heading for Baton Rouge. Can't think of a better way to travel than on the Southern Belle."

"Do you have business in Baton Rouge?"

"No, I have family members there. Actually, it's my wife's family, but she's gone now. Every now and then I check in on them – it helps me to stay connected to Elvida. That was the wife's name - Elvida, but I always called her 'Elvie.'"

"This is my first trip. I've never been to the South before."

"I'm not surprised, my dear, because you're grinning like a jack in the box. You will love the southern hospitality and everything there is to see in New Orleans. And oh, the food they serve! Fried chicken and catfish and pecan-everything. I go down there to fatten up," he chuckled.

"That's what I keep hearing. I can't wait."

"My Elvie and I last traveled this very train some nineteen-odd years ago. I had recently retired, and we wanted to participate in all the excitement surrounding the Miss Southern Belle contest. We rode from Kansas City down to Baton Rouge, and lo and behold, who won but Miss Margaret Landry from Baton Rouge! Elvie knew her family, so we all celebrated together. It was a high time!"

I nearly leaped out of my chair. I was so excited I couldn't contain myself. "You met her? You met Margaret Landry?"

"I sure did. I'm surprised you even know her name. It was a grand celebration. When Elvie and I boarded the train in Kansas City, there was such an air of excitement. At every train stop, a different Miss Southern Belle contestant boarded. As the train pulled into each main station along the way, there would often be bands playing and crowds gathered to cheer on their local contestant."

"How wonderful! I read about it, but it never seemed quite real to me."

"Oh, it was very real, my dear. The composer of the song 'The Southern Belle' was aboard with us. His name was Cecil Taylor. 'Not sure if he is still alive. It went a little like this," he crooned: *"'And I knew from the start, you had stolen my heart, SOUTH-ERN BELLE.'"*

"Wow, you have a really nice voice."

"I'm glad you think so. We all sang along that day. It was an atmosphere of great celebration. I am Reese Bennett, by the way - Shreveport born and raised."

As he offered his hand, I pressed his long fingers against mine. "Kat Caswell of Wabash, Indiana. Please tell me more, if you don't mind, Mr. Bennett. Did the Southern Belle contestants wear their gowns on the train?"

"Indeed, they did. They were dressed in old fashion southern garb - hoop skirts and great big picture hats. Some even carried frilly umbrellas. I wish Elvie were here now to describe those dresses to you. She could do a much better job. She took such delight in it all."

"I wish she were here too, Mr. Bennett."

"Oh, she's never far from me though. Never far. It took me a long while to get used to her absence. I tried to block out the memories but doing so makes the hole inside me feel even bigger. Now I let the memories sweep over me every chance I get. The love and the smiles were all part of my life - the best parts – so it just doesn't make any sense to try to forget."

"I suppose you're right. But it must hurt so much …"

"Sure. It takes bravery. You don't get over it, but you get through it. And now look where I am today - sitting here in this elegant car telling you all about Elvie and living the memories all over again. What a wonderful thing!"

I paused for a moment as I watched the scenery whiz by. I wondered if I could ever get to the place where Mr. Bennett was. I silently conversed with Jake all the time - in the present - but when I would think back on moments we shared together, it was still too painful to let my mind linger.

"I'm glad you joined me, Mr. Bennett," I smiled.

"I must say, it's very enjoyable to chat with you, Kat. A lot of folks think an old man is not worth wasting their time talking to. But us old folks have seen more of the world than most know."

"This is wonderful for me too, thank you, sir. Would you mind telling me what Margaret Landry was like?"

"Not at all. But I'm curious. If I may ask, why do you have such a keen interest in Miss Landry rather than in one of those young movie idols in the teen magazines?"

"They're okay, but to be perfectly honest, Senator Kennedy's wife Jacqueline is more my type. She's in all the magazines now, too. She's a photographer. But I'm interested in Miss Landry because when I first read about the contest, I really wanted to know her. I was just a little girl, and she was magical to me."

"She certainly did have a magic about her. She was as sweet as she could be, and so pretty, but not the kind of pretty that is overdone - just soft and natural. When she smiled, her face lit up, and that giggle of hers was infectious. She was so excited when she won that contest. Everyone who knew her was thrilled for her too. Only eighteen years old!"

It seemed impossible that the woman I had imagined to be my mother had been younger than my current nineteen years when I had first become captivated with her image. "Imagine having your face on the emblem of every Southern Belle train!"

"Some people are thrust into the spotlight, and they don't deserve or appreciate it. But according to folks who really knew her well, she never changed. She was always sweet and humble."

I loved Mr. Bennett's description of Margaret Landry. In the years since I discovered the truth about my mother, I had gradually retreated back into my imagination regarding who she was. My mother was still Miss Southern Belle. I knew it was far from the truth, but the image kept me from imagining the horrible way my mother's life ended. If I held on to the illusion, my mother would remain young and lovely ... and undamaged. My mother was the beautiful face proudly displayed on the

Southern Belle as she guided me toward New Orleans. She was with me.

Mr. Bennett rose from his seat. "I would be honored if you would allow me to buy you dinner in the dining car, Kat."

"Thank you, sir, but I have some food in my bag, and I-"

"Eat here in your seat and not experience the dining car on this magnificent train? I won't hear of it! Your company would be most appreciated. I insist."

"Well that would be just wonderful."

"Excellent. Shall we?"

As I followed Mr. Bennett to the dining car, my excitement mounted. I wondered if other passengers shared my anticipation about participating in such a unique experience. When a well-dressed male passenger and his glamorous female companion boarded at the next stop and followed us into the dining car, I sensed that the evening was just beginning.

CHAPTER FOURTEEN

"OH, WHAT A BEAUTIFUL TRAIN CAR!" I EXCLAIMED AS MR. Bennett and I entered the dining compartment. "It's just like I imagined it!" I was enthralled to see such a truly splendid room. The tables were covered with fine white linens, and there were flowers on every table. The graceful fabric draperies that lined the windows created a framework for the changing scenery. I watched in awe as waiters in white jackets took orders from the smiling patrons. The scene reminded me of those happy Texaco commercials on television. Instantly the sadness that was my constant companion receded into the background, and everything was momentarily beautiful and gay.

As we waited to be directed to a table, it occurred to me that perhaps I could get a job on a train. Maybe a hostess or a waiter? What if I could even work on the Southern Belle? The prospect was exciting.

I was about to ask Mr. Bennett for advice when the man behind him interrupted, "Excuse me, sir, but haven't we met?" His full face stretched even wider with an animated grin as he removed his jaunty fedora and thrust his hand at Mr. Bennett, who appeared to be thrown a bit off guard.

The affable man did not wait for Mr. Bennett's response. "Yes, by George, we have! Dexter Freeman Boudreaux and my wife, Lucille."

His companion, fashionably dressed in a red silk suit, smiled as she also offered her hand to Mr. Bennett. "Call me Lucy, please. And yes, I remember you. Reese, correct? We met in a restaurant in New Orleans a few years ago when you we were all there visiting. You were with your family, as I recall."

"Oh yes, of course!" Mr. Bennett exclaimed. "You're the couple I met at the Hotel Monteleone who was kind enough to tell us what sights to see. How nice to see you again!"

They were two of the most elegant people I had ever met. They both spoke in a soft drawl and carried themselves with a relaxed dignity.

Mrs. Boudreaux smoothed her blonde chignon and smiled, "Yes, yes! I remembered your name because Reese was also my granddaddy's name."

"Well, this trip just keeps getting nicer," Mr. Bennett smiled. "Please meet this delightful young woman who is traveling in the seat next to mine – Miss Kat Caswell of Wabash, Indiana."

Mr. Boudreaux chuckled as he thrust forth his hand. "Ah, quaint Wabash, Indiana – I've been through there. Wabash was the first electrically lighted city in the world to my recollection ... not that this old dinosaur was present at the lighting ceremony in the 1880's," he laughed.

"How do you do," I smiled. As I offered my hand, I was very self-conscious about my donated clothing, which was shabby compared to their elegant wardrobe. Dexter Boudreaux's flawlessly tailored suit was beige linen, and his shoes appeared to be crafted from the finest leather. Lucille's high heels and jeweled handbag matched her form-hugging suit. To me, they looked like royalty.

Dexter clapped Mr. Bennett on the back. "So how did you enjoy New Orleans? Of course, we prefer Shreveport, because it's our home, but New Orleans is a mighty seductress."

Before Mr. Bennett could answer, the hostess came to seat us.

"Excuse me," Mr. Bennett gestured apologetically, "but I think the hostess-"

Dexter held up a hand to stop us. "Please, you must sit at our table and be our guests. Let us offer you some Dixie hospitality. I insist. I want to hear about your trip, Reese. My wife and I never get tired of hearing about that dynamic city, do we, Lucy?"

Lucy's smile was dazzling, and her voice was like spring rain - soft and melodious. "It would be an honor, I'm sure."

"Kat?" Mr. Bennett politely looked at me for approval.

Although I felt shy and uncertain about being in their company, I was also excited to meet interesting people from a different part of the country.

"That would be very nice, thank you."

"It's settled then. Onward!" Mr. Boudreaux nodded enthusiastically as he signaled for us to follow the graceful hostess to the table.

Immediately upon being seated, Dexter ordered drinks all around. I was not old enough to be served alcohol, so I ordered lemonade. After our drinks arrived, Mr. Boudreaux insisted that I surreptitiously taste his mint julep, which was strong but delicious.

There was so much tableware I thought the waiter had made a mistake, but as the different courses progressed, I mimicked what Lucy did with her napkin, forks, and spoons. Lucy seemed aware I was studying her. When they presented us with a generous platter of oysters, she smiled at me before quietly sucking one down her throat. I stared at the coagulated blob before me. After a deep breath, I followed suit. Although I was immediately put off by the fishy taste and the slippery texture on my tongue, my brain warned my mouth that spitting the slimy remains onto the table would not be a good course of action. I swallowed, and then I planted a faint smile on my face.

"They're not for everyone," Lucy winked.

The waiter was extremely attentive. When he placed four large lobsters in front of us, I was completely baffled about what to do next. Some of the other patrons in the dining car looked our way and smiled, obviously impressed by each course brought to our table. Again, I followed the actions of my host and dipped my first piece of lobster into the hot butter before placing it in my mouth. The combined flavors burst on my tongue and were so delectable I wanted to hold the delicacy in my mouth forever. I was thrilled to experience such fine dining.

During dinner, Mr. Bennett enthusiastically gave his review of the glorious sights in New Orleans recommended to him by Dexter and Lucille. As he recounted his visit, I was enthralled to hear about landmarks like the old plantations and the magnificent old Victorian homes in the Garden District.

Even though I was a bit shy about partaking in the conversation, I mentioned my time spent in Franklin, Indiana, where there were also a lot of Victorian homes. By then, my dinner companions were full of good cheer, and they all expressed great interest in Franklin. After I described the Artcraft Theatre and the quaint town square, Mr. Boudreaux exclaimed, "Ah, a patriotic Yankee town. I like that a lot - especially a town with basketball fever and great popcorn!"

We all toasted Franklin, Indiana, and I found myself relaxed enough to keep the conversation going. "I'm so excited about seeing New Orleans. Tell me more, please, Mr. Boudreaux."

"You must see the cemeteries, Kat. Down in these parts, folks are buried above the ground. You should also take a boat ride on a bayou and feed the gators. That's a hoot. Just don't fall in unless you plan on a return trip to the cemetery." Mr. Boudreaux opened his eyes wide and made a gulping sound like an alligator swallowing.

Lucy giggled and dismissed him with a wave of her hand and then turned in my direction. "Oh, don't mind him. He loves to be dramatic. You must try a praline, dear, and be sure to order a beignet at Café du Monde while you're there. There's something special about beignets in the Vieux Carre."

"'Vieux Carre' - how exotic!"

"It means 'Old Square.' That's what I call myself," Mr. Bennett quipped, much to our enjoyment.

By the third course, Dexter Boudreaux had slipped me my own mint julep, so I was quite flushed, but I was having a high time. "I was about your age when I was at Tulane," he reminisced, "and the only teetotaler around was Bucky O'Neill from the Rough Riders. Of course, he was a statue, and I'm not sure he was sober either!" As we all laughed heartily, I felt lighter in spirit than I had in a very long time.

"Reese," Lucy asked, "did you have occasion to have Cajun food while in New Orleans?"

"I did indeed - unforgettable! It was at Tujagues on Decatur Street, which was one of your excellent recommendations, as I recall. We really enjoyed the crawfish and the shrimp remoulade, and then we finished off the meal with Cherries Jubilee. It was a feast."

Mr. Boudreaux, evidently very pleased their suggestions had been a hit with Mr. Bennett, slapped his hand on the table and signaled the waiter. "I suggest we relive the moment. Boy, if you please, we'd like two orders of Cherries Jubilee, and add two servings of your delicious bread pudding while you're at it. Oh, and another round of drinks, please."

Lucy excused herself for a moment as the men conversed. I focused my gaze on the beautiful Ozark Mountains, so different from the flat lands of Indiana. Small train depots flashed by as the mighty Southern Belle bypassed them for bigger stations. I loved the names of the towns we passed: Mulberry, Marble City, Poteau, and my favorite, Heavener.

After Lucy returned, she applied bright red lipstick before focusing her attention on me. She gently pulled my hair back and nodded. "Yes, that works. Kat, your hair looks lovely when pulled back a bit off your face. And you have such beautiful green eyes - you should set them off more. With a little fluff and perhaps more feminine clothing, you could be a model like Suzy Parker."

I was very flattered, especially to think that Lucy would take any interest in me at all. After living in boxcars, I had started to feel as neutered as Marie the rooster. It was nice to be reminded that there was still something female inside me somewhere.

Eventually Mr. Boudreaux also directed the conversation my way. "So now, Miss Kat, what do you plan to do in New Orleans? Do you have family there?"

"No sir, I plan to get a job as soon as I arrive."

Lucy immediately flashed me a look of concern. "But my dear, you don't have a job already set up?"

"No ma'am, but I can stay in a YWCA until something comes up." I was embarrassed to tell her the truth, so the lie came out of my mouth before I could think clearly. I had very little money left, and no defined plan. I couldn't tell her that, if necessary, I would find another encampment near the tracks. I knew they wouldn't approve ... or even believe me. How could I explain it to them? Was it only days ago when I last hid in the corner of a dirty boxcar? While sitting in the elegant dining car, the idea of it seemed even more preposterous to me than ever before.

"What kind of work are you looking for, Kat?"

"I was thinking maybe waitress work."

"Those jobs will not be plentiful down there," Lucy frowned. "Louisiana is in the heat of the season, so there will be fewer tourists this time of year, and many places close during the hot months. A lot of locals will be out of work until the weather cools off. Maybe you should consider something else?"

Mr. Boudreaux nodded in agreement. "Do you mind working with your hands? Just two days ago I met a real nice fella with a sugarcane field located not far from New Orleans near Bayou Lafourche. He claims they always need help. Apparently, they have a real good foreman, and from what he told me, they pay enough money to keep you going until you can get a good position in a restaurant."

Mr. Bennett's furled brow made it apparent to everyone that

he had his doubts. "But sugarcane, Dexter? Isn't that really tough work?"

"I suppose, but I was told some women do work in the fields. I think they do cleanup work and the like - and Kat seems young and strong. Right, Lucy?"

"I don't know. Are you sure, dear?"

"I was just proposing it as a good backup plan, my love - an insurance policy of sorts. Wait a minute now ..." Mr. Boudreaux paused as he reached into his pocket, "here - I kept the owner's card. Give it to the manager at the Hertizine plantation if you ever have a mind to do so. Look, he even wrote down the fella's name - Hank Sistrunk. Tell Sistrunk that I played cards with the owner and that his boss will be darn sure to remember me because I beat his keister at poker."

"Thank you, Mr. Boudreaux."

The conversation about sugarcane ended just as soon as the waiter set a bowl of Cherries Jubilee in front of me. We all dug in with relish, and I never wanted the trip to end.

When the meal finally came to a close and we had eaten enough to feel a gentle exhaustion sweep over us, we all expressed our pleasure with the evening's festivities and made plans to try to meet for tea in the salon car the following day. I thanked them all profusely as they rose to go to the Pullman sleeping cars. I turned back, knowing I would spend a long night upright in my seat, but compared with many of the places I had slept in the past weeks, it would be luxurious.

Mr. Boudreaux stopped me. "Kat, you're heading the wrong way, my dear."

"I'm back this way, sir. I didn't reserve a roomette."

"No? Well, you cannot sit up all night and be in any shape to look for jobs when you arrive in New Orleans. You wait right here."

Within minutes he was back, accompanied by a train attendant wearing a starched jacket, his arms full of white linens and a stack of pillows. "Everyone follow the colored man here," Mr.

Boudreaux commanded as he led us through the train car like a tour guide. "Lead on, boy. Kat, you will sleep well tonight."

Without hesitation, I turned on my heel and followed. I couldn't believe the sudden change in direction my life had taken. How could such a marvelous opportunity befall a college dropout who had been jumping trains and sleeping in hobo encampments? I was on my way to a Pullman car, where I would sleep in a bed on a majestic train that was taking me to New Orleans.

As we walked down the aisle, Mr. Bennett flashed a mischievous smile. He began to hum a tune, which I recognized immediately, so I gleefully joined in. By the time we entered the Pullman, we were humming a mighty fine rendition of "The Southern Belle."

CHAPTER FIFTEEN

IT DIDN'T SEEM POSSIBLE - I WAS IN A PULLMAN SLEEPER CAR! As I lounged on my bed, I relived in my mind all the details and events of the evening. The people, their dialect, the scenery – all were my first introduction to the South, and a great one at that.

One thing did strike me as odd, however. Although the passengers were very polite, they seemed to treat the Negroes as if they were of a different class. In Wabash, I had never heard anyone call a Negro, "boy," which made me feel very uncomfortable. The attendant, who appeared to be older than Mr. Boudreaux, had not reacted in any way to the use of that word, but the term seemed disrespectful to me. It also seemed incongruous to be coming from a man as friendly and educated as Mr. Boudreaux.

The waiter Mr. Boudreaux had addressed as "boy" was the same attendant who ushered me to my room. After he pulled down the berth with a simple tug of a strap and was satisfied my room was in order, he turned to leave. I was slightly embarrassed because I only had a few coins to tip him. "Thank you, sir."

"No need to call me sir, ma'am." He simply nodded and left. I had read about the racial unrest brewing in the South, but I was surprised to see the signs of inequality aboard such a majestic train. I wondered what to expect in New Orleans.

While relaxing on the bed, which was soft and spongy to the touch, I realized how grateful I was to have clean linens. The car also had a small toilet and sink. I was still too keyed up from dinner to try to sleep, so I was content to look out the window at the moonlit sky.

I thought of how my life had become a series of unexpected contrasts. It seemed too good to be true, but in spite of my good fortune, I was still worried about what was in store for me. It was not unlikely that I would be hopping cars again soon. I knew I didn't want to go back, but I didn't know where forward was. I remembered Jake telling me I needed to take more risks because I always played it too safe. Here I was with very little money left, and no safety net. *Look at me now, Jake.*

It was in that moment I realized how angry I was with Jake. It was more than pain. I could feel the anger, long suppressed, stir inside me. I had been struggling with it since the night he took his own life, but I had to fight through the pain first. As I tried to enjoy the luxury that surrounded me, I also felt resentment. Jake had chosen to leave me. He and I were closer to each other than to anyone else in our lives. *Why did you do it, Jake? Why? Did you think I would follow?*

The sudden change in train speed shifted my thoughts away from Jake. As I glanced out the window, I noticed we were traveling through a rural area. The lights from the train illuminated the small substation that bore a painted sign identifying the town as Wickes.

I was surprised when the engineer pulled the train whistle, because we were not scheduled to stop. All at once the lights from the station shed a back light on two male figures. To my shock, the men began running at full speed alongside the tracks. Train hoppers! My entire body went rigid with fear for them, knowing they were about to make the jump.

In my mind, I was running with them, as I tried to match the speed of the train and fight for footing while keeping focus on the boxcars with the hope of spotting an opening. Would they be able to find a grip in the dark, I wondered? As the train continued on past the station, the lights faded to a point where it was dangerously dark for any jumper to try to make his mark. *Don't do it*, I silently begged.

I fell back on the bed and pulled the sheets over my face. As I closed my eyes, the realization came over me: The lifestyle of the two drifters wasn't any different than mine. I had become one of them. It wasn't romantic or daring - it was dirty, frightening, and uncomfortable. The danger was ever-present, and although running from town to town felt like freedom, it was a dead end. Jake was wrong – he wasn't the one who was abnormal. *I'm the aberrant one, Jake.*

I couldn't fool myself any longer. Although I was riding in a luxurious sleeper car aboard the great Southern Belle, I was a train jumper - an itinerant drifter who was unemployed and squeaking by on charity. I knew I could not continue living as I was, because I would not survive. I lay awake for two hours before the train finally rocked me into a welcome sleep.

———

Early in the morning, we were pulling into Texarkana, Arkansas when I heard a knock at the door of my car. "May I offer you some coffee, ma'am?" The attendant presented a hot and milky cup of coffee and a croissant. Although I didn't usually drink coffee, I accepted it anyway. (I actually had two cups, just because I could.) I did not want to buy a proper breakfast, so I ate a bit of Margo's steak before I moved on to meet the others in the salon car. We had only a short time left together, and I wanted to savor every minute of it.

Mr. Boudreaux spotted me as I walked into the salon car and cheerfully called out, "Good morning, Miss Indiana."

Lucy smiled as Mr. Bennett scooted over to make room for

me in the booth. A platter of coffee cake, a deck of playing cards and a pitcher of mimosas were in the center of the table.

"Have you had breakfast?" Lucy inquired. She was dressed in a stunning yellow dress the color of the Sunliner convertible. The delicate white lace along the bodice brought to mind fields of Indiana daises in the springtime.

"Yes ma'am, thank you. Your dress is beautiful."

"Thank you, Kat. The men were just discussing business and beating me at hearts, so I'm glad a female companion has arrived."

"We don't want to bore you ladies with business," Mr. Boudreaux grinned.

"You couldn't possibly. However, please pardon me if I missed something earlier," I apologized to Mr. Boudreaux, "but what is it you do for a living, sir?"

"I'll tell you, but only if you promise to call me Dexter. Only my hired hands, my priest, and my parole officer call me 'Mr. Boudreaux.'" His laughter set the morning off to a great start." I'm an investor," he explained. "I invest money in other people's businesses when I think they have a good idea."

"He's very good at it," Lucy drawled. He has a surefire sense about what will be a success. Tell her what you're working on now, dear."

"As soon as we get into Shreveport, I'm meeting with some investors about a little thing called a Hula Hoop. We'll be selling them all over Louisiana."

"What is it?" Mr. Bennett asked.

"It's nothing more than a plastic hoop, Reese. You put it around your waist and then move your hips like you're doing the hula."

Mr. Boudreaux immediately stood up and began to do a hula movement, much to the delight of everyone in the salon car. He really got into it, and we were in hysterics.

"Mr. Boudreaux, you have rhythm! But why do you need a hoop to hula dance? You seem to be doing quite well without it."

"The idea is to see how long you can keep the hoop spinning around your middle without dropping it. It's harder than you may think, at least until you get the hang of it. Sounds silly, but kids are going to love it. Just you wait and see."

Lucy nodded enthusiastically. "Some folks tease him and tell him he's crazy when he backs something real new and different, don't they, sugar?"

"Yes-siree-bob. I got grief from some acquaintances for investing in Mr. Potato Head. But we all know how that turned out."

Reese whistled. "Mr. Potato Head? My nephew has one of those. He loves it. That's pretty impressive, Dexter. I'm sure your friends don't question you now."

"If they do, I gleefully remind them of how much they teased me about Mr. Potato Head before I whip into a little Gershwin song-"

Lucy cut him off mid-sentence and whipped into a familiar tune: "'*You say potato, I say pa-tah-toe...*'" We all joined in. As the Southern Belle continued south, we had a splendid time.

A short time after passing through Bloomberg, Texas, the conductor announced the next station. "Rodessa - entering Rodessa, Louisiana," he called. He pulled the word 'Louisiana' out of his chest like a piece of taffy as his words echoed throughout the train car. I couldn't believe we were finally in Louisiana.

As much as I enjoyed the train stops, I was actually sorry when we pulled into Shreveport mid-morning and had to part ways. With effusive expressions of gratitude and invitations like, "Look me up if you ever come back this way," my friends headed for the exit.

They all turned to wave one last time when Lucy Boudreaux unexpectedly headed back in my direction. She pressed a small velvet satchel into my hand.

"Lucy, what is this?"

"I didn't ask questions of you, Kat. I respect your privacy. But

I sense you're running from something. You take this and be safe. You're a lovely young lady, and it was my distinct honor to meet you. I sure I hope you find your way real soon."

I watched them on the platform as they retrieved their bags and shook hands. Lucy's yellow dress was the last glimpse I had of them as they disappeared into the crowd of travelers. I wanted to run after them, but I knew I had reached another ending. We were merry wayfarers who had passed alongside each other like the trains on the tracks going in different directions, destination unknown. I hadn't felt so alone since Jake left me behind, but I was yet to discover how much influence our meeting would have on my immediate future.

CHAPTER SIXTEEN

As much as I loved riding the Southern Belle, I knew I would be aboard almost another full day without the company of Mr. Bennett and Lucy and Dexter Boudreaux. For several hours, I sat in the observation car and read a book I found on the train, *From Russia with Love* by Ian Fleming. I really enjoyed the book, and James Bond was a great way to keep me distracted from my thoughts.

When I finally needed to give my eyes a break, I returned to the salon. People mingled about while the radios built into the sides of the train cars piped out popular tunes by the Everly Brothers and Bobby Darin.

Bobby Darin was just becoming popular back at Franklin College when Jake and I were there, and Jake did a great impression of Bobby singing "Splish Splash." As I pictured him in my mind, I could hear him singing, which brought a smile to my face. The memories of Jake's impersonations were a respite from the haunting and relentless visions of him illuminated by the oncoming train that savagely took his life. I sat down and closed my eyes as I listened to the music.

The nightmares about Jake had become part of my nightly torment. No matter how far I ran, they always accompanied me.

I often awakened in the night, still hearing the horrible sound of the impact the moment the train hit Jake.

The sounds were the worst part of the relentless mental persecution. After I had finally regained consciousness that night, I saw onlookers all around me, yelling and screaming. I was disoriented and in shock, and as I tried to sit up, someone forced me back down again. "Don't look. Lie still," a voice instructed. I pressed my cheek against the cold concrete sidewalk while panicked voices echoed off the train, which had come to an abrupt stop.

Slowly the high-pitched ambulance sirens grew closer, and the reality sunk in - Jake had stepped in front of a train. "Nooo," I screamed, "Nooo!" Over and over again my throat echoed my pleas as if it could somehow undo what had happened. I was totally disconnected from the voice, but I could not detach from the horror.

Although I could not see any of the carnage from where I lay on the sidewalk, I had seen my beloved friend as he was hurled into the air by the oncoming train, his limbs ripping off upon impact. The panic ruptured out of me with every scream. I tried to get up again to go help Jake.

"Jake! Don't leave me!" I cried out in my desperate hope he would answer.

The disembodied voice of the fireman leaning over me spoke again. "I'm sorry, miss, but he's gone." Everything went dark again, and I couldn't see Jake anymore.

———

After I finally managed to push the nightmarish memories out of my consciousness, I realized I had dozed off and had been crying in my sleep. I heard a voice close by.

"Are you all right, chere?"

I opened my eyes to see an odd woman sitting next to me. "Yes, I'm okay, thank you."

"Are you sure, sweetheart? Those sounds coming out of your throat were so frightening I thought I had mistakenly boarded the Orient Express."

"Oh, I am so sorry!"

"No need to apologize, child, unless you're the murderer. You need to relax. I just ordered us some tea."

CHAPTER SEVENTEEN

IT WAS STRANGE TO SEE A HUMAN BEING WITH BRIGHT ORANGE HAIR. My companion was very overweight and appeared to be in her fifties. The heavy lipstick that outlined her mouth matched her hair, and the effect was almost blinding. Her purple dress rustled every time she moved. She was a symphony of sound and a kaleidoscope of color. Nevertheless, I was immediately drawn to her. She had a warm smile, and everything about her countenance was pleasant and gentle.

"I'm Hilda. I came aboard back in Shreveport. Been walkin' around stretchin' my legs so my veins don't explode."

"Gee, that doesn't sound good."

"They haven't exploded yet, I'm happy to say. I've been havin' me a good ol' time playing cards in the salon, but after awhile, sittin' hurts my fanny, even though I have a heap of padding back there." Hilda made a comical face while stroking her vibrant bouffant into submission. "You going all the way to New Orleans?"

"Yes, I am. How did you guess?"

She let loose with a warm, rolling chuckle. "I didn't guess," she admitted. "You were dozing, so I asked the conductor if I should wake you up so you wouldn't miss your stop, but he assured me there was no reason because you're going all the way to New Orleans."

"Thank you for your concern."

"Sure, chere. What's your name?"

"Kat Caswell. Nice to meet you."

"'Kat Caswell.' That's snappy! You're coming from Kansas City?"

"Yes, ma'am."

"You live there?"

"No ma'am. I'm just going to New Orleans. It's my first trip."

Hilda paused a moment while she waited for more information. When I didn't elaborate, she raised one brow and gave me a shrewd look. "That well-used duffel bag you got tucked under your seat there tells me you've been travelin' around some already. I live in the French Quarter. You've heard of it?"

"I learned a little about it from some passengers who were on this train."

"It's a place full of intrigue. You'll love it! I'm just headin' back there."

"Were you doing business back in Shreveport?'

"Nope – I bought me a little vacation house in Caddo Parish. Real nice there. I lived there for a spell as a kid, but I really got to know Shreveport when I hitched up with one of my husbands. I've had four of 'em. They're easy to come by and way too hard to get rid of."

In spite of my anxiety, I found it easy to laugh with Hilda, who was jolly and light-hearted. "Thank you for the warning. I will remember that."

"What hotel did you book in New Orleans?"

When I hesitated, a knowing look spread across her plump face. "The YWCA, I'm guessing?" It was more of a statement than a question.

"Yes, ma'am."

"Hmm … ain't none of my business, but are you runnin' or are you being pulled?"

"I'm not sure I understand what you mean."

"See, sometimes we run. And other times when we listen to our instincts, we're *drawn* somewhere. I'm a strong believer in fate."

"I'll have to think about that one. Maybe it's both. My best friend and I have wanted to ride the Southern Belle and see the South since we were kids. And then recently I met a cowboy who told me New Orleans is a great place for someone who wants a new start. I figured New Orleans is about as far as I can go before I hit water."

"Thank God this train stops just short of that, darlin'! I may look like a floating device, but this ol' broad don't swim."

When Hilda laughed, her body gave a captivating performance. Her giant breasts bounced up and down in her dress like buoys, and her stomach vibrated under the purple fabric. The fat on her chin jiggled, while the flaccid skin on her arms flapped like wings. I was mesmerized.

After our tea arrived, we sat quietly and enjoyed the scenery before she spoke again. "That's a real pretty velvet satchel in your lap. Gift?"

"Yes, Ma'am."

"What's in it? I love surprises!" Her smile was all-encompassing.

"Gee, I don't know. I guess I should look."

"Well, yes you should! My curiosity is killing me. Let's have some fun. Open that dang thing!"

I reached for the bag in my lap. After everyone had disembarked, I was so deflated that I hadn't even opened the small bag Lucy had given me. While Hilda watched with curiosity, I peeked inside. The first thing I noticed was a lipstick. When I removed the lid, I was delighted to see a beautiful shade of coral.

"Oh, lookie there! It's a perfect shade for you, chere. Put some on." Hilda handed me a compact and watched in obvious pleasure as I colored my lips. "That color is a humdinger - it really brightens up that pretty face of yours."

I was delighted with my own image. It was such a contrast to what I had felt inside for so long. When I next reached into the bag, I found a very small bottle of perfume. I read the label and gasped.

"Will you just look at that, chere - Chanel N°5! Aren't we fancy! I wish I had friends like yours."

We both took a long whiff of the fragrance. I shook my head in wonder at the irony of wearing such an expensive perfume with my secondhand clothing, but I loved it. "Look, it says Paris on the bottle. It's an awfully nice gift," I agreed. When I peeked into the bag again, I discovered a twenty-dollar bill tucked inside. I was thrilled, and greatly relieved.

Hilda, still peering over my shoulder, shot me a grin. "That there cash oughta get you a few good nights at the YWCA on Gravier Street. It's not far from the station."

"Is it close enough to walk?"

"Yes, but we're gonna be arriving in the wee hours, so walking on dark streets you're not familiar with is not a good idea. Besides, sometimes the YWCA is full up with guests. I think we should call ahead of time before you go trottin' yourself down there for no reason. My friend Ethyline works there. She can tell us if they have a vacant room. I'll give her a call at the next station."

"Oh no, please don't. You could miss the train when we pull out again!"

"Who's getting off, chere? These train cars have phones. They hook 'em up whenever we pull into the big stations."

"They do? Wow!"

"Honey, this ain't a Greyhound. You're ridin' on the Southern Belle!"

There was a troubled expression on Hilda's face as she placed the phone back on its cradle and nodded to the attendant to signal her completion of the call.

"Honey, my friend informed me there are no rooms at the YWCA, which is exactly what I feared. There are a lot of unemployed workers this time of year - students and such - and they're all looking for inexpensive rooms until tourist season starts up again."

"Oh my gosh!"

"That there is a fly in the ointment."

"I'll be fine - thank you for calling, Hilda." I tried to hide my dismay, but I was really at a loss about what to do next. "I should never have assumed I could immediately find a place to stay."

"No one ever told you to call ahead when you're off to a new place?"

"It's just that ... well to be honest, my plans have been sort of spontaneous lately. I know that's foolish-"

"And I know it's none of my business, but how did you think you'd get by? No plans, no reservations - and if I have to say it - you don't seem to have much in the way of street smarts either, my dear girl."

"I've gotten by so far. But I haven't been traveling that long. I know I should have thought it through."

"No need to pay it any mind now. You'll stay with me."

"Oh please, that's totally unnecessary. I'll figure out something."

"Hush now, darlin' girl. You can pay your own way. I have a big ol' house over on Ursulines near Royal, and there's a comfortable room in the back. I already have a girl staying there. You can share the room with her and earn your keep until a room opens up at the YWCA. How does that suit you?"

"I suppose that would work," I agreed hesitantly. "But the girl - do you think she would she mind sharing her room?"

"She goes by the name of Leni, and I can't see why she would mind. She'd probably like the company. She's there temporarily, and she's about your age. Leni is doing domestic chores until my own girl, Dauphine, comes back from Georgia, where she's off tending to her sick mama. You girls can stay 'til she returns."

"That would be real nice."

"You can help Leni. She assists with laundry and dishes and tidying up - things of that sort. She even finally learned to cook and bake some. Her pecan pies are surefire mouthwatering."

"Oh, I would love to try some!"

"Can you cook at all? I have a lot of guests."

"Not really. I never had a mom, so I never learned many homemaking skills."

"I'm sure Leni can teach you. You got anything against Mexicans?"

"Excuse me?"

"Leni is from Mexico. Nuevo Laredo I think, or somewhere close to Texas. I hope you ain't sensitive to skin color. When I hire people, I pay no mind to what shade they are."

"No ma'am, I would have no problem with that."

Hilda nodded as she reached out to pat my hand. "Good, cuz in my house, the only color that matters is the right color lipstick."

"I've never had a Mexican friend. I think a lot of them work on the railroads and steel mills back home in Indiana, but there weren't any at my school. I come from a real small town."

"Small towns are wonderful, but your life is about to get bigger, Kat Caswell. Leni speaks English, and she's sweeter than Mississippi Mud Cake, but oh, that girl's a pistol!" Once again, Hilda's entire body accompanied her rollicking laughter. "It took me a while to convince her everything doesn't need to be wrapped in a tortilla, but now she's getting the hang of Southern cuisine."

"That sounds wonderful."

"What's wonderful is her fried biscuits and gumbo!"

"I've never tasted gumbo."

"We can fix that. And you're all good with colored people? I've got me some Negro help too."

"To be honest, Hilda, I've never had a Negro friend either, although I've talked to a few colored folks down by the railroad station as they were passing through."

"I'll be! How big is that hometown of yours? Can you see it from the road or is it hidden behind a haystack?"

"I guess it is pretty small," I chuckled. "But it's a real nice place. I never had anything against mixing with coloreds, but I just never connected much with people at all. I've only had one real friend ever."

"Hmm ... I was getting the feeling you're a bit of a loner. I'm pretty perceptive about people. But don't you worry, child, you'll like Leni a lot. One whiff of one of her pies will win you over."

"All this food talk is making me hungry," I groaned.

"Well then, let's order us some sandwiches."

"I think I'll just hold off awhile."

"Darlin', you said you was hungry, and now you'll eat. I don't eat alone. You'd be insulting me. If you're worried about finances, you can pay me from your first paycheck."

"Thank you."

"So, it seems my proposition sounds good to you? Not that you should be expectin' any other offers to come your way between here and New Orleans, eh?"

"Yes, thank you. I really appreciate the offer."

"I think you'll be real comfortable. You know, those YWCAs have a lot of rules - curfews, lights out, guest restrictions and the like. The only thing about my house is you never discuss any of my business or my guests with anybody. As they say, 'silence is golden.' We got a deal?"

I have always preferred privacy myself, so I was grateful for the offer. "Yes, Hilda, thank you very much. It's a deal."

———

We were both napping in our seats in the early hours of the morning when I was awakened by the voice of the conductor as he announced our destination: "New Orleans! Next stop, New Orleans!"

I nudged Hilda, who was sleeping soundly, her snores in rhythm with the rocking of the train. "Wake up, Hilda, we're almost there!"

When I stared out the window, I spotted Union Station ahead, its lights illuminating the sky above. Silhouettes of passengers stood out against the bright lights on the platforms alongside the bays. Even from a distance, I could sense the hustle and bustle of activity.

The noise level in the passenger car increased in anticipation of our arrival. As I leaned toward the window, my heart was beating rapidly. The lights of the city grew brighter - their radiance like a magnet pulling the steel train closer and closer. My excitement was hard to contain. *New Orleans! Jake, if only you could see this,* I thought wistfully.

When the train finally came to a stop, I experienced a great sense of relief. It was the end of the line, and I had made it. Maybe I could stop running. Maybe the constant ache in my chest would show mercy. Maybe I could stand still long enough to find my breath and a new direction.

Little did I know how seminal events in New Orleans would altar my life forever.

BOOK III

NEW ORLEANS

CHAPTER EIGHTEEN

THE MOMENT I STEPPED OFF THE SOUTHERN BELLE ONTO THE platform, I knew I was in a unique and mysterious city. The humid air had a sweet, unusual fragrance unlike anything I had ever inhaled.

Jazz notes flowed from inside the station where buskers entertained the travelers with a music style unfamiliar to me. It was something more than the blues and ragtime I had been exposed to in Franklin. My body instinctively kept time with the syncopated rhythms.

I noticed Hilda studying me, a broad grin of pleasure lighting her face. "Jazz," she smiled. "It's infectious, eh?"

After I hoisted my duffel over my shoulder, I accompanied Hilda while she gathered her bags. Several porters nodded to Hilda and called her by name.

"You must travel a lot," I observed. She answered only with a sly grin.

As soon as we exited the station, New Orleans lay before me. I wanted to run into the heart of it and take in her distinctive buildings and noisy streets all in one beat. Although I was exhausted from the long train ride, the city's exotic energy revived me.

I grabbed one of Hilda's bags and started toward the taxi line.

"This way, chere," She nodded toward a black Cadillac Eldorado waiting at the curb. A suit-clad, broad-shouldered man with dusky skin, who was relaxing alongside the car, waved the moment he spotted her.

"Wow," I exclaimed under my breath. "Your friend sure has a nice car!"

"Honey, this is *my* Caddie. Evens, say hello to my friend, Kat. She's going to be staying with us awhile."

"Hi, Kat." Evens tipped his hat, revealing a shiny bald head. "Nice trip, ma'am?" Evens inquired of Hilda. He had an unusual accent I had never heard before.

"Nice enough to meet my new friend here," she smiled. "Kat is gonna help out Leni. She's never been down in these parts before, so let's head for home and treat her to some real southern hospitality."

I commented very little as we made our way through New Orleans, because I was too absorbed by the scenery. After driving about ten minutes past businesses closed for the evening, we entered an area of streets lined by narrow, ornate cottages with gabled roofs and shuttered windows. Illuminated by old street lights, most of them appeared to be very old, but they were well-kept and constructed of brightly painted wood. The houses were positioned very close to the street - much different than the homes in Indiana. It was fascinating to see buildings so colorful and unusual.

"Welcome to the Vieux Carre, Miss Kat," Evens smiled as he looked at my reflection in the rearview mirror. "I remember my first impression when I arrived here from Haiti – heated me up like a rum kremas."

"I don't know what a kremas is, sir, but I'm sure getting a warm feeling all over."

Although it was the wee hours of the morning, the streets were warmly lit, and distant music was seeping over the rooftops. Evens pulled to the curb on a street that was not only beautiful, but quite mysterious. Some of the homes were free standing, but many were attached. "Here we are, ladies," he announced.

He dropped us off in front of a three-story brick house. There were pillars that reached from the street to the wrought iron second floor balcony above. Geraniums and sprawling ferns stretched lazily over the edges of the balcony.

At street level, the large, narrow windows were tightly shuttered. In the middle of the row of windows was a very tall door coated with black enamel paint and set off by two shiny brass door knockers shaped like lion heads.

Hilda nodded her head toward the door. "Like my knockers? They're my trademark. Two gorgeous knockers will open any door, honey." She laughed heartily at her own joke as she fumbled for her key.

While I waited for Hilda, I was somewhat apprehensive about lingering on the deserted street. Hilda saw me clutch my bag closer and chuckled. "Honey, this is an area of art galleries owned by queer gentlemen. The only thing that could happen to you here is they might tie you down and do your hair."

I burst into laughter at the image. "I love your humor, Hilda. You sure can lift a person's spirit!"

"That's good, because New Orleans is known for its spirit." Hilda was reaching for the knocker when the door abruptly opened. Standing in front of us was a tall, lanky man with molasses colored skin. His hair had broad licks of silver, and when he smiled, he flashed the whitest teeth imaginable. A crisp white shirt created a marked contrast to his black waistcoat. He was a stunning tapestry of black and white.

"Good evening, Madam," he greeted. "I trust you had a good trip. I'll call Quinton to collect your bags."

"Thank you, Alcide. This is Miss Kat Caswell. Ain't she a downright beauty?"

"She is indeed … if the young lady does not mind my saying so."

"Thank you, kindly." My face felt so warm my forehead was sweating.

"Oh, hell, she don't even know she's a beauty underneath those farmer clothes she's wearing. Please tell Leni to get this girl into something suitable in the morning."

I knew Hilda meant well, but I was not used to people looking at me. "Hilda," I demurred, "I have a change of clothes in my bag. Tomorrow, I will-"

"You'll what - put on another pair of them trousers that hang on you like yesterday's laundry? Sugar pie, you ain't in corn land anymore. You're in Dixie, where it's important to dress. Besides, it's time you start enjoyin' the fact that you're downright lovely."

"Thank you." It was a wonderful and unexpected change to be surrounded by beauty and genteel manners … and to actually feel feminine.

"Don't worry, my dear, we'll save the tiara and hoop skirts for a fancy occasion. Alcide, would you please show Kat to Leni's room?"

"It would be my pleasure," he nodded toward me before turning back to his employer. "I'll be back shortly with your nightcap, Miss Hilda." He was much more formal than Evens, but he was not intimidating. He reminded me of a finely carved obelisk, but his eyes revealed a gentle nature.

As we followed Alcide down a narrow hallway lined with a thick runner, I took in the details of my surroundings. Rooms lined each side of the hallway, and each was designed like a luxurious parlor, which was very odd compared to the Indiana homes I was familiar with. At the end of the hallway, we entered a magnificent room. The house, which had appeared smaller from the street, was deceptively large.

Pink silk fabric covered the walls of the room where we were standing, and a graceful, curved staircase led off to the right. On the opposite side, the room was lined with French doors that opened onto a patio dotted with flowering trees, each wound with strings of soft lights. The trees reached out to form a canopy over small tables and settees which were arranged in groups throughout the enchanting brick courtyard.

Voices wafted in on the late-night air. I could see silhouettes on the patio and a waiter serving drinks to two gentlemen, who puffed on cigars near a large fountain. A piano was at the far end of the patio, where a man played quiet tunes befitting the late-night hour.

Inside, the scent of sweet flowers permeated the room. "Oh, Hilda, how beautiful!" I exclaimed.

"I'm glad you approve, dear. Now you just follow Alcide, and I will show you more tomorrow in the daylight after we've both had some sleep and a delicious, fattening breakfast."

As she started for the stairway, I stopped her. "Wait, Hilda, you didn't mention you own a restaurant. I really think I can be of more help to you and earn my keep by serving. I'm a very good waitress, and I've had experience at-"

"Oh sweetheart," Hilda cut me off before I could ramble on any longer, "although we do serve light fare, this is not a restaurant. This is a club for gentlemen."

"A club?"

"Of sorts. This is a service establishment where we tend to all the needs of our very distinguished clientele. I am the proprietor."

I was astonished to a point of near silence. I looked at Alcide, whose face remained expressionless, and then back at Hilda again. She appeared to be very amused.

"You might want to take a breath and let the color come back to your face, chere," Hilda chuckled. "And relax - you'll only work in the back doing kitchen chores and the like. Welcome to Jolie Fleur. Good night, my dear."

My mouth was agape as I watched her leave. *How could you be so simpleminded, Kat!* I was amazed at my own stupidity. I wanted to run, but Alcide's strong hand on my elbow guided me up the stairs toward the back of the house.

"You are safe here, Miss Kat. Meeting Hilda was a blessing. Truly a blessing." I took a deep breath as Alcide knocked on Leni's door.

CHAPTER NINETEEN

"SORRY TO DISTURB YOU," ALCIDE APOLOGIZED TO THE GIRL standing in the doorway. "Miss Lenora Cruz, it is my pleasure to introduce you to Miss Kat Caswell, who will be residing with us for a time. Hilda assured her you would be willing to share your room, as it is has the extra alcove."

"Of course. Hi there. Please call me Leni like everyone else does – even Sir Alcide here." By the impish look on her face, I sensed that she found the formalities quite humorous.

"Pleased to meet you, Leni."

"We apologize to the young lady for the late-night arrival." Alcide made an exaggerated bow just to entertain her, causing us all to laugh.

"No problem at all. I was just reading *A Tale of Two Cities* and really enjoying it! Thank you for the book, Alcide. G'night." Leni did a mock-curtsy back at him before she pulled me into the room and closed the door.

I was immediately taken by her appearance. Her head barely reached my shoulders, but she was well-proportioned and very curvaceous. Her hair was even darker than mine, and her brown eyes were hooded with heavy lashes. Her nightgown exposed her creamy caramel-colored skin. Although not exactly beautiful, she was very striking.

"I'm sorry to disturb your reading."

"Oh please, amiga, I was just looking at movie star magazines. They are very informative, you know."

"Yep - higher education," I nodded enthusiastically.

"See – you understand me. Alcide is not as curious as I am to find out if Lana Turner really killed her Mafia boyfriend. He is self-educated, so he loves to share the books. I adore him and don't want to hurt his feelings, so don't tell him I use *A Tale of Two Cities* as a doorstop."

"I won't. I promise. But maybe *War and Peace* would be better for that," I giggled.

I was fascinated by the way she talked. She rolled her "r' sounds and sometimes added "the" in odd places. Her speech was musical and full of gaiety.

"I like you already! Put down your bag there," Leni instructed, pointing toward the alcove attached to the sleeping area. "There's another nice bed in there, and a sink and toilet down the hall. You can order the breakfast in the morning, or we can go downstairs together."

"Thank you."

"You're really bonita. I wish I had green eyes like yours."

"My friend always told me they look like lettuce."

"More like broccoli mixed with spinach."

"Great, I'm a walking vegetable platter."

"But such a pretty one! Before I grew tatas, my friend told me I was shaped like an eggplant."

"Now that's just cruel!"

"I agree. How old are you?"

"I just turned nineteen." I felt so comfortable with her that I ignored my usual instinct to remain silent. "How about you?"

"I'm eighteen, but Hilda says I'm old for my years. My dad lives back in Mexico, and there's no way I'm going there, so

Hilda is letting me work here awhile. I've been here three months now."

"Do you have to ... I mean, are you expected to-"

"To cuddle with the men? Only on the weekends."

"Oh my God!"

"Oh, chica, you are hilarious! You should see the look on your face. No, we're off-limits. Hilda is like a mother lion. I wouldn't know what to do anyway. I'm still a virgin. Are you?"

I was shocked at her question. Ben was the only person who had ever asked me about my virginity. Jake never had to ask, because he already knew. "Yes, I am, technically."

"Technically, huh? You won't lose your 'technical' purity here unless you bend over in front of the customers."

"Really?"

"Oh my gosh, you're really gonna have to learn when I'm kidding. Hilda would cut off any man's miembro if he touched one of us. And Alcide would drag the body down to Bourbon Street where no one would even notice for at least a month. You have nothing to worry about here." She turned and motioned toward the room with a dramatic flourish. "So how do you feel about big, fat feather beds?"

"Ah, that sounds heavenly."

"Com'on, let's get to bed. I have the day off tomorrow, so we can relax. I'll show you around the neighborhood a bit if you want unless you'd prefer to do something else."

"I think I'd prefer to stay here and read *A Tale of Two Cities*."

We stared at each other for a moment, and then we both fell into spasms of laughter.

"I really do like you! I'm so happy to have a new friend!" Leni smiled.

"So am I," I nodded. I was surprised at how much I meant it.

The next day, I awakened at dawn, despite having only a few hours of sleep. The air in my alcove was oppressive, and my skin felt hot and sticky. When I opened the window for some circulation, I discovered the courtyard was just below us. Even though it was early morning, the scene was quite cheerful. Piano music filled the courtyard as a small group of people milled about carrying beverages in china cups or crystal glasses.

I waited quietly in the alcove until Leni awakened. From my bed, I took in the details of the cozy room. The morning light trailed along the peach walls and skimmed across a large walnut chifforobe in the corner before settling on an ornate desk near the bed where Leni slept. The arch which separated my alcove from her section of the room was bordered on each side by two brass floor lamps topped with colorful glass shades. Oriental rugs, worn but genteel, covered the dark wood floors. I sat on the bed awhile, enjoying the peaceful feeling of waking in a room with such quiet elegance.

Leni finally opened her eyes and greeted me. "Oh good, you're still here."

"Good morning. I hope that's an observation and not a complaint. Is it always so hot this early in the day?"

"In the summer months, yes, chica. Our air conditioner is broken so Hilda is having it fixed this week. But you'll get used to it. 'Think of the heat as God's breath,' she always tells me."

"We get humidity where I'm from in Indiana, but dang it, this is like wearing a blanket in a hot shower."

"'Dang it'? You have a fun way of talking in Indiana. Maybe I'll start using that expression. I always say 'dadgummit' - learned it from the waiters. I've picked up some other words too, but I can't tell you those until I get to know you better. So, you teach me the Indiana English and I'll teach you the southern English, and maybe some Spanish."

"It's a deal. The only Spanish I remember from school is 'Donde está la biblioteca?'"

"That will come in handy when you need to find a library in an emergency."

"So, you speak Spanish and English?"

"Yes, and Alcide has been teaching me a little bit of French, mademoiselle. Alcide says I'm smarter than a Sunday suit, but I think he's just trying to encourage me."

"You're smarter than I am. When I was little, I thought all the French kids must be much more intelligent than American kids because they can all speak a foreign language - French."

"Ha! That makes sense in a strangely logical way. I thought American kids must be smarter than us Mexican kids because they were wise enough to be born in a rich country."

"I don't know about wise, but certainly very lucky. Last night you mentioned your dad is still in Mexico. So, I guess your mom is too?"

"No. Mama moved to Texas when she was pregnant with me, but my papa had to stay in Mexico. We had to go back to our village near Matamoros because my grandfather died. After they buried my abuelo, Mama insisted we return to America so we could have a better life, but when we tried to return, the guards stopped us at the border."

"Why?"

"I don't know. But my mama panicked because they started roughing her up. I tried to protect her, but she yelled at me to run."

"I can't even imagine such a terrifying situation. What did you do?"

"I ran because she insisted. I was sure they would shoot me in the back, but I ran like a scared rabbit. One guard caught me, so I bit him real hard 'til he lost his grip. I still remember how his hand smelled like cigarettes."

"Disgusting! What happened to your mom?"

"When I looked back, my mother was on the ground in the dirt, but I kept running, all the while thinking she would catch up with me. When she didn't come, I hid alongside the road for a long time until I managed to hitch a ride with some Mexican day workers, who took me back to where my mama and me were living near the Texas border."

"Did your mother ever come?"

"No. A week later, I heard what happened from a day worker who was staying in a trailer near ours. He told me they shot her dead."

"Oh my God!"

"If there *is* a God, He's nowhere near the border, amiga. Anyway, I ran away because I didn't want some strange family to take me in as a laborer. Sometimes I think I'm still waiting for Mama to catch up with me."

"I am so sorry, Leni! It must have been horrible to lose your mother. I never knew mine."

"Maybe not knowing is even worse. How about if we be like mothers to each other? Wouldn't that be good?"

"I would really like that. I just hope we can live here awhile."

"Hilda keeps finding work for me to do, and she will for you too. I swear she makes up jobs to keep me here. One day she asked me to watch TV to catch her up on her shows. She gave me some excuse that her mind was too tired to concentrate. Even Alcide rolled his eyes at that one."

"She sure is a character! What did you do before you came here?"

"I did everything from waiting the tables and ironing … and lots of picking whatever is in season. That's what brought me here. Those are some real hard jobs, but the farmers usually provide housing for the workers. A few months back, I couldn't find work, so I was sleeping on benches for a few hours at a time until la policia made me move. Hilda saw me singing for tips in front of a restaurant over in Jackson Square."

"You're a singer?"

"Madre de Dios, no, chica! Hilda came up to me and said, 'Child, I don't mean to insult you, but these unfortunate tourists are tipping you to *stop* this caterwauling.' I didn't know what the word meant, but I got the idea real fast, and I thought it was pretty funny. I had to agree - my voice sounds worse than howler monkeys in heat. After she bought me a hot dog from a nearby vendor, she said, 'What's your story, sweetheart?'"

"And you told her?"

"Sure. You know how she is - she can drag a conversation out of un hombre muerto. So, she brought me back here and took me in."

"Has she rescued others besides you and me ... and those poor tourists you tortured with your singing?"

"Oh, plenty! Alcide confided that when Hilda was a young teenager, she got pregnant, and so her mama threw her out of their home in Shreveport. She had no place to go until a hat maker named Fleur took her in. She lost the baby, but now she tries to help other needy folks just like Fleur did."

"Ah, now the name of this establishment makes even more sense. She is so kind. I've noticed she doesn't insult queers or women who sell their services to men, and she doesn't treat Negroes the way some people do."

"'Probably because the woman who took her in was Negro and Creole."

"Wow! Imagine a young white girl being raised by a colored woman in her era. I'm sure that was shocking."

"Yeah. She was treated worse than if she was mixed herself. Alcide told me so. He is Fleur's son."

"But-"

"I know - he treats her real formal when they're working, because that's how he likes to do. He once told me, 'Leni, I must set an example for all the working girls, even though it's hard for some to be dignified when they're buck naked.' That hombre can be a real jokester."

"He really does set a fine example. But I admit I was a little intimidated at first."

"Oh, don't be. In private, they are two silly old friends. You should see them late at night after they've had a few Sazerac cocktails! They are closer than brother and sister."

I felt a sudden pain in my chest as she described their relationship. Jake and I had been 'silly old friends,' too, and I missed him more than I thought was even possible. My internal conversations with Jake filled my waking moments, and I couldn't shake the sadness.

"Did I say something wrong? Your face just changed. I didn't mean to upset you. If I said something-"

"No, Leni, I'm just missing an old friend. But it's lovely to have a new friend," I added as I shook off the dark feeling and gazed back down into the courtyard where the gaiety provided a welcome distraction. "So, what's going on down there - is it a party?"

"Those are patrons from last night. They often linger for coffee and mimosas, which is a real tasty drink with champagne and orange juice if you've never had one. I sneak them all the time. You'll meet the girls soon. They live over in the other wing of the house."

I was a little shocked to see how revealing some of their outfits were. "That's some real skimpy lingerie. The ladies don't seem too shy about revealing so much of their, uh, assets!"

"I think you mean 'asses,'" she laughed. "Amiga, Hilda calls that 'marketing.' Look at the chubby girl over there by the magnolia tree. That's Mare. You can practically see clear through the gown she's wearing."

"Holy Hannah! I haven't seen mounds that big since I passed through the Ozarks," I giggled.

"Now you see what Hilda means. Mare's fanny doesn't need any more advertising than that. It speaks for itself."

"It sure does - in any language. So how do the Southerners say, 'I'm starving, let's eat'?"

"I could eat the north end of a southbound polecat."

"Well I could eat both ends. Let's go!"

"Okay, I'm going to get you some fresh clothes, and then, as

Alcide likes to say, 'We shall partake in the bounty of a delectable Southern buffet.' Jesús, how that man can talk!"

———

As we descended the curved staircase, I felt quite elegant. I had agreed to let Leni choose my wardrobe because she was so enthusiastic about making me look less road-weary. We were not the same size, so she had to rifle through a collection of clothes in the chifforobe until she found something suitable.

Leni chose a blush pink blouse with embroidered flowers around the scooped neckline, and a matching skirt of gauze cotton. The clothing was cooler than my usual garb, so I didn't object - a wise decision considering the rising temperature. I even applied some Chanel perfume and the lipstick Lucy had given me.

Something stirred inside me as I allowed some color to come back into my life. And when I saw my image in the mirror above the stairway, I was pleased to see a comely reflection. In spite of the numbness I had felt for so long, I was slowly connecting again with the Kat who had been shedding her tomboy persona until survival had become my only purpose. I liked the person who was looking back at me. I secretly wished Davey could see the young woman in the mirror.

Hilda greeted us at the bottom of the stairway with a broad smile. She was wrapped in a kimono made of fabric covered in iridescent flowers brighter than the pink silk wallpaper. In spite of the sadness that was always with me, it was hard not to be uplifted by so much good spirit.

"Good morning, Leni. I see you got our girl into a skirt. Good for you! Good morning, Kat. You look fetching. Did you sleep well?"

"Yes, thank you. It's so nice to be here, Hilda. I'm ready to start work as soon as you would like."

"Oh no, chere, not today. You take the day off with Leni. She will introduce you to our family. You help yourself to the buffet over there. The staff eats in the blue room. And this evening, I would like you both to join me at seven o'clock in the courtyard for a little music."

"Thank you Hilda, we will," Leni nodded, yanking my arm toward the food table. "I'm starving. Off we go."

"Try the grits, my lovelies," Hilda called after us as she headed for the courtyard.

I didn't have to serve myself, because Leni immediately fixed me a plate with more food than I could possibly eat. She piled on eggs, bacon, something that looked like Cream of Wheat, fruit, and biscuits. "Leni, that's enough food for three meals!" I protested.

"Look here now, you have to sample it all," she ordered as we entered a beautiful blue room with additional sets of French doors draped in white organza curtains. The carved wood furniture was highly polished, and a harp graced one corner of the room.

"This room is for the staff?"

"Sí. She separates us so the gentlemen know the hostesses from the staff, but we're all family to her."

"This table is big enough to be a skating rink."

"The house once belonged to a French general. Isn't it a *jolie maison*, as Alcide likes to say?"

"Very *jolie*," I repeated as I dug into what I thought was Cream of Wheat.

Leni slapped her hand on the table with glee when I made a face. "Grits," she chuckled, "they take some getting used to. But here now, just do what I do. First you load them up with butter. After they are drenched, you smother them to death with brown sugar and maple syrup. Now take a taste."

"Oh, they're yummy that way!"

"Great! Now try this beignet. Every morning Alcide and Evens go over to Café Du Monde to pick up an order for Hilda because they know she loves them so much. The café is famous."

"I heard someone talking about it on the train. Sure smells good. They look like fried dough."

"It sure ain't a hot dog. You're really quick in the morning, aren't you, chica?"

I playfully threw a piece of bacon at her, and then we continued to devour one of the best breakfasts I had ever tasted.

———

We spent my first day in New Orleans walking around Royal Street. By daylight, the street didn't look deserted, as it had when I arrived. The stores were open, and the shutters were turned back, so the street had come alive. Tourists were on the street peering into windows full of art and antiques more extraordinary than anything I had ever seen. We passed several bars that were already full of patrons.

"Folks here love their cocktails," Leni explained.

"So I noticed. And everywhere we go I hear music."

"Hilda told me if you don't like music, they'll put you on a river boat and send you back up the Mississippi where soulless Yankees go to die," she laughed. "Here they even play music and dance at funerals. It's a good place to die."

"New Orleans sure has a good attitude about living," I laughed.

"Damn straight, amiga. I'll show you more tomorrow, but let's head back to the house because it's time you meet Bertrand. He's the best jazz pianist in town. He won't play anywhere other than the Jolie Fleur."

"There's one thing I don't understand, Leni - is prostitution legal down here?"

"I really don't know, but I can tell you that lots of the policia come in as customers to visit the girls. Hilda knows them all, and I've seen her slip envelopes to a few. Alcide told me she has to 'cooperate to operate.'"

"So that's why she made me pledge not to gossip. I'm sure there are already enough bodies floating down the Mississippi."

"Dang it, you're catchin' on real quick, Indiana."

"Dadgummit, you're a real good teacher, bonita amiga."

———

By the time we returned to Jolie Fleur, showered, and grabbed a snack from the pantry, it was time to meet Hilda in the patio area. Inside the courtyard the scent of fresh flowers was intoxicating. Hilda, who was waiting at a table near the piano, signaled for us to join her.

As we approached, I was amazed and delighted to see bright red feathers in Hilda's hair. It was a fashion choice I had never seen before. Her vibrant lipstick was almost a perfect match to the feathers.

"Bertrand, please take a break and come over here," she called out to the pianist. "Sit, sit, girls. Kat, you are in for such a rare treat. This man is the most talented man I know. Come join us, Bertrand. Honor us with your presence."

Bertrand stopped playing and came to join us at our table. Even in the heat, he looked cool in his dark suit and fedora hat. Although he seemed to find his chair with ease, his dark glasses suggested he was blind. As he kissed Hilda on the cheek he drawled, "Good evening, ma chérie." His drawl was longer and more musical than the others.

"Kat, meet our Creole king of jazz," Hilda smiled as we shook hands.

"Hello my de-ah. It's always a pleasure to meet Hilda's new guests." Bertrand pulled a hand-rolled cigarette out of his pocket, lit it, and took a quick puff. "I hope you don't mind, Miss Kat, but I love me some whiskey and I love me l'herbe."

"You smoke herbs?"

"Oh yeah, chile … parsley, oregano, rosemary-"

When everyone laughed, it dawned on me that he was

smoking marijuana. My exposure to drugs in Indiana had been limited, so I had to wince at my own naiveté.

"I'm just teasin' you, chouboulout. So do you like jazz?"

"Oh yes. But I haven't been exposed to much."

"Jazz is in your soul. I tell ya, I've done riffed with the best jazz players in the world. I've had me a blessed life. My hero was Thelonius Monk. Him and Art Tatum. I learned my style from Thelonius - flat fingers and percussive as all hell." Bertrand slapped his fingers against the table as if playing a piano. The vibration was rhythmic and exciting.

"You really *are* good!" I exclaimed.

"I surely should be, cuz these fingers been doin' their thing for a whole lotta years now. I used to play with Dizzy and Charlie and the whole lot of 'em up in Harlem at a place called Minton's. You ever heard of it?"

"No sir, I haven't."

"It seems like you be needin' some jazz education, right Hilda?"

"Yes, and nobody can do it better than you can, Bertrand. You made me a believer the first time I ever heard you play over at Fritzel's Jazz Club. Of course, back in those days I thought you were blind, so I was even more impressed," she laughed as she signaled the waiter. "Whiskeys all around please, Jacques."

"I'm a handsome devil in these shades. You know these is just my signature look, ma chérie."

"And a mighty fine look it is. I never forget how lucky I am to have you playing for us in my humble establishment. Even Leni has become addicted to jazz. Right, little one?"

"I sure have. But I've been meaning to ask, Bertrand - how come you left New York? I thought you really liked it up north."

"I liked Harlem, dear. Oh Lordy, that's a place just full of soul. And they treat us colored folks better up there. But when New Orleans is in the blood, a body knows where home is."

"And you couldn't stay away from me." Hilda winked at Leni and me as Jacques delivered our drinks.

"Of course I couldn't, lovely Hilda. I sure didn't come back for the wages!" Bertrand leaned into me and chuckled, "She don't pay me enough to feed a parakeet."

"I heard that. Don't be a martyr. You make more in whiskey and tips here than you can get in wages *plus* tips anywhere else on Bourbon Street."

"That's sure enough factual. And truth be told, I wouldn't work anywhere else. The company is delicious, the Jameson keeps flowing, and I love me my Hilda." Bertrand raised his glass in a toast, and we all joined in.

"OK, so I want you to play some jazz favorites for the girls. How about doing some of Monk's tunes like 'Round Midnight' or 'In Walked Bud'?"

"At your service, madam." Bertrand stood up, tossed back his whiskey, and let out a long sigh of satisfaction. "Miss Leni, you mind yourself, you sassy child. Miss Kat, such a pleasure. Don't let this new friend of yours get y'all into trouble."

"Hey, hombre, I'm just a good Catholic girl, right, Hilda?"

"Yeah, but with more hankering for mischief than a liquored-up raccoon."

When Leni scrunched up her nose, Bertrand laughed heartily and tipped his hat.

While we sat listening to Bertrand on the piano, the whiskey and the music lulled me into a mellow mood and gave me momentary relief from anxiety. I was starting to understand why Jake had been drinking so much those last few months.

"One more round," Hilda ordered as she excused herself. "You two behave now. Guests are upon us."

Eventually some of the girls drifted into the courtyard. They were dressed in revealing garments, but they all behaved with an air of refinement. Leni pointed toward a redhead who had just entered. "That's Dersa. Sometimes late at night she joins Bertrand at the piano and sings some tunes. She really has a beautiful voice."

"It can't be as good as yours."

Leni kicked me under the table. "Be nice to me or I'll stand up and sing 'La Cucaracha.'"

We were having a jolly time when Alcide tapped her on the shoulder as a signal that it was almost time for us to leave. His timing was good, because I was already a bit tipsy from drinking more than I was used to.

Patrons of the establishment were flowing into the courtyard, and there was a bustle of activity. Hilda greeted her visitors in the manner of a high-class hostess as she ushered people into the room. More waiters made their way through the lounge with trays of colorful drinks.

I had never been exposed to anything like Jolie Fleur. Inside the stately walls of the residence, prostitution seemed almost genteel. Only one day earlier I had been shocked to discover I was in a place where women sold sex, but as I took in the festive ambiance, I realized how fortunate I was to be in a safe refuge. I had been shocked by so many other things in my life that I was able to accept the foreignness of my surroundings. And I knew I was simply following the direction of my breath in an effort to survive.

Leni smiled at me as if she could read my thoughts. "Hey you, all this is confusing, isn't it? I sometimes wonder how these nice people are considered sinful by some."

"I really don't know either, Leni. Out there maybe - but in here, everything seems respectable. I guess there is no guilt or sin in a place where there is no judgment. We could use more of that attitude everywhere. But it will take me some time to get used to this."

"If we're lucky, we will both be here long enough. Right now, Alcide is signaling it's time to skedoddle, noodle."

"Okay" I laughed. "I think the word is 'skedaddle,' but something tells me you already know that, you liquored up raccoon."

CHAPTER TWENTY

As the days turned into weeks, I settled into a routine at the Jolie Fleur. One of my favorite tasks was helping Jessie in the kitchen. Jessie was a tall, thin black woman with sparse gray hair who was energetic for her years. "I'm eighty years old," she announced one day. "But I've got me a long ways to go before anybody be plantin' these bones in no pine box. I might even get me another man ... as long as he don't wanna knock me up." She never cracked a smile, so it took me a while to catch on to her dry humor.

For me, washing dishes was very relaxing. When one of my blue moods set in, the warm water soothed me. The bad dreams were still frequent, and often I was very tired during the day, so Leni would sometimes pop in to perk me up. She cooked on weekends, but her current daytime chore was to help with the large piles of laundry. We still were able to spend much time together, as she often sneaked into the kitchen for snacks.

When Jessie saw Leni coming, she pretended to be annoyed, but she usually shoved a plate of chocolate croissants or cookies in front of her. "Y'all know you don't have to sneak, don't you, Miss Leni? Hilda don't care what you eat."

"Jessie, it's not as much fun if I don't sneak."

As I grew to know Leni better, I realized she was a person of contrasts. At times she seemed tough and mature, and other times she seemed very young and innocent, in spite of her feistiness. She looked younger than eighteen, but her self-assured nature often made me wish I had more life experience. Much of my security had come from Jake, but since losing him, I was often unsure of myself and off-balance. I admired Leni's spunk.

We always took our breaks and days off together. Within a month, I had seen most of the French Quarter on foot. Sometimes Evens would drive us around if he had to run errands for Hilda, but we didn't have extra money to go out much at night, and Leni always seemed anxious to get back. We listened to records in our room, and Leni taught me all the words to "La Bamba," a Top 40 hit by Richie Valens, who was a favorite of Leni's.

We spent hours talking. Leni was sometimes blunt, which could throw me off my guard, but her face was honest and kind, so I never felt threatened. "How come you never tell me about your other girlfriends?" she asked one evening.

"I never really had any close girlfriends."

"So how 'bout you tell me about why you didn't have girlfriends. You're a real easy person to like, Indiana." (She had only recently started calling me "Indiana," which I found quite humorous.)

"I was a tomboy, for one thing, so I was more interested in boy-like activities. But there were a few girls at school I liked well enough. One girl named Louise even went to college with me for a while."

"You went to college? What a waste of money!"

"Huh?"

"Look where it got you. You're living in a whorehouse."

I burst into laughter. "Good point, listillo."

"You're calling *me* a wise guy? I think I've taught you too much Spanish!"

"I'm a fast learner. Anyway, I was only there one year. I liked

Louise a lot, but we really didn't have anything in common. When I was young, I didn't have girls at my house for sleepovers because my dad drank all the time. The place was a mess, and I was always embarrassed to have anybody see where I lived. I had a lot more in common with my friend, Jake ... but Jake died."

"Oh, that's terrible! What happened?"

"I just can't, Leni ... I can't talk about him."

Leni's eyes gently searched my face. "Okay, I understand. That must be the sadness I see inside you all the time. You never talk about your family either. I worry your sadness is going to take you away from me. Maybe you'll go home, and I will just be a memory."

"No, that won't happen. Even though I did have a home of sorts, I'm running, too - just like you are. My dad is mostly absent. And now Jake is gone, so I can't go back there."

"You never talk about your mother. You never say her name. You only told me you never knew her."

"I only had a photograph. Her name was Marie. She died in a hospital for mentally ill people." I was surprised at how the information escaped my mouth as easily as exhaling. I was so shocked to hear the words aloud that I started shaking.

Leni threw her arms around my shoulders and drew me close. When I started to pull away, she held on even tighter. I finally gave in to her tenderness and relaxed into her embrace.

"Shh, Indiana, you and I will be each other's home."

———

The nights were not as hot as they had been, so the employees often gathered in the courtyard late at night after most of the patrons had retired to the guest rooms with the girls. Some patrons, however, lingered to play Bourré, a trick-taking game with seven players. Alcide was a master. He won hand after hand, and because it was a dollar ante betting game, he pocketed a lot of money.

"This is how Alcide gets his cash to buy all those publications with those fifteen-dollar words in 'em," Leni whispered. "He has a roomful of books."

"So that's where the damn biblioteca is!"

"It's about time you figured it out. You are so funny, mi hermana loca."

After we got to know the game a little better, Leni and I began to suspect he actually threw a hand every once in a while just to keep the other players happy. "Exceedingly well played, sir," he would say, which was always an indication to us that he had thrown a hand.

Old Jessie sometimes sat in on the game too. She was a crackerjack player who won a lot of hands herself. "Old ain't stupid," she would grin, "and youth don't mean shit next to experience. Now, somebody top off my bourbon and deal. This hand ain't gonna play itself."

Card playing for money was off limits to Leni and me according to Hilda. She was very protective that way. We had to stay away from the patrons unless Alcide was with us, because a lot of people came and went throughout the days and evenings.

One night while the others were playing cards, I excused myself from the group to wash some of the night dishes in order to get a head start on the next day's chores. I had my back to the door when I heard the click of the door latch. I turned around just as a delivery man stepped inside lugging a bucket of crawfish. He looked me up and down lasciviously and licked his lips.

I was disgusted. More and more often since becoming increasingly relaxed in a safe refuge, I enjoyed being noticed by men, but I couldn't understand why some men felt it was appropriate to acknowledge the wonderful differences between the sexes by crossing unspoken boundaries. I ignored his gaze and gestured toward the workstation, where I pushed aside the other containers of food stacked on the counter. As I was directing him where to set the bucket, he reached out and grabbed my privates.

I yelled and whipped around just fast enough to watch his face turn white. Hilda had grabbed his testicles from behind and was holding a knife up to his throat with her opposite hand. "Snip snip," she quietly threatened. The guy was shaking so hard I thought he was going to lurch onto the blade and slit his own throat.

Hilda kept the knife steady. "Now we're going to walk together like this over to the door. Just me and you now. Then you're gonna try to get out that door without pissing your pants. And you're never going to come back unless you plan on sacrificing these two little limp biscuits in my hand here. Isn't that right now?"

"Yes, yes!"

"What did you say, you slimy little reptile?" When she squeezed harder, he gasped, but he managed to spit out the words.

"MA'AM! Yes, MA'AM!"

"See how nice it is when everyone uses their good southern manners?" She shoved him out the door, tossed the knife into the sink, and shot me a sly grin. "Now that's how you do it at Jolie Fleur, sweet-cakes."

––––––

Leni and I loved old Jessie. When she wasn't playing Bourré with Alcide and Evens, she would sometimes come to our room and play board games.

During a relaxing game of Monopoly, we were surprised to learn she had once been a hairdresser. "I even had my own place," she told us as she rolled the dice. "I did white people's hair and colored folks' hair too. That's how I met Hilda. She was a real steady customer. Always plump and pretty. Over the years, bendin' over so much got real hard on me, and she done noticed. That good woman insisted I close up shop and come to work in the kitchen here."

"That's because you're a darn good cook. You taught me a lot." Leni caressed Jessie's hand affectionately as she advanced her shoe around the Monopoly board.

"Forget kitchen work," Jessie teased. "I keep tellin' Hilda I can put out for the men if they pay me good. Exceptin' I'm old in my bones, so I gave her orders to let me know when she finds a sucker who's willing to let me sleep through it."

"The fat politician who always visits Dersa probably would." Leni flashed a devilish smile as she passed a bottle of brandy to Jessie. "Dersa says there is more life in an armchair."

Jessie took a swig of brandy as she threw down her Monopoly money to buy Park Place. "I reckon we all have our stories. Didya know Evens was in jail awhile after he come up here from Haiti? Hilda told me they done laid a bum rap on him. Nice way to welcome a soul to Louisiana! Damn po-lice and them immigration bullies ain't kind to nobody."

"Can we please talk about something else?" Leni threw the dice down so hard they flew off the board.

Jessie reached out to pat Leni's hand. "Didn't mean to tread on soft ground, honey chile. You wanna tell us where all that fire done come from?"

"Oh, Jessie, I'm sorry. You didn't say anything wrong. It's just that I've had some real bad experiences myself. A lot of people think brown people should just go back to Mexico or wherever, even if it means starving."

"That ain't gonna happen while Hilda and Alcide and me be suckin' air. You belong right here with us, girl. You know we gonna protect ya."

I had gotten to know Leni well enough to see her mood had shifted. She seemed distracted as she pretended to count her paper money. "You okay?" I asked.

"Yes. It's your turn to roll, please."

I picked up the dice and rolled so we could continue the game. Leni pretended to be engaged, but she was quieter than usual during the rest of the evening. There was a lot more about Leni I had yet to learn.

CHAPTER TWENTY-ONE

As Thanksgiving approached, I became very nostalgic. I had wanted to get as far away from my past as I could, somehow believing the pain would disappear with time and distance, yet the memory of the colors and the scent of bucolic Indiana autumns made me long for home.

One night when Leni was asleep and the activity in the house had subsided, I sneaked into the parlor to make a collect phone call. I hadn't spoken to my father since before Jake died, although I had left messages of my well-being from time to time. I didn't know if he even cared, but for some reason I couldn't let go.

After the phone rang several times, I was ready to hang up just as my father finally answered the phone. His words were slurred when he told the operator he would accept the call, but I was still happy to hear his voice.

"Kat? Kathleen is that you?"

"Yes, Dad. You don't have to yell. It's me."

"How are you? I've been so worried!"

"You have? I'm sorry, Dad. I left word with Louise's mother to tell you I'm safe."

"Yes, yes - she called. She said you were traveling with friends."

"That's right. I just needed to get away. I'm in New Orleans."

"You dropped out of college?"

"Just for the time being. I'll probably go back." As soon as I heard my own words, I knew they were not true. I couldn't be in Franklin without Jake. And my last memories of Franklin were too gruesome to relive.

"But your scholarships-"

"I can get them reinstated, don't you worry. Do you know if the Jacksons are well?"

"Yes. They come by periodically to say hello. They've had a real hard time of it since the accident. How could Jake fall in front of a train, Kat? What were you two doing by the tracks at night?"

"No! Please do not talk about that night. Please, Dad. I'm begging you. It just happened. It was a dangerous railroad crossing. Accidents happen!"

"All right - no need to get upset now. I guess we all just have to accept it. You know, I never understood that boy's sense of humor, but everybody loved Jake. I did too, Kat."

There was a long silence on the other end of the phone. "Dad, are you there?" I was ready to disconnect when I heard faint whimpering. I was so shocked to realize my father was crying that a sudden wave of nausea rushed through me.

"Dad, please, let's not talk about it. I've got to go. I really have to hang up. Please call the Jacksons and tell them I'm doing fine, and I miss them. And please take care of yourself. Please, Dad."

"Yes. Kat, wait. Please wait. I just want to say ... I admit I drink ... too much, I know. I'm so sorry about that. I'm no damn good, but I'm still your father.

"Yes, you are my father. And you're a good person, Dad. I really have to go. You take care. Happy Thanksgiving."

"Happy Thanksgiving, Kit-Kat."

After I placed the phone back in the cradle, I was quite shaken. As I leaned up against the wall for support, I noticed Hilda standing in the doorway. When she held out her arms, I ran to her.

CHAPTER TWENTY-TWO

The day Hilda informed Leni and me that her regular helper, Dauphine, would not be returning from Georgia, we were overjoyed. The room was now truly ours, and we were considered a permanent part of the staff. By then we had stayed on for almost seven months and we were about to ring in 1959.

Although no one could ever replace Jake, Leni and I had become very close. She was what I imagined a sister to be like. Sometimes we would disagree about insignificant things, but we were each other's confidantes and protectors.

Leni taught me how to knit, so as Christmas approached, we spent our evenings making scarves of very fine wool for Alcide, Jessie, Evens, Quinton, and of course Hilda. Each scarf was wrapped in leftover silk wallpaper swatches Hilda had stored in a closet. We also found a colorful antique brooch at Keil's Antiques on Royal Street, which we each chipped in on as an extra gift for Hilda to let her know how much we cared for her and appreciated her giving us a home.

The Jolie Fleur really did feel like a home to both of us, and Hilda and the staff were our family. Although I missed Jake and thought about him every day, each month that passed brought me more peace. I still experienced vivid nightmares of the actual moment Jake stepped in front of the train, but with each new morning, I was able to shake off the darkness faster than I had when I first arrived.

One nightmare was particularly horrible. In my dream, I ran to pull Jake back from the tracks, but instead, he yanked me under the train. Leni heard me scream and came to my bed to wake me. Without asking questions, she stroked my back until I grew calm again.

We had an unspoken understanding about what subjects were off-limits. I shared information with her about Jake, but I never told her he committed suicide. I did finally tell her he fell in front of a train, and I know she suspected it was not an accident, but she never pried. Likewise, I understood she never wanted to discuss her younger years. It was almost as though her life started around the time her mother was killed at the border. She once showed me a photo of her and her grandfather, which confused me, because I thought she first saw him at his funeral. I decided not to press her for details.

Thanksgiving had been a joyous and festive event where everyone who worked at Jolie Fleur gathered in the courtyard for a massive feast. Jessie cooked all day and Alcide brought in heaping amounts of food that Hilda had ordered from Antoine's Restaurant on St. Louis Street. Leni spent three days making pies and even taught me how to make a decent crust. It was hard work, but we all had a great time.

We helped Hilda and the girls decorate the house in festive Christmas decor that included two towering Christmas trees displayed in the middle of the courtyard and in the foyer. One was decorated completely in silver garland and glass ornaments, while the other was entirely red and covered in silk poinsettias and velvet bows.

Dersa had her own tree in her quarters in the opposite wing of the house. She decorated the tree with strips of police tape that warned: CRIME SCENE – DO NOT CROSS. Elves were hanging from nooses that had been strategically placed all over the branches, and the Christmas angel atop the tree was head-less. It was such a hit that we all posed by the tree for photos.

Almost every day, gifts were delivered to the Jolie Fleur - flowers, alcohol, sweets, nuts, and even a box of lobsters that Hilda shared with everyone. Leni and I couldn't believe our bounty.

One night we were digging into a whiskey bread pudding from Commander's Palace - a gift from a judge who was a frequent visitor - when Leni asked, "Did you ever read that book about Eloise who lives in a hotel in New York? This must be what that life is like."

"Yes, but I doubt the Plaza in New York allowed Eloise to traipse around in sleazy lingerie." When Leni spit out her bread pudding, we both fell into hysterics.

Before Christmas, we took a few days off to visit some of the old plantation homes along the levee. The antebellum homes were magnificent, but the contrast between the masters' homes and the remaining slave quarters was so unpleasant, we decided the bayous would be of more interest.

In the bayou, the moss-draped trees and the mysterious waterways were very different from anything I had ever seen in the Midwest. We paid for a boat ride, hoping to catch a glimpse of a dormant gator or two. As the boat moved through the bayou, it parted the green water silk before us. Much to our delight, our guide nudged a sleeping alligator, who opened his jaws in protest. We screamed, but we loved it. We both found the experience to be fascinating.

Our plan was to do some more sightseeing after Christmas, but Leni seldom wanted to venture far from Royal Street. I would have liked to explore some of the other nearby towns, but I enjoyed her company so much I did not mind staying close to the French Quarter, which was always an exciting place to be.

Many of the girls who worked at the Jolie Fleur decided to go home for Christmas, so Hilda planned a great Christmas celebra-tion for those who remained. She scattered glitter all over our hair and made us don Santa hats before treating our small group to Christmas dinner at Galatoire's on Bourbon Street. Our meal was a true feast, and each of us received a bonus check and all sorts of extra treats such as chocolates, pralines, and bottles of whiskey.

Bertrand joined us for Christmas dinner and regaled us with stories of the great jazz clubs in New York. "One night after I had me an intimate convocation with ol' Jack Daniels, I couldn't keep this here body attached to my piano seat. So, I shook off my shoes and socks, draped my sorry bones atop the bench and played with my toes, all the while accompanied by Charlie Parker hisself. Charlie was as pie-eyed as Cooter Brown, so he never done noticed my peculiar affectation. Our tips just kept a'comin' all night, and these here talented toes got me a standing ovation."

His wild tales prompted some animated storytelling by Hilda and Alcide, too. "Alcide," Hilda recalled, "remember the time Mare's mother showed up at the house on a surprise visit? We didn't know it, but Mare had told her very Catholic mother she did laundry in a church-sponsored home for orphan girls. Laundry! I nearly busted out of my girdle when I found out!"

Hilda began laughing so hard that her Santa hat set sail into the butter bowl and she could barely finish her story. Her breasts were threatening to pop out of her dress as usual. Just watching her tell a story was enough to get everyone laughing. The words never mattered because her performances were legendary.

"I told Alcide to run upstairs and tell all the girls to grab their laundry and dump it into piles in Mare's room and then disappear while I tried to stall her mother. When we finally went upstairs, the room was filled with more laundry than you can imagine." Hilda gasped for breath. "I can't breathe – you have to tell them the rest, Alcide!"

Alcide, normally dignified and composed, had to cover his mouth to keep from losing his last bite of shrimp etouffee. "Hilda's attempt to cover almost worked until Mare's mother noticed the piles of laundry consisted of everything from lacy corsets and girdles to bras and crotch-less panties. Hilda, you must do your impression of Mare's mother."

Hilda stood up and whipped into an imitation of a right-eously offended southern woman. "Mother Mary and all the saints, please tell me what those strange split-panties are!" I told her they were designed to keep ladies cool in August. She was so impressed she asked if she could take a pair home. Of course I obliged. Mare said that after that her dad seemed happier than he had ever been, but they couldn't keep her mother out of the confessional booth." By then we were all cheering and asking for more amusing anecdotes while Hilda ordered another round of drinks so we could toast Mare and her befuddled mother.

After dinner we went to a great blues joint where Bertrand knew all the musicians. He got up and jammed with the band while we danced in any empty space we could find. Leni kept whooping, "Arriba! Arriba!" Soon we all were shouting any Spanish word we had ever heard - from cucaracha and fiesta to piñata and mariachi. Someone would yell a word and we would all follow suit. Before long we were making up words like 'imadrunko' and 'gottapeeo' until we were exhausted by our own alcohol-fueled antics.

Christmas with my rag-tag group of friends was its own perfect gift. I looked around the dance floor at my companions and felt a sense of bliss. I had found a new family, and I loved each one of them. I felt a sense of *home* that I had never felt before. I felt whole again.

We all made a vow to repeat the night's activities on New Year's Eve ... but we never got that chance.

———

The following day was a black day for Leni and me. After we awakened, we decided to hang a photo Alcide had snapped of us and presented as a Christmas gift. In the photo, Leni and I were standing under the magnolia tree in the courtyard, each of us wearing floppy felt hats we had found in a thrift store. It was a great photo, so Alcide had the image enlarged before mounting it in an ornate gold frame.

It was early in the morning, so neither of us was dressed when we heard someone knock loudly on our door. Leni was in the alcove, so I answered. Standing in front of me were two strange men. Hilda and Alcide were behind them, and I noticed that Hilda, who looked pale and shaken, was tightly clutching Alcide's arm. When Alcide gave me a warning look, I instinctively stepped further into the doorway to prevent the strangers from entering. Behind me I could hear the chifforobe door open and close, but I remained frozen.

The taller and more menacing man pulled out a badge and announced, "Immigration. We are looking for Leanora Cruz. We have received information about illegals being harbored in this establishment. Anyone without papers will be arrested. Identification please."

My heart was pounding, but I tried to act as casual and cooperative as possible while I fabricated a cover. "Yes, sir. I am Kathleen Leanora Cruz Caswell. I have an American Drivers License and I am from Indiana. I am hardly illegal, so I'm afraid your information is incorrect."

"Show me some identification," he grunted.

My handbag was on a table right next to the door, so I was able to reach into my purse without allowing them room to pass. I paused for a moment, trying to formulate my next lie as I shoved my driver's license into his hand.

"This says you are Kathleen Caswell."

"Yes, that is correct. My mother's name was Kathleen Leanora Cruz. I am named after her. Of course, she took my father's name, Caswell. In Indiana they only put your first and last names on licenses. But I suppose you already know that, sir. My friends call me Leni. I guess that's where your misinformation came from."

"You don't look Mexican to me," the shorter man snapped as he took the license and copied down the numbers.

"I'm not sure what you were expecting." I nodded a polite thank you as I took my license back. "My mother is only half Mexican and my father is Caucasian, so of course I am light skinned. Did you expect me to be wearing a big sombrero?"

The room went almost silent until Alcide stifled a snicker. I was shocked at the words that had flown out of my mouth without any good sense attached, and I feared the immigration officer would take offense at my cheekiness. While each second passed, I nervously tried to build my story and was terrified of what might happen next.

By that time, Jessie had come upstairs and was standing in the hallway behind Hilda. She had overheard us and quickly assessed the predicament I was in. "Leni," she snapped at me, "as soon as you finish socializing, I really need you down in the kitchen." She gave me a cautious look as she anchored herself by the doorway.

The lead officer seemed very suspicious. He glanced at Jessie before turning back to me. "I'd like to come in and see your room, miss."

I saw Hilda shaking her head in panic, but I didn't know what to do.

"Of course you may look around." I smiled weakly and stepped back into the room a few steps without fully allowing him to pass. "But you can see my entire room from right here. So, unless you plan to arrest me, I respectfully ask you to just take your time and look around from where you are. I believe that's fair, don't you? I certainly have nothing to hide."

He was not happy with my suggestion, but he seemed reluctant to push very hard, so he stepped just inside the doorway and looked around. Alcide was practically holding Hilda upright, and Jessie was still lingering by the doorway to see what might happen next.

The officer seemed satisfied until his eyes zoned in on the

bed. I knew Leni must be hiding in the wardrobe, but she had left the photo of us exposed. "Do you have a roommate?" he inquired.

The image in the photo was not clear from where we were standing, but I was afraid he would demand I show it to him. My hands were starting to shake from panic. I didn't think I could carry on the bluff any longer until Jessie pushed her way into the room.

"I'm her roommate, and it's burning my butt that Leni here ain't down in the kitchen working her shift because you're holdin' her up, Mr. Whoever-you-be." Jessie glanced at the bed and promptly walked over and took a seat.

The second officer looked at her with a disdainful look on his face before moving closer to me. "You have a colored roommate?"

"That's right," Jessie snapped. "We're all hired help here, and there ain't no extra rooms for us coloreds."

"I guess anything goes in a whorehouse," he sneered.

Jessie reclined on the bed and allowed her long apron to cover the photo. "My color don't rub off. I'm eighty years old, so I can't be sleeping in no damn shed!"

"Okay, we're leaving. But if our Indiana bureau cannot verify your records, miss, you can be sure we will be back."

"Let's go," the smaller one nodded. "I don't want to be in this brothel any longer than necessary."

"And we are all grateful for that," Hilda snapped.

I closed the door as Alcide and Hilda escorted the immigration officers back down the stairs. I was shaking so hard I started to pant. Jessie looked at me and put her finger over her lips. She ran to the front window and waited until they left to signal that we were clear.

The second she nodded, I ran to the wardrobe and yanked open the door. Leni had covered herself with blankets, which I yanked off her to help her breathe. She was crying softly. "I'm so sorry," she repeated, "I'm so sorry."

"Why are you in trouble, Leni? Why are they looking for you?"

"They're looking for all of us."

"Who is 'us'?"

"Immigration has been ordered to step up the hunt for all Mexicans without legal documents."

"But you were born in Texas, so maybe all we need to do is get you a Social Security card or something. I'm sure we can get this all straightened out."

"No, Kat, we can't. I was born in Mexico."

"Oh, no!"

"It's true. We crossed through the desert without papers. Please don't be angry, Kat – we were desperate for work. My mother died just trying to provide me with food – and a future. I had nowhere to go after she died, so I stayed and found whatever work I could get in order to survive. I have a fake identification card that I bought in Texas. I was too scared to tell anyone - even you."

"Jesus, Leni!"

"I'm so sorry, but please don't let them send me back there, Kat. I have no one other than the family I have here. I'm begging you - please!"

Leni immediately lapsed into Spanish and continued sobbing. She struggled with me as I tried to pull her out of the wardrobe.

When I turned to look at Jessie for help, Jessie slowly shook her head in concern. "I'll get Hilda. Those men be comin' back."

———

Hilda was already at our door. "We have to work fast, chere. Start packing her things into a bag. This is all the cash I've got on hand, so put this in her bag." She handed me a roll of bills. "Leni is going to have to lie low until things cool down. Right now, I need you to get her ready to go. Tomorrow morning, we will decide what to do. I have to figure out a way to keep you out of trouble too. You did a great job of buying time, but they'll know damn soon you were lying, sugar."

"Did you know Leni was wanted by immigration, Hilda?"

"I suspected. But that doesn't matter. This young girl is going to be sent to a foreign place where she doesn't know anyone and doesn't have a soul to take her in. We have to figure out something fast."

"Leni," she ordered, "stop crying and get up on out of there. I'm going down to make some phone calls. Jessie, I want you to start packing food. Right now, everyone - that's a damn order!"

As I was helping Leni up out of the wardrobe, Hilda turned to exit. She stopped momentarily to steady herself against the door frame. "No damnable horse's ass is going to come into my house and take any of you away from me!"

I looked back at Leni, who was dead white and trembling. She shook her head in surrender. "She can't stop them, Kat. No one can stop them. Not even Hilda."

———

Leni was quiet all day. She kept looking out the window, and she couldn't stop shaking. Her usual feistiness had disappeared, and she looked smaller and younger to me than she ever had.

Jessie brought hot tea to our room, and Alcide checked on us every hour. From time to time throughout the day, I met with Hilda in the hallway. She told me she still hadn't been able to reach anybody who would help.

"Damn judges and local officials come here all the time for private leisure activities, but when I need help, there's always a limit. They're telling me they have no control over immigration officers. I think I've got you covered, though, Kat - I've got a sheriff who will say you were just scared, and he'll get some money into the right hands. But I'll need more time to get it done. And I've got to get Leni situated somewhere else for her own protection."

"Do you know someone who will take her in?"

"That there's the problem. No one wants to mess with the illegals, or they could get into serious legal trouble themselves. I don't think she should use public transportation but I'm gonna try to get her up to that house in Shreveport I just bought. She can hide out there awhile. Evens left for the holidays this morning, and Alcide doesn't have a license to drive. I'm trying to arrange a ride now. I'll update you as soon as I know something. It's about a five-hour drive, so just have her ready to go."

Leni and I went to bed that night not knowing what the next morning would bring. Leni wouldn't say much other than, "I'm so sorry, Kat. I'm so sorry."

———

I tried to sleep that night, but the sound of Leni's constant crying was devastating. I had finally dozed off when I heard Leni rustling around. When I opened my eyes, I was startled to see she was dressed and heading for the door with her bag in hand.

"Where are you going, Leni?" I demanded.

"Shh, amiga. Go back to sleep."

"You're leaving? You were just going to go and not tell me?"

"I left you a note. I can't stay any longer, Kat. If they catch me here, Hilda could lose everything. I can't do that to her. She has been like a mother to me. I'll find you again as soon as I can."

"No, I'll help you, Leni. I promise I'll help you."

"You don't understand - no one can help me. You can't get involved. I did a very bad thing. I didn't just bite the border guard who grabbed me - I stabbed his arm with my penknife. That's assault - a bad crime in America, and they want to put me in jail!"

"Oh no, Leni!"

"He was hurting me, and I was terrified. And I watched them

attack my mother! They've been trying to catch up with me ever since. If you try to hide me, it's the same thing as helping an escaped convict. You could get into serious trouble, and I would rather die than have that happen."

"Well, you're not going without me, Leni - you stay right there dammit. You will not leave me behind!" I leaped out of bed and grabbed my clothes from the chair.

"No, mi hermana, I can survive on my own."

"Leni, if you walk out that door I'm going to scream and wake everyone up." I started throwing things into my travel bag as quickly as I could. When I had what I needed, I headed for the door. "Okay partner, let's get out of here."

"Are you sure?"

"I've never been more sure of anything in my life. We're family. 'Me, Tonto.'"

"Is a Me-Tonto good?"

"Damn right it is."

Leni paused as she pulled out the wad of money Hilda had given her. She placed it by the letter she had written and left on the desk.

"Leni, we're going to need that money."

"But it's not mine, chica. Hilda will need to pay people off so she doesn't get shut down. I've already caused enough trouble. No more."

"Okay, I understand. Where are you planning to go?"

"I'm going to hide on the streets until I figure something out."

"Hilda has a house in Shreveport-"

"No, that's too much risk for her, Kat. I won't do it."

"Wait!" After I rifled through my bag, I pulled out the business card Mr. Boudreaux had given me. "This is a sugarcane plantation I heard about from a man on the train. He swears they always need workers. Do you think they would ask you for papers?"

"I don't know. Farmers usually hire Mexicans on the Bracero program because those migrants have permits, but I don't think they check too close because they need labor. Do you know how to get there?"

"It's south of Bayou Lafourche, about sixty miles from here. I looked it up once. It's near the train line, so we can walk along the tracks as far as possible, and after that, maybe we can hitch a ride. We can follow the rails and stay out of sight."

"I'm so scared, Kat. Will we be safe?"

"Safer than we are here. But we have to move fast, Leni – we have to disappear." When I said the words, I had no idea how true they would be.

BOOK IV

LENI

CHAPTER TWENTY-THREE

On many occasions since my arrival in New Orleans, I had walked to the nearest railroad tracks during my free time. Watching the trains pass gave me a sense of peace, even though the feeling was always tinged with sadness. Out of habit, I had studied the train routes and schedules. Even without Jake, the routine was comforting. The night Leni and I left the Jolie Fleur, I knew it would be easy to identify which track to follow toward Houma and Bayou Lafourche from Union Station.

It was too risky for Leni to try to train hop with me, so we walked for the better part of two and a half days. At night we found places to sleep near the tracks, and I taught Leni how to use what we had with us to prepare a bed and to protect herself. We were both terrified of snakes but with good fortune, we were able to avoid them - until the second day.

We were following the rails late in the day when, to our horror, we encountered a long rattlesnake stretched along the tracks. I was walking with a stick in hand, as Jake had always insisted, but it seemed like meager protection when facing an angry, venomous snake.

The second we saw the snake, I shoved Leni behind me and told her to stay very still. I heard her whimper in terror, but I held her steady and spoke as calmly as my nerves would allow. "Don't move, Leni, do not move."

As the rattler moved closer to the rail, the threatening vibration of the oncoming train spooked it. The snake instantly coiled into striking position and lifted its rattle, emitting an ominous hissing sound. Unfortunately, the rail did not become its focus for attack – we did.

I was so terrified I wanted to run, but I kept my body in front of Leni's and did not flinch. We were frozen in position for so long I was afraid my knees were going to buckle, but the snake finally lost interest. It uncoiled and slithered down the embankment into the tall grass just as the train appeared in the distance. I could feel Leni reach up to cover her mouth to keep from screaming as it retreated.

When the rattler disappeared from view, we both broke into tears from pent-up fear. Leni rubbed her chest and spoke in hushed tones as if she were afraid the snake would hear her and return. "Are we too young to have a heart attack, Kat?"

"No, and we're not too old to cry like babies either."

"Do you think snakes are attracted to pee?" she asked.

"I hope not, or we both are doomed," I laughed.

After walking a bit farther, we were still so nervous we vowed to find a house close to the tracks where we could sleep that night on a porch or patio rather than on the ground. We managed to find a vacant shed for shelter before moving on the following day.

As we continued our trek, I noticed Leni had lost her usual spunky spirit. She was quieter than usual, although she could still make me laugh.

As we walked the final stretch into Bayou Lafourche, I tried to lighten the mood. "Leni, you were so white after we saw that rattlesnake, you didn't even look Mexican."

"No? Did you expect me to be wearing a big sombrero?" The smirk on her face was downright comical.

"So, you heard that, huh?"

Leni laughed aloud. "You could do stand-up comedy, amiga!"

"I'm glad you find me so amusing."

"I do, but my feet don't. Are we almost there, Me-Tonto?"

———

Once we were near Bayou Lafourche, we were able to get specific instructions to the sugarcane plantation, so Leni and I followed the road along the river. Everywhere we looked, there were acres of lush green cane farms. The entire area was like a tropical jungle, dense with brown ridged stalks that resembled tall bamboo plants with bright green leaves feathering out of their tops.

As soon as we spotted the sign to Hertizine plantation, we departed the river road and waved to the driver of an old blue Chevy truck that was stopped near a wooden gate at the end of a dirt lane.

As we approached the truck, a young man, who appeared to be in his late twenties, flashed us a suggestive grin. "Are you two cupcakes needin' a ride?"

"No thanks." My senses were immediately on alert, but I decided it was best to remain polite. "Can you tell me where we go to sign up for work?"

"Work? If the boss is hirin' sweet things like you, then me and the other boys are gonna be as happy as possums on a sweet tater. Just take yourselves right on over there to that old trailer. Manager is back there."

"A guy named Sistrunk?"

"Yup - ya got the right place. Wes Jarrell at your service. You two like to party?"

"No. My father is a police officer, so he doesn't allow it," I snapped.

"Yeah - aren't they all, sugar?" he winked as he tipped his hat.

"Thanks for your help." I grabbed Leni's arm and turned to

go in the opposite direction as Wes revved the truck and drove off.

"Where are you going, Kat? He said to go this way."

"No, let's keep looking. I don't have a good feeling about this place."

"I've seen worse places. We're about out of money, and I need to hide some place like this where those immigration hombres can't find me. I don't want you to have hardship because of me. Maybe you can find work in that little town we passed through, huh? That would be nicer than working the fields. And you can just let me know where you are so we can sneak to see each other?"

"There's no way I'm going to do that. We have to stay together, Leni. And we can live cheaper that way too."

"Didn't you say this place might be able to put us up?"

"Yes, okay, come on. Let's at least check it out. But I really think we should keep to ourselves as much as we can. And let's keep our bags packed until we can really check out the situation here."

———

Hank Sistrunk immediately struck me as an amiable guy. He had a broad smile, and although he was paunchy, his ruddy face was so jovial that it made him oddly attractive. I liked him immediately.

Leni and I both relaxed as we settled into chairs across from a paper-strewn desk in the field trailer. He handed us two cold sodas just before he sat down and propped his feet up on the desk.

"So how did you come about travelin' all the way out here to these parts?"

I slid the business card across the desk. "A man on the train gave me this. Dexter Boudreaux. He is sure the owner of the cane farm will remember him."

"Boudreaux? The Potato Head guy?" He let out a hearty guffaw that made Leni's eyes grow huge.

"He has a head shaped like a potato?" she giggled.

"Ha! No, Miss … Leni, is it? Well, I can't say what his head is shaped like, but he's an investor. And he's also a really great poker player, I hear. My boss told me all about Boudreaux. He described in detail how he nearly lost his shirt *and* his pants to the guy in a card game on the train from Shreveport a while back. 'Thought he might have to exit the train in his altogether! It was mighty nice of him to send you our way."

"So, you do hire females, sir?" I asked. I didn't mean to be so abrupt, but I wanted to get directly to the point of our long trip out to Bayou Lafourche.

"Sure, I can use two tough girls … and no questions asked." He glanced at Leni and then looked back at me. "Miss Kat - if you don't mind my calling you that - we don't put female workers on the really tough physical jobs like chopping the plants with machetes and the like, but there's a lot of other work to be done in the cane field - things like cleaning up the debris and piling it into trucks. You think you two are up to that?"

"Yes, sir!" we answered in unison.

Leni leaned forward so she could get a better view of the cane field through the trailer window. "Do you have living quarters for your workers?"

"We kinda do, but the housing is quite dilapidated, ladies. I'm not sure the old place would suit you. The building is original to the plantation. It's got a metal roof and no air conditioning. The bathroom area has a pull shower with cold water only, and a toilet and small sink in the corner of the room - that type of thing. The place does have a hot plate to warm up soup and the like. Honestly, it's a real shack. Usually there are mostly men workin' the fields, so their accommodations have been fixed up better.

Leni shifted in her chair. "We can make do. But would we have roommates?" Leni tried to ask as offhandedly as she could, but her concern was not well-hidden, as she had grown much more wary of meeting strangers.

"The place is empty now. We were puttin' up a few of our extra men in there until a week or so ago, but they moved on to pick fruit. They left the blankets and cots clean, but it is mighty rough living. Are you sure-"

"Sounds like camping." Leni cut him off before he could talk himself out of letting us stay. "We can handle that, Mr. Sistrunk."

"OK, but you'll need to get you some supplies. I think the men left some soup and instant coffee. There's a tiny refrigerator in there - not sure if it still runs. You can get more supplies about a mile from here. 'You sure you don't want to look for a room in town?"

"No, we need to save our money. We'd like to stay here, sir," Leni reiterated. "Just please tell me there aren't any snakes."

"None that are on the payroll," he smiled.

"Come on, I'll get you set up and show you where you can throw your belongings. You can start training tomorrow, and you just let me know if you need anything." He turned a framed photo in our direction. "You know, I have a real fine girl of my own. She's all grown up now and works on a Mississippi river boat. 'Miss her a lot. I sure admire enterprising young ladies like y'all. You've got a fan right here, yes-siree. Let me know whenever I can be of help."

"That's nice to know, Mr. Sistrunk," I smiled as I looked at the photo.

"Just 'Hank' will do."

"Thank you, Hank. We also just met one of your workers named Wes."

"Sorry to hear that. I call him 'Waste.' If he behaved like a moron, just pay him no attention. But stay away from him. He did some time for brawlin' in a bar, so his daddy, who belongs to the same club as the owner here, wanted him to do some hard labor to get him back on the right track. He called in a favor with my boss, it seems. I didn't get a say. Lucky for all of us, he's out of here at the end of February. Him and his dingleberry sidekick are both a real pain in my butt. Of course, you never heard that from me."

"I'm sorry sir," I smiled as I held my hand to my ear, "I think I missed something - I couldn't hear what you were saying."

"That's a good one! I sure do like your wit. Come on, let's get you settled. The first few days are always real hard, and you're gonna have some mighty sore muscles. You'll need to rest up."

"Thank you," I said. "One other thing, Hank ... could you not mention to anyone that we are here?'

Hank paused, and then he nodded knowingly. "I ain't never seen the likes of you. Com'on, Buckingham Palace awaits."

CHAPTER TWENTY-FOUR

ALTHOUGH WE WERE NOT ASSIGNED TO CANE CHOPPING DETAIL, THE work was strenuous. We had to bend over constantly to gather and then tie the piles of cane leaves all day long. The farm was smaller than some of the bigger farms that had automated equipment, so the stronger workers cut the cane by hand. We followed the choppers down the rows as they cut the stalks with their machetes, which was a labor-intensive job that required a lot of strength. The cutters had to be careful not to chop into the soil, and most of them had developed an exact technique and rhythm.

Hank told us if we wanted to switch up our work while our bodies adjusted to the labor, we could take shifts that allowed us to sit and strip the cane after it was cut. The alternation between stripping and cleaning up debris gave our backs a break. It didn't take us long to learn to wear hats and keep our bodies covered to protect ourselves from the sun. We were deep in harvest season, and although the weather had cooled some, the days were still very hot.

Leni and I kept to ourselves in spite of attempts at conversation by Wes and his crude friend Zack. We were more cordial with some of the others because Wes and Zack's remarks were often lewd and offensive.

One day, Hank, who usually supervised in another part of the field, tracked Leni and me down in order to teach us the most effective way to strip stalks. He got behind me and lifted my arm in an upward motion as part of his demonstration.

Hank's strong arms on mine created an invisible wall of protection from all the threat that constantly surrounded Leni and me. I had become so accustomed to being on the run that I felt a momentary relief from the constant anxiety. I allowed myself to accept being safeguarded by someone else, and Hank was a kind, fatherly figure who made me feel safe in spite of my vulnerability.

Wes, who was chopping cane in the row next to ours, stopped to watch the demonstration. "That's real good teachin' there, boss. Go on and get in there real close and rub up behind her and she'll get the hang of it real fast."

The moment I heard his voice, a beautiful and innocent moment was destroyed. I pulled away from Hank abruptly.

"'Glad to help you out with that if you like. I can teach her friend, too," Wes oozed.

"Shut your trap," Hank snapped. "Don't think I won't fire you just because your daddy knows some higher-ups around here. You've been a tick in my shorts a lot lately, boy. Use a civil lip around these girls, or you and me are gonna have a real throw-down."

"Yes, sir. I was just havin' me a little fun."

"You get on over to the next row and stay over there."

Wes tipped his hat and gave Leni a suggestive look before he retreated.

"That boy has no respect for women. And he thinks he's better than all the Negroes and Mexicans who work circles around him. You two stay away from him - especially you, Leni."

"Cochino," Leni said under her breath.

After Hank left us, I asked her what "cochino" meant.

Without answering, she made a pig face and snorted loudly. It was a darn good barnyard impression, so I caught on real fast.

From that moment on, whenever we saw Wes approaching, we snorted to each other as a signal. The closer he got, the more we snorted until we had to suppress our laughter. He always looked confused because he could never figure why we were laughing. He kept his distance for a while, and we kept ours.

———

At night we always returned to the cabin, which truly was a shack. It looked to be turn of the century construction. The walls consisted of rough wood planks, and in some areas, enough daylight entered through the gaps to streak the worn floors. The tin roof overhead had no insulation, and on the few nights it rained, the noise was so loud we could hardly sleep. Leni insisted that Santa's reindeer would have caused less "clatter."

Nevertheless, exhaustion always took over.

The toilet, sink, and small cooking setup were all in the same small area. There was a space heater and a hot plate, but if we plugged them in at the same time, the electricity would go out, accompanied by sparks and a popping sound that terrified us. In a short time, we learned to drink cold instant coffee and to exist on bread and cheese and the stale crackers we found in the cupboard. For something sweet, we sometimes chewed on pieces of sugar cane we brought home from the field. The stalks were woody in texture and not as sweet as I expected, but I enjoyed the mild flavor.

We also had a few uninvited roommates. Whenever a mouse ran through the cabin, Leni threw everything she was able to pick up. I was glad she couldn't lift me, too, or I would have sustained a concussion.

"Indiana, this is not like camping at all. It's more like a prison in Tijuana. And it's so quiet, just like a cemetery. I miss the noise of the French Quarter."

"I do, too. But this place does have its good points."

"Oh, yeah? Like what?"

"Well, you could sit on the hot plate with one foot in the sink and one foot in the toilet, and then you can plug the toaster into the outlet for an instant blowout if you ever decide you want to lose your virginity."

"Great idea. I'm going to name the hot plate Elvis. He can warm my fanny anytime."

By the end of the day, we were usually too tired to play with the deck of cards I carried in my travel bag. Many times, we were even too spent to talk. Every day after work, we threw ourselves onto our cots and just stared up at the stained ceiling, making a game out of defining who the water spots looked like. Leni was sure she spotted Queen Elizabeth on our ceiling, but I insisted that the pinkish discoloration looked more like Nikita Khrushchev. "You may be right - he *is* big, ugly, and red," she laughed.

The cabin that quartered the men was across the field from ours. We often heard boisterous activity in the evening, and we knew they indulged in a lot of alcohol, because we had seen several men stumbling around in the moonlit field.

One night Wes and his friend Zack banged on our door, but we pretended not to be there. They had a loud transistor radio with them, and it was obvious they were drunk when they yelled at us to come out and dance. I heard the words 'puta,' and 'furcia,' - words Leni told me were slang for 'whore.' I also knew it was Wes who was hurling the insults.

We grabbed some heavy pans and waited by the door just in case they became more aggressive, but eventually they went away. Afterward, we fell back down onto our mattresses, grateful to have survived an especially long day.

"What does 'Wes' mean in Spanish, Leni – 'jackass'?"

"I'm pretty sure it means 'Foreskin.' Madre de Dios, Kat, I hurt all over!"

"Me too. I've never worked so hard in my life. How long do you think we need to stay in hiding?"

"I've been hiding since I left Mexico. I hate it that you're going through this, too. You really don't have to stay."

"Yes, I do - they're after me too, for sheltering you and for lying to immigration officials, Leni. And I'm sure I did not win the Miss Congeniality award for my sombrero comment," I grimaced.

"I would vote for you! Kat, Hilda assured us it's really me they want. You are not their priority. Get out of this dump while you can. I can take care of myself."

"We've had this conversation before, and I'm not going to change my mind. I'm here until you think the heat has let up so we can head back to the Jolie Fleur."

"But that could be at least six months."

"We can make it … if the killer mosquitoes don't get us first. Leni, you never told me why you and your mom left Mexico. I really don't know anything about your country."

"America is really my country, compadre. Mexico has very nice people, but it's a very poor place where I lived, and very dirty, because there was no place for trash or human waste in our village. It was not even a village. It was more like a hillside of shacks."

"Did you live in a house?"

"It was a shack like this one - a chabola with big cucarachas … and we were always hungry. I told you I had a dad, but I lied, and I'm so sorry. The truth is, he left us when I was young. I believe that maybe he really is still in Mexico somewhere, so I convinced myself it wasn't a lie. My mom had a hard time taking care of us because there was very little work."

"Why didn't you go somewhere else?"

"No car, chica. No transportation at all. A few men had trucks, but no money for gasoline. We were abandoned in a slum. I always ask God why I was born in a barrio he rejected … but still no answers."

"I'm sorry, Leni. So how did you finally get away from there?"

"When I turned thirteen, the drought got worse, and the local fruit farmer who sometimes gave us work in a good season went out of business that year. We were begging for food in the street, but everyone else was in the same situation, so no one could help us."

"You didn't have food?"

"Not much. I was hungry all the time. But one day my mother met a man in a car who had detoured off the main road somehow, so he was looking for directions. When she asked him for a ride, he promised he would take us as far as the Texas border. I thought her plan was to look for work in a border town, but she decided if we had to be alone and desperate, it was best to start again in America because we heard it was a magical place - a cuerno de la abundancia. I think you say 'cornucopia.'"

"Hmm ... yes, I suppose if you squint your eyes right now and look around this lovely pigsty, you will see it's a cornucopia of delights."

"Ha! I'd have to claw the eyeballs out to make that happen. But believe me, it's still better than where I was born."

"Could you speak English when you got here?"

"I learned some from my mother, but I picked up most of the English in Texas. For the first two years I did migrant labor. I only had a few years of school, so one of the women taught me to read and write because she knew I wanted to learn. We called our lessons the 'Agrarian Academy.' In every town we found discarded books, so I read a lot – the *Bible* and lots of Steinbeck and Hemingway books, and even Shakespeare and Dickens ... but not *A Tale of Two Cities* yet," she grinned. "The gossip magazines are just for the photos. Anyway, after living in so many migrant shacks, I know how to adapt."

"All right, we will work a few more months, and when you feel safe enough, we'll leave this glorious cornucopia behind. In the meantime, let's call Hilda to see if anyone came back around."

"And we keep saving our money for emergencies?"

"Oh, yes. But this entire situation is an emergency. I sure hope it doesn't get any worse than this."

I immediately wanted to retract my words. I had a dark feeling that I was tempting fate.

CHAPTER TWENTY-FIVE

1960 HAD ROLLED IN AND JANUARY HAD PASSED, BUT LENI AND I barely took notice. Although our bodies had acclimated somewhat to the hard labor, we were still tired all the time. It seemed as though all we did was work. Whenever we had a bit of leftover energy, we walked a mile to the road stop for supplies.

Near the end of February, after Mardi Gras was over and the city's festivities had died down, we hoped enough time had passed to allow for our safe return to New Orleans. We decided to call Alcide from the road stop to get an update, because we were just biding our time in hopes the men from immigration would lose interest.

Leni and I both crammed into the phone booth by the gun and bait shop to place the call. As we pressed our heads against the earpiece, the smell of stale of beer and vomit made us both recoil. I was about to suggest we call back another time when Alcide finally picked up.

He was very happy to hear from us, but he also seemed unusually anxious. "I'm very glad you two are safe for now. But please stay where you are. Things still aren't good here. Immigration has been back several times. Remember Dersa? They apprehended her and sent her back to Guatemala. She has been here her entire life, but she was born there, so they sent her back. She doesn't even speak Spanish! The whole thing sticks in your throat like a hair in a biscuit."

"Is it the same men who keep coming back?" Leni asked.

"Yes, Leni. They claim you assaulted an officer, and they know you were here. Their intent is to make Hilda pay for hiring illegal workers."

"Oh, no! Everyone's troubles are my entire fault!" she cried.

"Don't you fret about that. Hilda insists they are no match for her, and I think we can all agree on that. However, they do have us on temporary shutdown."

"No one is working?"

"Quite the contrary. They forgot we have a back door, so we are surviving just fine. Some of the same people who have been putting on the pressure still come around as customers. Damn hypocrites. We expect them to back off in a few months after enough money gets spread around, but right now they're trying to send a message. Hilda thinks if they apprehend Leni, they'll forget about you, Kat. You're bait to them."

"Damn bullies! Was Hilda mad at us for leaving without warning?"

"No, she was just worried sick. We all have been. She loves you two girls, and she'll be very disappointed she wasn't here to talk to you. But just stay safe where you are. This may take time to blow over. We're sure the person who gave the tip-off to immigration was a customer, and if that client is still coming around, you're not safe, Leni."

The phone abruptly started clicking over Alcide's words just as a recorded voice requested that we deposit more money or be disconnected. "We're out of dimes, Alcide. Please give our love to Hilda and Jessie and the others."

"Yes, I will, Kat. You must promise to stay out of sight. But please stay in touch. And Leni, I'm collecting movie star magazines for you and-"

The phone line went dead. "We lost him." My heart was still clinging to the sound of his voice as I placed the phone back on the receiver and opened the door of the phone booth. Neither of us had noticed the blue Chevy truck that had pulled into the parking lot during our call.

"Hey girls, how about a ride back?" Wes called out as he approached the booth. Zack can drive, and Leni, you can ride on my lap. It's a real bouncy road, so I'm sure you'll enjoy it, yeah?"

Leni stepped back into the booth. I pushed the glass door closed and stood my ground outside the booth. "Thank you, Wes, but we prefer to walk."

"Oh, so my company is not good enough for you and your little Mexican friend?"

"It's not that at all, Wes. We appreciate your offer. We just really need the exercise and fresh air."

"You don't get enough of that out in the field? Or are you just a little too highfalutin for us?"

"That's not it at all. We like to walk and get out because our bunk house smells like dirty feet. Why don't you go on ahead, and maybe we can get together later this week before you leave."

"Yeah? Well, that's mighty friendly of y'all. I knew you'd warm up sooner or later. I'll plan something real special for us. 'Later, gator." He winked at Leni before heading back to his truck.

Leni waited until the truck was out of sight before she exited the phone booth again. "Oh God - he is such a disgusting pig! Thank you for always protecting me."

"Let's just go along with him one more week until he leaves."

Leni nodded. "'Now is the winter of our discontent.'"

"Shakespeare?"

"Yep. He knew about tragedy, sí? I often repeat that line in my head to remind myself that the bad is temporary. After winter comes the spring, no? But I just don't know how long we can we make it here, hermana. I don't feel safe."

"Leni, you're tough. Don't give up now. We have to hang in

there as long as it takes." There was no way I could tell her I was
as discouraged as she was.

CHAPTER TWENTY-SIX

WE WORKED VERY HARD THAT WEEK BECAUSE WE WERE AT THE height of the harvest and still waiting for new crew workers who had not yet arrived. Wes and his friend Zack had requested to extend their employment, but Hank refused. Leni and I were more than happy to put in extra hours just to cover the shortage rather than have Wes stay on. Wes's reputation for slacking off and being a mean drunk left us with no doubt that many other workers felt the same way.

Since our encounter at the road stop, we had managed to avoid Wes almost completely. Finally, it was Wes's last day of employment, so Leni and I planned to have our own little celebration after work. I prayed he would leave before either of us encountered him again, but luck was not on my side. Late in the afternoon, Wes emerged from a wall of cane and caught up with me in the row where I was piling cane leaves. I wasn't fearful, because other laborers were working the same row, but his presence revolted me and made me nervous.

"So, are you gonna miss me, baby?" He sidled up to me and flashed me a grin that was so oily I could barely stand to look at him.

"Only two hours left on your shift, Wes, but I think I can stand the pain."

"You and your little chiquita friend promised you were gonna party with us, remember? I got me some Jack and a few other surprises."

"Thank you, Wes. But I'm afraid that's not going to work out after all. Tonight, we both have a meeting with Hank, so we can't meet you."

"Really? Well now, that's a real disappointment."

"Yes, I'm sorry, but he is the boss, so what can we do? But I do wish you the very best of luck. Leni is helping out in the office today, but I'm sure she would wish you good luck too. I've got to get back to work now."

He looked at me strangely, but before he could protest, the foreman yelled at everybody to pick up some speed because clouds were rolling in. Wes made a strange clicking sound with his tongue, which was as lascivious as it was threatening, before he finally slithered off. I was grateful Leni hadn't been there to hear his cheeky comments, because he rattled her even more than he did me.

After Wes was out of view, I reflected on the many ironies in my life. I recalled how my female needs had been awakened again at the Jolie Fleur, where I sometimes thought longingly about being held and comforted by someone of the opposite sex, and I learned that femininity was not something to suppress or to be afraid of. However, the thought of a man like Wes touching me filled me with repulsion.

As I stripped my last batch of cane stalks that day, I realized how tired I was of living in an environment better suited for tough men. The skin on my hands was so cracked that every time it healed over, the flesh would open up again. I always felt dirty, and my eyes burned with sweat. My back ached so much that it felt better to stay hunched over rather than to try to stand upright. I was covered with bug bites so red and inflamed that I could not scratch them without drawing blood. But worse than the physical issues were the looming threats that kept Leni and me on the run.

I missed the Jolie Fleur, hot showers, and a soft bed. But what I missed most was Hilda, and Alcide ... and always Jake. I stopped working for a moment and tried to shake off my mood. I knew I couldn't let anyone see me surrender to the sadness.

I had never minded hard work, but I hated uncertainty. Even after I ran away from Franklin, the uncertainty was different. Whatever was to come was always a result of my free choice, even without a plan. But now Leni and I were someone's pawns, and I knew that could not continue.

By the end of my shift, I had made a decision to find a way to hide in plain sight. It was time for Leni and me to leave Bayou Lafourche.

———

When I met Leni back at the cabin, which we had dubbed "The Hole," I told her I wanted to discuss a new plan with her. "Leni, we've made it this far, but now I think it's time to move on."

"Gracias a Dios! I have tried to be as tough as you are, Indiana, but I can't stand it here any longer. I am so relieved! I am going to nominate you as a saint."

"Thanks. You Catholics must set a low bar ... but I might look good on a gold neck-chain. Let's walk over to the road stop and pick up a few snacks and come back and devise our new plan. I'm going to take a quick shower."

Before I finished towel-drying my hair, I noticed that Leni had fallen into a peaceful sleep on her cot, so I didn't bother to wake her up. I grabbed my walking stick and headed down the dirt road, taking advantage of the alone time to formulate my plan. I wondered if there was a way to get back to Margo, who lived in a small enough town for us to board there awhile in freedom while waiting to return to New Orleans. But after thinking it through, I realized I couldn't contact her or even the

Jacksons without exposing them to problems for sheltering Leni. The situation would be no different than at Jolie Fleur.

By the time I reached the road stop, I had played out all the scenarios in my head and had dismissed them all, but I was still determined. As I was about to enter the store, Wes zipped by in his blue truck. The truck slowed down before revving up again. Terrified that he may have seen me, I stepped inside and quickly shut the door. I paused briefly to see if he would turn around and come back. To my relief, the truck kept going. "I hope you drive into the bayou and a gator eats your johnson," I uttered under my breath.

I lingered awhile inside the road stop. After setting some chips and soft drinks on the counter by the cash register, I grabbed a Hollywood gossip magazine for Leni and handed it to the clerk who was always pleasant and conversational.

"I see you like them movie star stories," he commented.

"Nah, I really prefer taxidermy magazines."

For a moment, he looked at me curiously, and then he shook his head and shot me a wry smile. "You're puttin' me on, girl. But I get it. I'd like to stuff a few people myself."

"Yep - some critters are just better hanging on a wall!"

I flipped through a few more magazines until my gaze landed on a cover with a photo of a ranch and horses. I thought of Davey and wondered if I could locate him. While I tried to think through the possibilities of heading to Texas, something in the back of my mind tried to scratch its way to the surface.

As I stared at the magazine rack, my upbeat mood was overtaken by an ominous feeling. Then it occurred to me - Wes had seen me, but for some reason he had not stopped to harass me. "Oh no, God!" The rush of cold panic made my heart pound so hard I could barely catch my breath. "God no, please!" I threw the magazines down and grabbed my walking stick.

"You all right, miss?"

"No, no I'm not. I'm so sorry, but I have to go!"

Why didn't I see it before? Wes didn't turn around when he

saw me because he had something else in mind. He kept going because he knew Leni was alone! I pushed open the door and started running.

———

Darkness had already set in, which made it difficult to navigate the ruts along the dirt road. I ran as fast as I could, but after a hard day of labor, I had to struggle against the weight of my legs. When I was turning the final bend in the road and could see a light from inside our cabin, I lost my footing in a crevice in the ground. As I fell forward onto the hard surface, a gripping pain seared through my left hand. After I caught my breath, I managed to upright myself and started to run again. My pant leg was torn, and I could feel blood seeping into the fabric, but I kept going.

As I got closer to the house, I had a momentary sense of relief because I did not immediately see Wes's Chevy truck. But when I glanced out into the trees, I spotted the truck parked facing an exit road that cut through the cane field. I felt a rush of acid in my throat as I forced myself to cover the remaining distance to the cabin. Upon approaching the porch, I heard muffled sounds coming from inside the cabin.

"Leni!" I yelled. "Leni, are you in there?" I tried the door, but it was locked from the inside. The tattered shade on front window was pulled down which prevented me from seeing into the shack.

I ran to the back of the house and tried the other exit, but that was locked too. "Leni," I screamed again, "Are you okay? Do you need help?" There was one small window in the back that was too high to reach, so I pushed an abandoned rain barrel in front of it. Pain crawled from my hand up my left arm, but I was in such a panic I barely flinched.

In spite of my injuries, I managed to hoist myself up. When I looked in, I was so shocked that I reared back and almost fell off the barrel. Wes was on top of Leni. Something was shoved in her mouth to prevent her from screaming, and her eyes were glazed over. I was overwhelmed by horror to see Wes brutally violating Leni.

Leni wasn't moving, and for a moment I thought she was dead. I started screaming as though my words could stop him. "Nooo! Stop! Stop!"

Wes didn't flinch. I lost total awareness of my whereabouts and fell off the barrel. After I sprang to my feet, I ran back around to the front of the house and threw a brick through the window. Before I could climb through the broken glass, the door opened, and Wes stumbled out.

With one arm, I picked up my walking stick and slammed it as hard as I could across his sweat-covered face. He yelled and reeled backwards with his hands against his cheek.

"You rotten-" Wes stopped long enough to spit out a mouthful of blood.

"I'm calling the police," I screamed.

"No, you won't," he slurred. "You won't call anyone cuz you two are runnin' or you wouldn't be working in a place like this. Right, girlie?"

"I'm going for help!"

"You call the cops and they're gonna send her little puta ass back to Tijuana or wherever dump she came from. Nobody gives a shit about wetbacks."

"Get out!" I screamed. "Get out!"

Before he could move, I picked up my stick again and bashed it across the opposite side of his face. The sound of his jaw breaking resonated in the night air as he fell to the ground with his legs askew. I ran to him, raised the stick, and jammed it as hard as I could into his groin. Wes's entire body flexed from the shock of the pain before he rolled to his side and howled into the dirt.

After I ran back into the house and locked the door, I shoved a cabinet in front of it. "Leni, are you okay? Oh, Leni! Somebody help us!" I was screaming and crying, but Leni remained completely still. The gag around her mouth was so tight I could barely get it off. Even after I removed it, she lay there in silence. Tears poured out of her eyes, but she continued to stare at the ceiling.

I sat on the floor next to her and gently pushed her hair back from her face. The sight of her was horrifying. Leni's clothes were torn, and there was blood on her sheets. Her face showed signs of swelling, so I knew Wes had beaten her into submission. I grabbed a blanket to cover her and placed a pillow under her head. "I'm going for help, Leni. You're going to be all right, I promise."

Leni lifted one arm and grabbed my hand before I could stand up. "Stay." Her voice was barely above a whisper.

"Leni, he's gone. I heard his truck leave. I'll lock you in. I have to go for help."

"No."

"I know you're frightened, but I have to get you help. You can't walk and-"

"No! Don't tell anyone."

I was so frantic I was almost hysterical. "But what he did to you was-"

"No one will care."

"Yes they will! He can't get away with this!"

"Yes, he can. He's a white boy. And I'm an illegal. They'll send me back and I'll be all alone. Please, I'm begging you." With that, she turned to her side and placed her head in my lap.

A few minutes later we heard a knock at the door. I started to panic, but Leni reached up and placed her hand over my mouth. I heard the voice of one the workers calling to us from the other side of the door. "Anybody home? It's me, Clarence. Are you two all right in there?"

Leni gave me a pleading look before she slowly removed her hand from my mouth so I could answer.

"Yes, Clarence, we're fine, thank you."

"We thought we heard someone yelling."

"Sorry to disturb you. Leni just got some bad news is all."

"I'm sorry to hear that. I see you got yourselves a broken window."

"Yeah. It's been that way awhile. I've been meaning to take care of it. There's some extra tin roofing out back I'll nail up over it tomorrow."

"Well, you might wanna sweep up the glass out here. You take care of your friend, and just give a shout if me and the guys can help."

"Thank you, but there's nothing anyone can do."

I lay down next to Leni and held her close to me. I had never felt so helpless. The brutality was too much to absorb. Together, yet suddenly more separate than we had ever been, Leni and I cried through the night.

CHAPTER TWENTY-SEVEN

IT TOOK DAYS FOR LENI TO SPEAK AGAIN, BUT I COULD OFTEN HEAR her sobbing into her pillow. I was sick with grief for her. I could not get the image of Wes raping Leni out of my mind. When I lay in bed, I saw it happen over and over again. I could feel his hands on me, too. I knew I was also vulnerable and able to be overpowered by someone as ruthless as Wes.

I could not change the brutal events of that night, and I did not know how to help Leni heal. No matter how many times I pleaded with her to let me go to the police, she refused. "They'll help me today, but they'll have me arrested tomorrow," was her only response.

After Wes attacked Leni, I did not want to leave her alone to go to work, but she dismissed my protests and insisted it was necessary to avoid the inevitable questions. There was a small toolbox in the cabin, so I nailed metal across the broken window, and then I instructed her to push the dresser against the door upon my departure. Reluctantly, I left her to fend for herself.

When I saw Hank in the field, I called him over to tell him that Leni had an emergency back in New Orleans and couldn't work for a while. He seemed genuinely concerned. "I am so sorry to hear that. Is she coming back?"

"Yes, she will. I'm just not sure when."

"Did something happen to you? You're limping and I noticed you favoring that left arm of yours. Did you have some kind of accident?"

"Yes," I lied. "I was walking home in the dark and a car side-swiped me."

"For chrissakes, Kat! Did you get a license number?"

"No, it was too dark, but everything's fine. It's really no big deal. I'm just sore."

"Maybe you need to take a little break from the field. To tell you the truth, I need some help in the office, so how 'bout you give me a hand for a few days 'til you feel right again. What do ya say?"

"That would be swell, Hank. I really appreciate it."

"You know, Clarence told me that him and the guys heard some yelling over at your cabin and were concerned."

"Yes, that was right after Leni received the bad news."

"Uh-huh." Hank scratched his head and looked down at his rough hands. "You know if there's a problem, you can come to me, don't you?"

"Yes, I know, Hank. No need to worry. Thank you."

"Kat, please don't wait until it's too late."

Although I quietly nodded in agreement and gratitude, I wondered if it was already too late. When Wes violated Leni, he violated me too. She was my beloved sister, and I had absorbed her fear, pain, and humiliation. Now we were both hiding like injured animals.

———

During the days I worked in the office, Leni stayed in the cabin. She seldom ever talked, so I tried to give her space. I knew she was still in shock and would need time to heal before we could leave, but as the months passed, I became more concerned.

She often sat on her cot staring off into space. When I tried to talk to her, she responded to my questions with as few words as possible. She was emotionless, and her once animated face no longer showed much expression. The light in her was going out, and I didn't know how to stop it from happening.

Sometimes Leni sat out on the porch, but eventually she stayed in her bed most of the day. Once in a while I could get her to eat soup, but she had very little appetite. When I tried to distract her with Hollywood gossip magazines, she would flip through the pages and then lie back on her cot with the magazines pressed to her chest.

We had been taking hot showers in the worker bath structure located in the field, but now we were too fearful to go in there in case Wes came back around, so we returned to heating water on the stove for bathing. It was inconvenient, and I never felt completely clean. As much as I was worried about leaving Leni, work helped relieve my growing sense of claustrophobia. My only goal was to help Leni recover enough so we could find our way out of there.

One day as I was working in the trailer office, Hank came in and threw his hat down on the desk. "Kat, something is stickin' in my craw, and I need to talk to you. I know Leni is back. The other day when I drove by your cabin, she was sittin' on the porch. I waved and called to her, but she got up and walked inside without sayin' a word. Did I do something to offend her?"

"No, Hank. It's thoughtful of you to ask. She's just in mourning." It wasn't a lie - Leni was mourning. We both were. Something inside Leni was dying. We had nowhere to go, and there was no one who could really help us.

"Kat, I can't keep her on the payroll if she doesn't work. But she can stay with you in the cabin until we need the space. You know where I am when you're ready to come to me."

"Thank you. Excuse me, Hank, but I have to use the bathroom." I nodded in apology as I abruptly exited the trailer. I did not want him to see me cry.

―――――

Leni was growing thin and gaunt. Autumn was now upon us and the new harvest had begun. The days were still warm, yet Leni piled on layers of clothing and stayed under her blanket.

"Leni," I told her one night during a prolonged silence, "when my leg was injured, Hank gave me the name of a retired doctor who lives nearby. I think we should go talk to him to see if he can help you get through this. It has been almost eight months, and I know what happened to you is too horrible for words and will leave terrible scars, but you *must* get better. And you are - I think you're getting worse. I want to talk to a professional."

"No. Don't call. Are you still my Me-Tonto?"

"Leni Cruz, how can you even ask me that? Of course I am."

"No doctors. No questions."

―――――

I did not know how long we could go on the way we were. The shack had become a tomb for both of us, and we had not received the all-clear from Alcide. Hilda was paying off people to find out who had tipped off immigration about Leni, but she still had no answers and was afraid if Leni were seen, someone at immigration would learn of her whereabouts. I was growing desperate for a solution.

I thought if Leni could get her strength back, maybe we could go to Texas. On many Sunday afternoons on my days off, I had Hank drop me off at the nearest library so I could research newspapers that announced local rodeos. Finally, in late October, I found what I was looking for. It was an announcement in an Austin newspaper for a nearby rodeo. Davey's name was on the bill.

Seeing Davey's name in print gave me more hope than I had in months. Leni and I had been saving all our wages in an empty beef stew can, and although I knew it was a long shot, I thought if we had enough money to get to Texas, Davey might have some connections to help her get a new identity. Most importantly, I knew he could be trusted not to talk. Leni mentioned she had crossed the border near Nuevo Laredo, so Texas would be no safer than New Orleans, but with a new identity, we could move on quickly to California or to Canada or somewhere else far away from the authorities who were hunting her.

It was a long walk back to the cabin, but once I arrived, I was in good spirits at the promise of a new start. However, when I opened the door, I almost passed out.

CHAPTER TWENTY-EIGHT

THE FIRST THING I SAW WAS THE BLOOD. LENI WAS SITTING UP ON her cot with a blank look on her face. A blood-soaked blanket covered her groin, and another blanket was draped over her chest. "God help us!" I gasped. "We need to get a doctor - you're hemorrhaging!"

Leni shook her head resolutely. "No! Flush it down the toilet." She lifted up the blanket to reveal a bloody mass that lay between her thighs. I was so horrified I froze.

"Leni, don't move. We need to get help now!"

As I turned to run for help, she called out to me.

"Kat, stop! I need you. Please help me. I think it's alive."

When I turned to face her, she lowered the blanket that covered her chest. Something was moving in her arms. I couldn't make sense of what she was saying or of what had happened. I slowly walked to her side and looked down at the object she was holding. I was so stunned that it took all my willpower to keep from collapsing. Leni was holding a tiny baby.

"Oh, Jesus! Where did, how-" The shock was so great, I couldn't finish my sentence.

"Please flush that." Leni nodded to the mass between her legs. "I bit the cord."

"How in God's name ... I don't understand. How did you do this alone, Leni?"

"I saw how the migrants did it in the fields. So much pain ... but it was fast. Take what's left."

"Are you sure the baby is alive?" I was afraid to touch the small object she clutched to her breast.

"Yes. It has to suckle."

"Jesus, Leni, you had a baby! This is more than we can deal with. Why didn't you tell me?"

Leni bit her lip firmly, and with the back of her hand, she swiped at her eyes. "I wasn't sure. And if I didn't believe it, maybe it wouldn't be true. Maybe it would go away ..."

"But it *is* true, Len. We have to get you to a hospital."

"No, I can do this. Just help me."

The baby let out a cry, which alarmed me even more. "I have no idea what to do," I protested as I backed away.

"Here," she instructed. "Wash it and wrap it tight. I already cleaned its mouth and patted its back."

When she handed the child to me, she looked away. I took it from her arms and stared at the tiny bundle. Although the child was small, it was breathing without effort, and everything seemed intact. "It's a boy." Although I was in shock, I looked at the tiny little creature in wonder.

With the child in hand, I filled a pot with water to heat on the hot plate. Once the water was warm, I gently washed the baby and held it close to my heart as I rifled through our bags for the softest pieces of clothing I could find. After tying a kerchief between the baby's legs in a makeshift diaper, I wrapped the child in one of Leni's gauze skirts before returning him to her arms. I was shocked by how small and delicate he was.

There was blood on her mouth from biting the cord, so I washed her face with a warm cloth as she mechanically put the baby to her breast. She nodded again at the bloody blankets as though she couldn't bear to look at them any longer.

"Okay," I nodded. After I gathered the soiled bedding, I threw an extra cover over her and flushed the mass before I ran outside to bury the blanket that neither of us could bear to look at. There was nothing to use to dig a hole, so I shoved the bedding into the abandoned rain barrel and ran back inside.

As I entered the cabin again, the baby was making little noises as though announcing his presence.

I was frantic. "What are we going to do, Leni? Haven't we had enough?"

"We try to bear it. This is our winter of discontent."

I wondered if spring would ever come.

———

Three weeks passed with Leni holed up in the cabin with the baby as I worked in the cane field and tried to act as if everything was normal. Several times I walked to the road stop to pick up supplies. Without questioning me, Rick, the road stop manager, ordered infant formula, bottles, diapers and pins, and plastic pants. Much of the money we had saved was going to the care of the child, but I was relieved to know we could buy what was necessary.

Leni wasn't producing much milk, so we had to supplement the baby's feeding to keep it from crying all the time, but the child seemed to adapt to the routine. The diapers were much too big, so they leaked. As a result, I was constantly washing diapers and bedding in a tub of water by the sink. I made a bed for the baby by padding a drawer in the bureau. The baby was so small that I was always afraid to handle him, but I clutched him to me whenever he cried out.

Leni started to eat a little bit more and looked less wan than she had prior to the baby's arrival. She got out of bed more often in order to help with the wash and to heat canned food for dinner. It was strange to see how she tended to the baby as if he were a delicate plant assigned to her as her responsibility. She took care of the baby and kept him fed, but she didn't engage

with the child in any way other than to satisfy the basic require-
ments for his survival. Whenever she was done feeding, she
handed off the child to me or placed him in the drawer. I was the
one who soothed the baby when he was awake and tucked the
child in at night.

I was fascinated by the baby and studied his every movement, but I completely understood Leni's disconnect. I knew that
every time she looked at the baby she relived being raped. The
child was a result of a vicious assault, and she was unable to see
or feel anything beyond that.

I was still in shock and wandered around the cabin like a
robot. We were on the run, and our lives were out of control, yet
now we had another living being we had to care for. During
those three weeks, we did not think or talk about the next step -
we just got up every morning and did what we had to do to get
through the day. But at the end of the third week, we were forced
to make a decision.

———

After barely mustering up enough energy at the end of the
workday to pick up supplies at the road stop, I exited the store.
It had been a long day, and I couldn't wait to have a bite to eat at
the cabin before collapsing on the cot. The baby had been
waking us up at night, and I was operating on very little sleep,
so I looked forward to a relaxing walk back to the cabin while
enjoying the quiet of the evening. Much to my shock, as I closed
the door of the shop behind me and turned around, l saw Wes's
blue Chevy truck parked in front of the entrance. I was so terrified I was paralyzed.

At first, I wasn't sure it was Wes because his face looked so
distorted. He leaned out the window and snarled, "What's the
matter - don't recognize me?" His mouth made a strange movement as he spoke, and the fresh scars on the side of his face
pulled his skin taught. "Why are you lookin' at me like that? You

did this to me, you bitch. Two surgeries on my jaw and it still ain't right. You think you're not gonna pay for this?"

I was too frightened to speak, and I didn't know which way to run. Just as I was about to scream for help, Hank pulled into the parking lot directly behind Wes's truck. "Over here, Hank," I yelled. Shaking with terror, I turned to wave to Hank to let Wes know we were not alone.

Wes looked in his rearview mirror and revved the engine. "You've done used up all your lives, Kitty Kat. Keep a look over your shoulder cuz I'll be back," he growled as he peeled out of the parking lot.

I was shaking uncontrollably when I ran to Hank's truck. Without even asking, I jumped into the passenger side of the cab. "Please take me back to the cabin, Hank. Please?

"What's wrong? I recognize that truck. Was that sumbitch fixin' to mess with you?"

"It doesn't matter. Leni and I have to leave. I'm sorry, but I have to quit my job. Can you take us to the train station?"

"I don't like what's going on here, Kat."

"Hank, you told me that you would help. With all respect, the best thing you can do is to get us out of here and not ask questions. Please … for Leni's sake."

Hank's brow furled, but he nodded his head in agreement. "Understood." We pulled out of the parking lot and headed down the dirt road. "I'll be sorry to see you go, Kat. You're a damn good worker and a real strong girl. Let's go by the trailer so I can get your wages."

"No, there's no time. Just forget it. I honestly don't care."

"Hmm, sounds like you're in a real rush. Well, here then." Hank reached into his pocket and pulled out some bills. "You can take whatever cash I have."

As soon as we reached the cabin, I jumped out of the truck. "Thank you, Hank. Just give us ten minutes - that's all we need."

I threw open the door to the cabin and yelled to Leni. "Hank is waiting in the truck. Wes is back. We have to go. Now, Leni,

NOW! You grab your bag with your clothes and grab the stew can full of money. I'll get the baby's things. Don't take anything you don't need."

Leni's eyes were wide with terror, but she did not ask any questions. We frantically shoved clothes into our bags, and I gathered up any additional baby supplies I could find.

"Get into the truck, Leni. I'll bring the child. Tell Hank I'll be right out."

When I made a quick last-minute check of our quarters, I spotted my walking stick propped by the door. It had saved me from snakes and had given me strength when my legs were too tired to walk, and it had been my only weapon against Wes. I touched it with my hand one last time. "Thank you for taking care of me, Jake." I turned and walked out the door.

Leni was already in the backseat of the truck, so I climbed back into the front passenger side. When Hank saw the baby, his jaw went slack with shock.

"What in Hades-"

I gave him a look of warning and glanced toward Leni, who was huddled in the corner of the seat behind him.

After a moment of confusion, Hank nodded silently. "I'll drop you off at the local station. Get yourselves to New Orleans. You can transfer anywhere you want to go from there. As far as I know, I never met you and you were never here, should anybody come asking."

Hank looked in the rearview mirror at Leni before returning his gaze back at me and the baby. "Wes?" he mouthed. I looked down at my hands and remained silent. Hank clenched his jaw, nodded and kept driving. When we got to the parking lot of the station he pulled to a stop.

"Thank you for your kindness, Hank." I opened the door and turned back to Leni. "Let's go, Leni." Leni mumbled her thanks without making eye contact with Hank.

"You girls call me when you settle, okay?"

We nodded as we quickly grabbed our bags. When we turned

to leave, Hank leaned out his window. "Just so you know – the boys and me have a way of takin' care of brutes with a mind to hurt others, and I guaran-damn-tee you, we're gonna. No sumbitch is gonna harm you again. I'll be here if you ever need help." His jaw was set with anger, and I knew he meant it.

I gave a quick wave and shoved Leni toward the entrance to the station.

———

We stopped in the rest room long enough for Leni to try to nurse the baby. She was so unnerved that her breasts were practically dry, so I fed the baby some formula before approaching the ticket counter. "Leni, I need the stew can," I told her. I took out enough money to cover our tickets before shoving the can back into her bag. "We have to put this all behind us now."

I purchased tickets to New Orleans, where we could connect to the Kansas City line. "We're going to be all right now, Leni." I was trying to convince myself as much as I was trying to assure her. Our goal had been to hide, but I knew that our next move was something we should have done long before things had become so bad. We needed to go almost anywhere other than where we had been, and I had faith that if we could just reach New Orleans, the Southern Belle would lead us to safety.

———

The train ride was long and arduous with a baby, but the elegant accommodations on the Southern Belle were a joyous contrast to where we had been living.

As we took our seats, I felt a most amazing sense of freedom come over me. "It's over," I told Leni. "We are free now."

I was so elated to be rid of the threat that shadowed us, I was able to overlook Leni's continuous refusal to hold the baby other than to feed him. Even during feeding, she almost never looked at him. She hadn't named him and continued to refer to him as "el niño." I was the one who tended to him most often, but I believed that as time passed, she would change her feelings and begin to connect.

"Look, Leni, he looks like you," I commented, but she turned her head away, demoralized and ashamed. I ached inside knowing how she was still suffering.

When the baby woke up, I picked him up and walked him around a bit to get him to go back to sleep. I had begun to talk to him as much as possible, because I wanted him to know he was not alone. I enjoyed how he responded by nuzzling into my chest, and I loved the way the little guy smelled. He was a pure and innocent being, in spite of the way in which he was conceived, and I wanted him to know that. And I prayed Leni would one day be well enough to accept that. *Give her time, Kat,* I often told myself. *She is broken.*

After he snuggled back down in his blanket, I purchased some sandwiches and took them back to where we were sitting. "I hope you're starting to relax some, Leni. Isn't this train car beautiful?"

"Made in America. Magical." Leni forced a slight smile, but her voice was emotionless.

The train attendants were so accommodating that we actually got a bit of rest. They heated up bottles for us and disposed of the cloth diapers to avoid any odor. A female attendant replaced our cloth diapers with extra diapers from the train's emergency supply.

The greatest treat was when a kind woman from Cleveland offered to let us spend a few hours in her Pullman car while she played cards in the salon. The time alone allowed us to lay the baby down and rest awhile. I tried to distract Leni by telling her all about my first trip on the Southern Belle, but I knew she wasn't listening to my patter. She stared out the window as though she were somewhere else. It terrified me to witness how vacant she had become. I had witnessed the same thing with Jake, and my heart was breaking.

After another stretch of silence, I could no longer hide my concern. "Leni, I feel like you're slipping away. I know how much you have been through, but please try to fight back. Don't let him take any more from you than he already has. We will see Hilda again somehow. And right now, we are finally safe."

"What is safe?" Leni's empty stare told me she was retreating farther into some remote place in her mind as the train put more distance between us and Louisiana.

———

After an exhausting trip, we finally arrived in Kansas City. Immediately upon entering the bustling train station, I felt an exhilarating sense of hope. While cradling the baby in the crook of my elbow, I planted Leni in a seat in a corner of the station and handed her a leftover sandwich from her bag before shoving the bag under her seat with my foot. I then readjusted my own satchel on my shoulder. "I'm getting good at this balancing act," I bragged. "Please eat something while I take the baby to change his diaper and try to find more formula. We're almost out. Will you be all right on your own?"

"Sí, mi amiga." When a rare smile lit up her face, I was filled with a sense of joy and relief because I hadn't seen her smile in so long.

After I bought formula and some extra diapers at a drug store in the station, I finished using the bathroom and headed back to the passenger area to discuss our next move with Leni. I had used up most of the money Hank had given me, and I knew we needed to take stock of our remaining funds. My plan was to call Hilda and Alcide. Hilda once told me she knew a lot of people in Kansas City, so I had faith she would help us figure something out. For the moment, the most important thing was that we were out of Louisiana, and we were safe.

When I rounded the ticket counter, I could see the corner of the room where I had left Leni. She had moved, so I wondered if she had come looking for me. When I got to the seat, I set the baby on an adjacent chair as my eyes scanned the waiting room. I couldn't see her anywhere in the station, so I was unsure whether I should wait or go looking for her.

I was so confused it took me several minutes to realize that her bag was gone too. On the seat where she had been sitting was a thin piece of cardboard that had been torn off the sandwich box. A sudden rush of nausea gripped me the moment I noticed the words scrawled in Leni's familiar penmanship. With shaking hands, I picked up the paper. On it she had written:

Forgive me, my forever Me-Tonto. I will love you always - Leni.

Leni was gone.

BOOK V

WHISTLE STOP

CHAPTER TWENTY-NINE

Too numb to move, I sat in my seat in the Kansas City train station staring at Leni's sleeping baby lying in my lap. We had both been abandoned, and my heartbreak caused such physical pain, I thought if I moved, I might break.

I was more worried for Leni than angry. *Why did you go, Leni?* I asked myself the same question over and over again - even though I knew the answer. The harsh circumstances and constant terror of being a fugitive, and the helplessness of being brutalized with no recourse had destroyed her spirit and sent her into the depths of a depression she could no longer manage. I had stood by and watched helplessly as the flame inside her was snuffed out. She was my companion, my sister, my Jake, and the pain of mourning her loss was overwhelming.

Even as I feared the worst for Leni, I was worried about the baby as well. It was clear to me that her impulse to run was meant to relieve me of any further obligation to her. She trusted me to find a home for the baby - a baby she wanted to survive but could not look at without constantly having to relive an assault that had snuffed out the flame inside her. She would always see Wes's face every time she looked at the child, and as brave as she was, that was the one thing she could not handle.

I knew her decision to run was impulsive rather than planned, and when she left, she was not conscious of the fact that almost all our money was in the stew can, which was in her bag. I still had some bills left in my pocket from what Hank had given me, but it wasn't enough money to get me far. Luckily, I had purchased supplies for the baby before Leni disappeared, but I knew they wouldn't last.

Out of desperation, I considered calling the Jacksons. With Leni gone, there would no longer be a threat from immigration, but I still wasn't prepared to face them, or burden them - especially with a mixed-race baby I was not ready to explain.

When the baby woke up, I fed him and changed his diaper as he lay in my lap. I was captivated by the way he sucked his little fingers with such contentment. He made happiness look so easy, and I hoped he would always find bliss. "I'll see that you are well cared for, little one. Maybe I can find a place to take you in. I won't let anything happen to you."

I reached into my pocket and counted my remaining money. I was thankful the seat I had chosen in the depot waiting room was far away from others. I fought against bouts of crying as I struggled to pull myself together. As soon as I rocked the baby back to sleep, I hoisted my bag back over my shoulder and walked to the ticket window. After I studied the information about trains going in and out of Kansas City, I still was unsure of my next move, but staying in one place was not an option.

When I stepped up to the ticket window, I placed all my money on the counter. "I'd like a ticket to-" My eyes grew wide when I realized I was talking to Mary, the seamstress who had once frequented the hobo camp. "Oh, good heavens, it's you!"

"I remember you," she nodded. "I still have that pink thimble you gave me. It's Kat, right?"

"Yes, Ma'am. Wow! You're working here now?"

"Yes I am. I finally caught me a break."

"That's wonderful, Mary. How did all this happen?"

"A good Samaritan gave me a boost."

"Really?"

"Sure thing. A real nice lady saw me hopping trains and decided I was too old for such shenanigans. She helped me get cleaned up and find a job. I have too much arthritis in my fingers to be a seamstress these days, but this job suits me fine."

"I'm so happy to hear that. The lady who helped you – by any chance did she live in a farmhouse by the depot and wear a canvas hat with fishing hooks?"

"By golly, she did! You know she told me one time about a real nice young gal she met, but she wouldn't give a name. All she told me was that the girl was from Indiana, so I always wondered if that was you."

"Yes, I met her. Angels like Margo have a way of getting around, it seems. I've been thinking about dropping in to see her."

"In Mississippi?"

"Mississippi?"

"Yes, she had a little health scare, but she's doing fine - thought it best to move in with her daughter though. Here, I'll jot down her phone number in Jackson just in case you ever want to give her a call. I'm sure she'd be plum tickled. Is that little sleepy baby yours? What a cutie!"

The baby was stirring slightly, so I rocked him back to sleep. "He really is cute, isn't he? And he's a real sweet baby. I'm minding him for my friend." I placed my money on the counter and glanced again at the schedule posted overhead. "How far east will this take me?" I wasn't sure where I was going, but I knew in what direction my instincts were pulling me.

Mary counted the money. "This will get you about as far as St. Louis. Do you need to go farther than that?"

"I'm not sure yet. But I think so."

She nodded as though she understood my hesitation. After fumbling through the wastebasket, she plopped a discarded train ticket on the counter. "Look here - a gentleman just bought two transfers out of St. Louis, but sometimes the machine pops out an extra, so we just toss them out. So how 'bout you buy a ticket to St Louis just to keep the record straight, then you use this transfer ticket to get you out of St. Louis. It will take you as far as Lafayette. I hope that helps some."

"Thank you, Mary. I'm very grateful. I wish you much success in your new job."

"You are very welcome, my dear. You take care of that sweet little baby ... and your sweet little self too."

I looked down at the ticket. "Come on, baby boy, we're off to find you a safe home." I was torn, because I had become attached to the little baby in my charge and did not want to bid goodbye to him. But I also knew that Leni was counting on me to find someone who could provide him with the best life possible. In my mind, I knew what I had to do, but I was apprehensive about my ability to see it through. I was in turmoil as I headed for the platform to wait for my train out of Kansas City.

Without Leni, a part of me was missing. The ache in my heart was almost unbearable, but the baby in my arms kept me moving forward. *Leni, you were always the one with all the gusto and courage until someone robbed that from you. I miss you so much, and I really need you right now.*

My tears were welling up again, but when the baby moved in my arms, I pulled myself together and shifted position so I could make him more comfortable. When he looked at me, I could see Leni in his eyes, and I knew I had to protect him. I trembled as I waited on the platform because I knew what lay ahead, but I stepped up onto the train platform and boarded the Missouri River Eagle just as the conductor yelled, "All aboard!"

Soon we would connect with a train that was as much a part of me as Jake and Leni and all the people I had ever loved - the great Wabash Cannonball.

———

Lafayette was the end of the line for me. I made sure the baby was fed and had a clean diaper just before I got off the train. I didn't linger in the station because I was afraid I would lose my courage.

After exiting the depot, I skirted around to a street that ran parallel with the tracks and walked for at least two miles before doubling back to the tracks in an area overgrown with shrubs and weeds. As I leaned against a spindly tree, I checked the baby to make sure he was happy. He was starting to smile, which amazed me. I brushed my lips against his forehead and smiled back.

After I made sure no one else was in view, I opened my shirt and tucked the infant inside next to my chest before buttoning my shirt back up as far as his neck. I then wrapped a thin blanket and several scarves around him and me, binding us together. The bindings felt bulky and awkward, but I knew he was securely strapped to my chest. I could feel his little heart beating against my bare chest breathing life into me and firing my determination.

As I waited by the brush, I tried to swallow my fear. "You can do this, Kat. You can do this," I repeated. When I heard the next train coming down the line, I threw my bag over my shoulder and secured the bottom part of the bag tightly to my waist. After I took a deep breath, I started running.

The train was far enough out of the station that it was starting to pick up a little speed. Although I was out of practice, as soon as I started running, I regained my speed and rhythm. *Please, dear God, let there be a car.*

The train was still picking up speed when I saw an open boxcar approaching. Just as the boxcar reached me, I stretched up and grabbed the handle alongside the door. After I swung up, my legs followed suit. I thought I was clear, but suddenly my momentum stopped, and I was momentarily suspended halfway out of the boxcar.

My canvas bag had caught onto the edge of the door and

flipped me face down, so I was facing the tracks below. Everything suddenly became a terrifying blur. Using my foot, I wedged myself against the door and pushed. When the door didn't give, I began to scream. The train was going faster, and I was losing my grip as the wind beat against my face. The tracks raced below me as I dangled helplessly from the side of the car.

With all my strength, I shoved my foot behind me one more time. The door finally gave way. I rolled into the car onto my back. The baby was crying, so I held him tightly as I lay on the floor of the car trying to catch my breath and quiet my heartbeat.

I untied some of the scarves from around my waist and pulled the little boy out of my shirt. "There, there," I cooed as I tried to slow my own breathing. "See, I knew we could do it. I'm really good at jumping. I admit we had a little hiccup there, but we did it. You did a real good job yourself. I promised I would find you a safe home, little fella, and I don't break my promises."

———

As I lay on the floor of the train car with the baby on my chest, I knew it was time to make one of the greatest decisions of my life. The rumble of the Wabash Cannonball calmed me while I contemplated every stop on the route that lay before me.

My thoughts also kept returning to Franklin, the town I loved until it took Jake from me. I knew the Logansport depot would be coming up soon. If I got off there, I could head south to Franklin where I was sure I could get a job in the café below the apartment Jake and I once shared. But could I bear to be in Franklin without him? It was time to gather the courage to face whatever challenges were in front of me, and that included dealing with all the pain I had tried to leave behind. "I'm still here, Jake," I whispered.

The train rocked back-and-forth easing me into a quiet calm I hadn't felt since before Jake died. The Cannonball had been there for me when I needed to run. And she was there now when I needed her to lead me to a place of rest.

"Okay, baby. This is the last stop."

———

After opening my duffel, I scooped out a section in the middle of my belongings and used the remaining diapers and clothing to pad every side of the bag. I then placed the baby in the middle of the bag and zipped it just enough to hold him inside without closing off his air supply. He looked at me as though he trusted me, and without any protestation, he closed his eyes and went back to sleep.

I pushed the door of the boxcar open just far enough to watch the scenery and depot signs as we passed. Jake and I had studied the rails so long I recognized where we were. And I finally knew where I was going.

Just after we pulled out of the Peru, Indiana, train station, I readied myself. The miles passed, and as the train pulled closer to the next depot and started into the curve, I was prepared for the moment the hobo encampment would come into view.

My sense of relief was greater than my fear as I held onto the railing alongside the boxcar door and leaned out as far as I could. With one of Hilda's bright scarves in hand, I signaled for help. Several encampment dwellers were milling about, but I was still too far away to recognize any of them. I continued to wave and shout, although I knew my voice could not be heard over the rumble of the train.

As the train moved nearer the encampment, I finally recognized one of the men in the field. It was one-arm Joe. A look of recognition and shock crossed his face when he saw me. When I signaled again, he suddenly started running toward the tracks. I continued waving the scarf until he got alongside my box car. Luckily, the train was slowing, so Joe was able to keep up.

I always believed I could jump aboard a train with the baby, but leaping off would be almost impossible without rolling, and I was terrified I could crush him. My only solution was to provide the baby with a soft cushion with no body weight to press against him.

Reaching back into the box car, I picked up my bag. I signaled to Joe to catch it, and then I pounded my heart to tell him how precious the parcel was. I'm sure he didn't hear me, but I kept yelling, "Don't drop him! Don't drop him!"

While Joe kept pace alongside the car, he signaled for me to release my bundle. Joe continued to wave his arm to tell me it was okay to let go. I sent a silent plea to God and dropped the duffel. With his one powerful arm, Joe skillfully caught the bag and pressed it into his body.

The train continued on its path toward the station. I was about to jump off when I looked back and saw Joe stumble on the loose stones that lined the track. I gasped as his feet gave way and he fell backwards. His body bounced as his back hit hard against the uneven ground. Joe raised his knees and dug his feet into the gravel to keep from rolling down the embankment, and then he thrust the bag upward to protect it from impact. He lay on the ground with the bag over his head, grinning in triumph.

I jumped. After hitting the ground hard, I ran as fast as I could to cover the distance between us. When I got to Joe, I threw myself on him and yanked open the bag. I cried out with relief as a sweet and content baby smiled up at me.

"Say hello to Joe, baby," I smiled. "And welcome to Wabash."

CHAPTER THIRTY

THE OLD BOARDS CREAKED IN GREETING AS I STEPPED UP ONTO THE porch. I reached under the porcelain rabbit that had once held a healthy fern - now nothing more than a pot of dirt - but the key was still there.

Shreds of screening still stubbornly clung to the door as a reminder of the night my father crashed into it and ripped it out of its metal frame. When I stepped inside, I felt a great sense of satisfaction to see that everything was pretty much the same. The smell of cigarettes lingered in the air, and the living room was strewn with paperwork and anything else that had been left where it was last used.

As I walked down the hallway into the kitchen, I heard a familiar voice, "Who's there?"

"Hi, Dad," I smiled. He was sitting at the kitchen table drinking a cup of coffee and reading the paper.

When he looked up, his mouth broke into a broad grin. "Well, well, well … aren't you a sight for sore eyes!"

"So are you." After I set my bag on the table, I draped myself around his shoulders. It was wonderful to breathe in his familiar scent.

He leaned his face into my arm, which was the closest thing

to a nurturing hug I ever remember receiving from my father. "It has been too long, Kat, but I always knew you would come back. I've been waiting for you, girl."

"That's nice to hear. How are you doing, Dad? I didn't expect to find you home on a weekday."

"Today is my day off. I have a new job now - the plant laid most of us off. Can you stay awhile?"

"Sure, if you'll have us."

"Us?"

I lifted the baby out of the bag and held him in my arms for my father to see.

"Is that yours?"

As I looked down at the baby, I searched for the answer I already knew. I had promised I would find the best person to care for him, which is exactly what Leni wanted. "Yes. Yes, he's mine, Dad. He's mine."

"So, it's a boy. What's his name?"

I pulled the baby closer to me and looked at his bright eyes, which seemed so full of life and wonder. "You have never told me your name, little friend." I paused for only a moment before I answered. "It's Jake, Dad. Jake Cruz Caswell."

"Jake Cruz Caswell. That seems right-fitting and proper. Can I hold him?"

When my father saw me hesitate, he nodded in understanding. "I know, I know. I don't have a real good track record. And I'm not gonna sit here and fib to you by sayin' I don't drink anymore. But I've got it under control now, Kat - except for on an occasional Saturday night. I promised Jackson I'd stay sober."

"George Jackson?"

"Yep. When I got laid off, he gave me a job down at his dealership prepping new cars. He pays me a real fair salary, and I'm right grateful to be given the chance."

"That's great, Dad."

"He's a good man. He even lent me some money until I got caught up with the mortgage. After I got laid off, I got an offer to buy the house, but I wanted to keep it so you would have a place to come home to. How old are you now, girl? I can't keep track." "I'm almost twenty-one," I smiled. "But I sure feel a lot older." "We all do. But at least we still have our hair. Ol' George Jackson has lost all of his," he laughed. "And speaking of Jackson, why don't you hand me that little guy now and go take a gander out the back window to see if it all looks the same to you."

When I placed little Jake in my father's arms, I was filled with emotion to see how gently he handled him. I stared at them both for a minute, amazed at how content they both seemed.

"More chickens, I'll bet!" I laughed as I walked to the window. When I peeked out, I was both startled and thrilled at what I saw. In our brown and overgrown backyard, the contrasting color was incongruous. I immediately started laughing. "Oh, Dad - it can't be-"

"It sure is."

"Well, Dad, as you would say, that's right-fitting and proper."

I walked back over to the table and reached into my bag. For the first time since the night Jake committed suicide, I unzipped the small pocket on the side of the duffel and gently removed Jake's beret. Then I placed the beret on my head and tipped it over my right eye just as he had always done. "Marilyn is back, Jake," I murmured.

When I looked back up at my dad, he and baby Jake were both smiling. "Okay, little boy," I smiled. "I'm going to give you a bit of lunch, and then I'm going to take you and your grandpa for the ride of your lives in a 1952 Ford Crestline Sunliner convertible that's the brightest damn sunshine yellow you'll ever see in your life."

EPILOGUE

Wabash, Indiana
1967

NOW THAT I AM TWENTY-EIGHT YEARS OLD, I HAVE FINALLY COME TO
the realization that Wabash will always be my home. The Jacksons are still my second family, and they treat Jake as if he's their
own grandson. It warms my heart to see how happy he makes
them. Mr. Jackson offered me a job in the office at the dealership,
where I have been working for more than six years.

My boy often comes to the office so he can help his grandpa
and learn all he can about cars. I still have Marilyn, and Jake is
learning to appreciate her cheerful but fading beauty. He also
likes his Spanish instruction and piano lessons, and just like me,
he loves trains. Sometimes we walk down to the rails to count
cars or to tell tales about the faces in the windows as the
passenger cars speed by. Naturally, he has yet to discover how
complicated their true stories may be, or how far-reaching their
travels may take them. In time, I will tell him.

Periodically, I call Margo in Mississippi to check up on her.
She says she misses her farmhouse by the tracks, but she still
wears her silly hat just to remind herself of home. She told me

the people in Jackson look at her like she's senile, but of course she loves that.

Once in a while I walk down to the hobo encampment and drop off fresh fruit and other food items, including eggs. (Yep – Dad adopted a few more chickens, much to Jake's delight.) Pete and some of the regulars still come and go, and new faces appear daily. One-arm Joe said they never see Doc anymore. According to Joe, Doc felt he was getting too old to hitch rides on trains, so he went back to Scranton permanently. Joe also told me that Charles was in a Veteran's Hospital for more treatment for his facial disfigurement. I was sad not to see Doc and Charles, but Joe promised to pass on any other news that should come his way.

I've made one trip back to New Orleans since I left. Jake was five years old at the time, so I took him with me aboard the Southern Belle. He was very excited, and it was so rewarding to experience it through his eyes: "Look, Mom, I can pull down the bed all by myself! And I can watch the people and the trees go by while I'm sleeping! This sure is a fancy train."

"That's right, Jakey. The Southern Belle is first-class. And just wait until you taste the breakfast grits. We can add lots of butter and brown sugar and maple syrup. You'll love them!"

Hilda and Alcide and the entire group were thrilled to see me and to meet Jake. Bertrand held Jake on his lap and taught him a few jazz notes, and of course Jessie stuffed us both with bread pudding. We all had a long cry when I told them what happened to Leni, but we were determined to shake it off so Jake could have a great time.

I spent a week at the Jolie Fleur, and I finally got to see Mardi Gras. Without Leni, it was bittersweet, but I was so happy to make new memories with my son. Alcide sent us home with a selection of books, and Hilda loaded my suitcase with bright scarves and a roll of cash.

Before returning to Wabash, I called Hank to thank him for everything and to let him know that things have worked out.

Without offering any details, he assured me that Wes had been convicted of possession of drugs and would be in prison for a long time. I had my suspicions about how that all came about, but I knew not to ask for any more information than Hank had already offered.

When we left, I had to promise Jake we could visit again next year - if he would please stop talking about pralines and alligators for at least a day or two.

When Ben is in town, he also drops by to visit. He is now a history professor at Wabash College in Crawfordsville. I was really surprised the first time he showed up right before Jake's first birthday. I was on the front porch watering the new plant in the porcelain rabbit when I looked up and saw a strapping figure get out of a Ford Thunderbird.

"Nice ride," I applauded.

"I heard you were back, Kat. It has been a long time."

"Yes, it has."

Jake was asleep, so I led Ben to the back yard where we spent the afternoon catching up. It was wonderful to hear Ben laugh, as it had always been so easy for us to humor each other. While we talked, we gazed across the field beyond. Periodically we could see the Wabash Cannonball pass by, always on schedule, and always heralded by a resonant whistle.

"It hurt me so much when you ran away, Kat, but I think I understand why you never reached out to me again."

"I'm truly sorry. I was so naïve back in those days. I didn't understand about you and Jake."

Ben held up his hand. "Before you go any further, I have to tell you that Jake didn't understand either. We were kids, Kat. And we did experiment a little - but it wasn't for me. When I explained that to Jake, he just couldn't accept it. And he couldn't believe that it didn't matter to me if that's the lifestyle he wanted and needed. I tried to tell him that he would always be my best friend, no matter what."

"He was so confused."

"Kat, I tried to tell him he was born that way, and all God's creatures are by His design. But he was too angry with God to believe me. I even tried to persuade him to move to a bigger city where he could find a community where he would be accepted."

"Jake just wanted to be like everyone else. Inside he was struggling so much. He couldn't trust that we would accept him the way he was, because he couldn't accept himself. His death was devastating."

"I know. It tore me apart. I dropped out of Purdue because of it."

"You did?"

"Yes, I stayed out for a year. Eventually I transferred to Wabash College over in Crawfordsville. It's a great school, but because I lost a year, I'm just finishing up now."

"How wonderful that you are graduating! I would love to come to the ceremony.'

"Yes, please do."

"Do you ever hear from Louise?"

"Yes, I run into her occasionally when we're both in Wabash at the same time. She graduated from Franklin and moved to Indianapolis. She's engaged to a dentist, and she is still just as lutitidinous as she always has been."

It was bittersweet but satisfying to hear her nickname once more. "And now she'll always have someone to glue her crowns back on," I laughed. "If you run into her again, please tell her I'd love to see her."

"I will. Is it true you have a baby?"

"Yes, he's inside sleeping. He's about to turn one year old. His name is Jake."

"Wow. Jake, huh? That's real nice, Kat. Really nice. And the father?"

"No father. Jake has me."

"That's all he needs. You are more than enough."

"Thank you, Ben." I knew Ben's words were true. All my life I had been looking for a mother, not realizing that although I would never find one, I was learning how to *become* one. And I was enough - enough for little Jake, and enough for myself.

"Can I meet Jake sometime - maybe drop around and give you a hand whenever you need it?"

"Yes, thank you, Ben. That would be lovely. It's healthy for Jake to hang around good men. I've had a few dates since returning home, but none that kept me interested."

"I get it. Me, too, Kat. Maybe we both still have a lot of healing to do. So, you were on the road for quite a while, huh?"

"Yes. Someday I'll tell you all about it."

And I kept my promise.

———

Over the years, I have shared with Ben the details of my time on the road and on the rails. And I have told him all about Leni - her laugh, her spunk, her spirit, and most of all, her bravery. I even described the day that two truculent immigration officials finally tracked me down at our home in Wabash. They were no longer interested in me, but they wanted to know if I had been in contact with Leni. According to immigration, Leni was spotted near New Orleans and was still on the run. After I convinced them I hadn't been in touch with her, I closed the door and sighed with relief and joy. They were looking for Leni, which means she is still out there somewhere.

I look at my son Jake, and I know Leni is with me always. I have never seen or heard from her again, but I sleep well at night knowing she is still free. Against all odds, her spirit could not be broken, and that spirit will always live in Jake.

Every night I whisper into my pillow, "May God keep you safe, precious Leni. Via con Dios, mi hermana."

THE END

MUSIC REFERENCES

Dresser, Paul. "On the Banks of the Wabash, Far Away." Howley, Haviland and Company. 1897. Sheet Music.

Gershwin, George, Gershwin, Ira. "Let's Call the Whole Thing Off. Chappell & Co., Inc., 1937. Record.

Hanley, James F., MacDonald, Ballard. "Back Home Again in Indiana." Shapiro, Bernstein & Co., 1917. Sheet Music

Roff, J.A., "The Great Island Rock Route." (Early version of "The Wabash Cannonball"). Publisher name unlisted. 1882. Sheet Music.

Taylor, Cecil. "The Southern Belle." Kansas City Southern Lines, 1940. Sheet Music.

ACKNOWLEDGMENTS

There are certain wonderful people in my life who make the often-exhausting effort of writing a novel worthwhile. Their encouragement, support, and unwavering belief in my ability to create compelling stories keeps me sane – although some may wish to debate that point.

Kristin Banta, Antony Bland, Jan Pastras, and Dmitry Arbuck are always my first go-to team. They are fair and honest critics who set the bar high while still treading lightly on my tender author ego. They have read every book I have ever written – probably more times than they ever hoped to - and their thoughts and ideas are an inextricable part of all my novels. This book is yours, and I love you all.

Antony's guidance with story development was invaluable in helping me to find my direction in writing The Train Jumper. Dmitry Arbuck's brilliant and insightful notes helped me to flesh out the character of Kat, which made the book so much better for it. To them, I wish to say that I am grateful beyond words for your insights and for your selfless gift of time.

My introduction to Franklin came via my dear sister, Lisa Leggington, as well as our great friend, Kathy Neff, who not only introduced me to their charming town, but also assisted me in historical references and location research. Their love of Franklin was a great inspiration for this book, and I am truly indebted to you for your assistance and enthusiasm. I promise to take you to the Artcraft the next time I am in town. Popcorn for all!

Mr. Elwood Neff of Franklin, Indiana, spurred my imagination with the miniature railroad village he so painstakingly created, which was remarkable in detail and workmanship. I really wish everyone could experience the pleasure I did when he shared his magical train town with me. A very special thanks to Mr. Neff.

The Johnson County Museum of History in Franklin, Indiana, was of great assistance in my research. I want to extend a sincere thank you to museum director, David Pfeiffer, and to museum researchers Linda Talley, Genealogy Librarian, and Jane Hughey, Education Coordinator, and Rob Shilts. Your time, effort and knowledge helped to create an historical representation of Franklin so readers can love and appreciate your wonderful town as much as I do.

My earliest exposure to railroad history and travel came from my grandfather, Leland Bennett, who worked on the Pennsylvania Railroad and regaled me with stories. I still have his commemorative pocket watch, which is very precious to me.

There exists a group of supporters who wait for each of my books and cheer me along the way. Their support is so precious to me that I want to acknowledge them herein: Aileen Casadevall, Cecilia Samaja, Jean Chouquette, Patrick Martin, Craig Nadeau, Janet Sullivan, Roy Rentner, Kathy Szymanski Knight, Linda MacNeal Rentner, Janet Menetski Marinari, Debora Van Duren, Joey King, Richard Kuhlman, Marcia Russell, Sheryl Mahoney Jackson, and most of all, Diane Meyer Simon.

Thank you to my publisher, Next Chapter Publishing, for always keeping the faith.

Lastly, I'd like to thank my dog, Buddy. He keeps me company through the late-night hours, and he never complains when I talk to myself in different voices. (It's an author thing, not a sanity issue. I hope.) Peace and love.

Gwen Banta
Los Angeles, California
2022

ABOUT THE AUTHOR

 Gwen Banta was born in Binghamton, New York, and educated in Indianapolis, Indiana, where she received B.A. and M.S. degrees from Butler University. She is a member of Kappa Delta Pi International Honorary Society in Education. She also received a language certification from The Defense Language Institute in Monterey, California.

The author has received numerous awards for her fiction, including: Opus Magnum Discovery Award (Honorable Mention); Winner - Unpublished Stories: Great Northwest Book Festival, Los Angeles Book Festival, Pacific Rim Book Festival, San Francisco Book Festival, Great Southeast Book Festival, London Book Festival, and the Paris Book Festival.

Gwen has also written several screenplays. Her screenplay, *Skies A' Fallin*, is currently under option to an independent producer. Awards for her screenplays include: Writer's Project Semi-Finalist, Columbine International Screenwriting Competition Finalist, Ohio Film Festival Semi-Finalist, and People's Pilot Semi-Finalist.

The stage play, *The Fly Strip*, based on *The Remarkable Journey of Weed Clapper* and co-written by Richard Kuhlman, is currently scheduled for publication

An award-winning actress of stage, screen, and television,

Gwen is a member of SAG-AFTRA and Actors' Equity Association. She is a supporter of Global Green International, Project Angel Food, The Elizabeth Glaser Pediatric Aids Foundation, and St. Jude Children's Research Hospital. She resides in Los Angeles with her dog, Buddy, who is a major fan of her books - as long as there is food involved.

———

To learn more about Gwen Banta and discover more Next Chapter authors, visit our website at www.nextchapter.pub.

REVIEWS FOR THE TRAIN JUMPER

Winner: Paris Book Festival 2021
Honorable Mention – London Book Festival 2022
Honorable Mention – Los Angeles Book Festival 2022
Honorable Mention – Hollywood Book Festival - 2021

Gerard Way, My Chemical Romance, author/creator of "The Umbrella Academy"

"Gwen Banta has a resonant voice, one that pulls you into highways and bus terminals. For anyone who ever wanted to disappear, or feels as if they already have…"

Dmitry Arbuck, Author of "Mastermind"

"Gwen Banta continues her phenomenal writing, captivating readers with stories of real people and events. In her latest book, Gwen masterfully proves that there is nothing more fascinating in life than life itself. The Train Jumper is a delightful and deeply touching story. I highly recommend it."

DONOVAN'S LITERARY SERVICES

"Banta demonstrates ... a wry sense of humor which deftly captures small-town atmosphere and interpersonal relationships. [Kat's] chosen mode of transport brings trains and their culture to life. *The Train Jumper* strikes ... a balance that vibrates with the click clack of the train and a track Kat follows to a very different destiny far from her hometown roots."

Readers Favorite, 5 Stars - Pikasho Deka

"The Train Jumper is a thoughtful coming-of-age story filled with heartbreak, humor, and adventure. Author Gwen Banta's moving tale of a young woman's self-discovery journey showcases the human spirit's indomitable power to overcome overwhelming odds."

The Train Jumper
ISBN: 978-4-82414-337-2

Published by
Next Chapter
2-5-6 SANNO
SANNO BRIDGE
143-0023 Ota-Ku, Tokyo
+818035793528

29th July 2022